Previous fiction by the author:

The Artichoke Queen

One Summer on Cutthroat Lake

Owen Duffy

Livingston Press
The University of West Alabama

Hardcover binding by: HF Group
Typesetting and page layout: Sarah Coffey, Joe Taylor
Proofreading: Barbara Anderson, Jayla Gellington, Erin Watt,
Joe Taylor, Tricia Taylor, Ashley McMinn, Maddy Owen
Cover layout: Katie O'Day
Cover photo: Jason Ross

One Summer on Cutthroat Lake

Owen Duffy

For Liz

Book One:

Cowgirl Ballads and Trail Songs

To make a prairie it takes a clover and one bee, —
One clover, and a bee,
And revery.
The revery alone will do
If bees are few.

—Emily Dickinson, from *Nature*

One

Spring, 1946: Denver, Colorado

The passengers waiting for the train to Braxton, Wyoming, let out a collective sigh as the conductor announced that it had been delayed due to weather. A snowstorm, he said, on their intended route. This news came after the train had already been late to arrive, and those waiting in the lounge area, their suits and skirts wrinkled and disheveled, a cloud of cigarette smoke hanging above them, were told to wait for further instruction. Outside, the gleaming locomotive sat parked under a powder blue sky. As if in defeat, it chugged to a halt and released several long jets of steam.

The woman seated nearest the large windows stared out at the train with sharp gray eyes. She was in her late twenties, dressed in a brown wool suit, with a fur collar and matching hat. She wore silk stockings and heels, a dash of dark red lipstick. Her nails were neatly pointed in a matching shade, and a large diamond ring hung from her left hand.

It was the fourth train she'd taken since five days prior. From New York, to Chicago, to Saint Louis, to Denver. There'd been a lot of time to burn. And she'd used it wisely. On long distance phone calls back to New York, to her attorney, her banker, and then ahead to Braxton to make sure all arrangements were in place for her arrival.

She tapped her cigarette in the pedestal ashtray she'd been sharing with a businessman in a gray Western style suit beside her. He wore a Stetson hat and sat reclined with his cowboy boots crossed at the ankle.

"Train travel," he said in a soft drawl, to no one in particular. "A thing of the past. Flew up here from Dallas myself on a DC-3. Ever been on one?" He glanced at her but didn't wait for a response. "Well, it's the future. I tell you, we wouldn't be worrying about a little old snowstorm. We'd already *be* in Braxton."

1

She glanced back at him. She didn't mind him talking, even if to himself. All the passengers in the waiting area had started to stretch and converse. There was little else to do.

"I know what you're thinking," he said, tilting back his hat. "A snowstorm is a snowstorm. But an airplane, boy. It can fly around it. Over it. Under it."

There was a pause as the train's luggage compartments were closed. For a moment it seemed the conversation was over, as since New York she'd made every effort to avoid any social entanglements, but here she could no longer help herself.

"Where," she said finally, "are you going to land an airliner in Braxton? A cow pasture?"

The question hung in the air. He sat up slowly and knocked some ashes off his boots. Even if she was being disagreeable, she didn't much care. When she looked over, however, she saw that he was grinning brightly, and realized that he'd craftily lured her into conversation.

"Where did you come from, if you don't mind me asking?" The man's voice adopted a more serious tone as he studied her. "I'd say New York City by the look of you."

"You guessed right," she said, continuing to look forward as the conductor on the platform, hands behind his back, instructed the porters to shut the passenger car doors.

"Traveling alone?"

At this she too looked at him closely. His suit looked expensive. And he was handsome, she supposed. Clean shaven. Mid-thirties. He looked like a wealthy cowboy. New to money perhaps, but still hanging onto his old ways.

She turned back to the window. "My husband is meeting me in Braxton."

"Vacation?"

"That's right."

He leaned closer, as if to say it was an odd time to vacation in Braxton, and odd for a woman of her class to be traveling alone, but before he spoke she cut him off.

"He's coming from Los Angeles, where he's been on business."

He turned at the sound of the passenger doors slamming shut. "Looks like we won't be getting out of here anytime soon," he sighed. "If it wouldn't offend your husband, I could keep you company tonight, perhaps dinner? I know Denver well."

She glared at him. This was exactly what she'd hoped to avoid. And who, exactly, did he think he was? Surely he could see that she was self-sufficient, not used to others handling her affairs. And he seemed the type that would hold every door, make all her arrangements, loop his arm through hers—when she was doing just fine, thank you.

She blew out a thin stream of smoke and crushed her cigarette. Then she ceremoniously slipped on a pair of gloves and began to gather her things.

"I don't think so, but thank you anyway," she said, and—to her own surprise—thrust out her now gloved hand, which he took and held firmly.

"Will Heaton," he said, still holding her hand, as if allowing the sound of his name to breathe, and give her time to recognize it. "And I didn't get your name."

"Because I didn't give it," she said, slowly retrieving her hand. She'd heard of him. A magazine perhaps. A film reel about Texas oil barons or cattle kings. Something of the sort.

"Well, good luck in Denver," he said, tipping his hat forward and resuming his slouch, her slight having done nothing to dampen his spirits. "I hope your husband makes it alright," he added from under his hat.

"Thank you," she said, before turning and walking across the room, with the odd feeling that he wasn't just looking at her, but right through her.

After she spoke with the ticketing agent, the passengers seated nearby watched the production of her luggage being retrieved from the First Class car. If it was an embarrassment, as the porters dragged it from the train's belly, then stacked it neatly on a dolly, she showed not the faintest blush.

As her bags were wheeled in, she turned on her heel and walked briskly past the waiting area, past Will Heaton, who was now stretched out with his hat over his face, his pant leg riding up so she could see the long pearl handled knife tucked in his boot.

Some turned to watch her exit, as if wondering who she was, or where she thought she was going. There was only one way to Braxton, and this was it.

The porter struggled to keep up with her luggage, consisting of a matching set of three Louis Vuitton suitcases, a small trunk, and a valise. He pushed it out to the curb, where she instructed him to put it in the nearest cab, before placing a silver dollar in his hand. She climbed in, peeled off her gloves, and ordered the driver to take her to the nearest automobile sales lot.

He spun around and looked at her blearily. "In case you didn't notice, there ain't many lots back open yet. Rationing hasn't been over here but six months." He pointed at the gasoline rationing sticker in the corner of his window.

"I don't much care," she replied. "As long as it has a car for sale. Old or new."

He looked back at her again, where she was, at the moment, gazing out the window, before she turned and narrowed her eyes at him, which made him snap around in his seat.

"Yes ma'am," he muttered, putting the cab in gear.

They pulled up outside a downtown DeSoto dealer minutes later, where she went into the sparkling showroom and said to the young salesman who came to wait on her: "I'll take that one." Her bare finger was pointed at a new cream-colored convertible which sat by the street-side window under a swath of bright lights.

His mouth hung open only a moment before he snapped it shut, nodded, and said, "I'll write it up."

After the paperwork was done, she produced half the value of the car in cash and the rest in a check drawn on the account of a Thomas D. Gladinger of Fifth Avenue, New York City. The salesman and an associate rolled open, with great effort, the large glass showroom doors and drove the car out into the brisk late March air.

"Here you are Miss Gladinger," the salesman said, opening the car's door, as his associate began to raise the canvas top.

"No," she told him, "I'd prefer it down."

The two men looked at one another.

4

"But ma'am, it's not yet fifty degrees. You'll freeze."

She flashed the same look at them as she had the cab driver, and the man fastened the top back down.

As soon as her luggage was secure in the trunk she surged forward, only to slam on the brakes a moment later, and turn to the two men who were still standing there watching her.

"Do you by chance have a map?"

They said it was a six-hour drive to Braxton on the westerly route, through Pocatello and Idaho Falls. It was there she stopped for lunch at a café, placed a phone call ahead from the booth by the door, then had the DeSoto gassed up as she sat there in the clear midday light.

She drove with the map on her lap, the heater blasting. Soon she saw the familiar image of the Tetons Mountains and the ranges that extended beyond to the north and west, into Idaho and Montana. Those old valley homes and surrounding ranches she passed, cattle grazing in the fields, spoke of a long bitter winter having come to an end. The Snake River, winding down from the north, ran high with spring snow melt. She paused on the bridge spanning it—and without fanfare—plucked the wedding ring from her finger and flung it in the water.

A herd of cattle drinking on the banks looked up at the sound of the splash, which was not unlike a fish jumping. She shrugged and pulled her hat down further on her head.

"Don't be too impressed," she said to the cows, as they turned their indolent gaze towards her. "It was only paste."

While it had been meant as a deterrent on her trip west, and was foolish to dispense with it now, she'd long dreamt of throwing her wedding ring in the East River. Only thrift had kept it from happening; the real diamond she'd sold back to a jeweler on Park Avenue who'd made it for her husband years before. The remainder of that balance was secure in her purse. By all accounts, she'd earned every cent of it.

Braxton, as she pulled in two hours before dusk, with its tired wood buildings and faded advertisement signs, looked less of the tourist trap of old and more of a regular cattle town—a café, a filling station, a church, a grammar and high school—which must've suffered, she reasoned, from poor attendance this time of year due to ranching.

Her foot pressed the brake, and she came to a halt in the middle of the dirt road and glanced at the street signs, working the stem of her sunglasses between her teeth. A truck behind her honked and pulled around, but when the young driver caught sight of her in the DeSoto, he pushed back his hat, as if in disbelief, before he slowly drove away.

COME ON IN!

The rusty sign hanging above the café across the street beckoned in the breeze. She glanced at her watch, then pitched the map in the seat beside her. A coffee sounded mighty good.

The place was half-full, ranchers and their wives huddled at small tables. Every shade of denim was represented, every degree of wind-burned face. And every one of them lifted when the door slammed shut behind her. She stood there in a block of pale sunlight, all eyes on her. Had there been a jukebox, she was sure its needle would have lifted from the record, only to continue playing after she'd gone.

"And what brings you to town?" the waitress asked after she'd found an empty stool at the counter and the coffee was being poured.

She flashed a thin smile. "Business," she replied, removing her gloves and setting them neatly beside her.

"Pie?" the waitress asked.

"No," the woman said, lighting a cigarette, "thank you."

When she looked over her shoulder, heads turned away, and the murmur of conversation, present when she first stepped in, resumed. Of course it was the kind of place where everyone knew everyone; a stranger here stood out. Here, even the cut of the pearl button shirt, or the silver belly hat one wore, especially if it didn't look like the type on display in the clothing store she'd passed— *Rafters*—would give the impression that a person wasn't from around there. And the way she was dressed, she thought, in an outfit she'd purchased not the week before on Madison Avenue, she may as well have come from Mars.

Or Philadelphia, to be more accurate about it. At least, she'd grown up there. Summered in the country on her grandparents' farm. Riding horses, mending fences, milking cows. Her grandmother taught her it was okay for a lady to get her hands dirty; unlike a man, she always said, dirt would wash off with a little soap and water.

It would be years before she knew what her grandmother meant. She met her husband to-be on a family trip to New York City when she was eighteen. In the dining room at the Edison Hotel, to be exact. He was the son of E.G. Gladinger, a wealthy Boston candy confectioner. Taffy and other kinds of candy no one ate much anymore. *No matter*, her mother whispered, grasping her hand under the table. *The money has already been made.*

Had her mother not practically *forced* her to go on a date with Thomas, imploring her that this was her best chance, her best chance at anything other than the life of a woman of modest means and education, with a father whose health was failing no less, she may have been sitting in a dowdy café back in Pennsylvania this very afternoon, not unlike the one she was in now. May have even been serving the coffee.

"Looks like we got snow a-comin' our way," someone nearby said to no one in particular, breaking her train of thought. "Spoke with a friend in Laramie this morning. Said they had six-foot snow drifts and fifty mile an hour winds."

She laughed aloud, thinking of all those passengers still waiting back in Denver. The other diners went quiet again, looking at her with expressions that slowly turned from quizzical to suspicious, as if suddenly realizing why a woman like her was in their town: she was quite surely here on business, or to be more precise about it, she was here to buy their land. All of it she could.

They must've known people like her were coming. Braxton had once been home to lavish dude ranches, catering to the wealthy elite, who wanted to come play cowboy for the summer while swathed in luxury. But its golden era had been waning since the twenties, and the few ranches that didn't go under during The Great Depression or the ensuing war were now derelict. Left to rot.

Cattle and grain prices were down, but tourism was on the

upswing. And they'd be coming by car, by train, and indeed by airplane now. They'd soon flood back to Braxton for its fresh air, unrivaled mountain views, and the romance of the Old West. The only people here now were weary ranchers, selling off land for pennies on the dollar. For those who'd defaulted on their loans, deals could be struck with the banks—she wasn't a mercenary, but she suspected that train in Denver had been full of them.

This wasn't all business to her, however. She'd spent a summer in Braxton with her family when she was twelve. It was all a big to-do: most of the preeminent families in Philadelphia at that time summered out there. References had been required, and it was through a well-positioned family friend that they'd been placed on one of the finest ranches, *The Flying U*. Her father must've been stretched to the limit bringing their family out that year—but he'd managed, and it had been the happiest time in her life.

She'd ridden horses all that summer, stopping only to watch cowboys round up cattle and wrangle horses. She'd secretly fallen for one of those cowboys, and although she was young and he was much older—and the feelings were of course completely unrequited—memories of that summer were still close, and she thought of that time fondly.

It was only after she returned home that she received a postcard from a fellow guest—a boy who she suspected had a thing for her—reporting that her cowboy had been killed in a rodeo accident. She'd walked around in a daze afterwards, heartbroken; he was the first person she'd ever cared about in that way. And by cruel fate, he was also the first person she'd ever known who'd died.

It was all too tragically romantic, she supposed now. But was it a sin to want a little of that romance again? A little of that magic? And was it foolhardy to think that she could buy it back? She didn't much care.

Her husband had hated fresh air. Hated mountains. Hated the beach too. She felt like a room that hadn't seen daylight in years. At last she'd pulled back the drapes and opened the windows and a beautiful, glorious breeze was blowing in.

Thomas would hate that she was here. Would hate that she was buying land. Especially with money that had once been his. She found herself grinning deliciously as she sipped the last of her coffee and headed out the door. It would be a one-two punch to a man who had only months before, punched the wind out of her…

The main strip in Braxton hadn't changed since she'd visited in the early thirties. The buildings wore the same faux pioneer façade, the streets were still unpaved. The same tacky casinos, bars, hotels, and restaurants remained. But they were mostly empty now and bespoke a desperate kind of hope. This was in many ways a ghost town, and the souls of the tourists who'd once filled these haunts since the last century would not be returning to pump nickels into the slot machines, slosh beer on the barroom floors, or unload their wallets for a family steak dinner.

It seemed as if the town had forgotten what made it great in the first place. In this, she seemed to have found a companion. She'd lost herself in marriage—given the best of herself and thought it gone. Here, there was hope she could get it back; and a little hope, she'd realized lately, could carry a person a long way.

And if by chance she appeared fearless to anyone watching, as she walked across the street from the café towards a little hardware store that day, it was also just a façade. She was deeply afraid of failing here too. Petrified. Friends and family back home called her crazy, and maybe she was. Maybe she was the only person who was coming back here. Maybe she was buying land nobody wanted. Maybe that train in Denver had been full of speculators who'd take one look at this town and turn around.

A hand-painted sign hung in the *Hickens' Hardware* display window:

LAND FOR SALE
INQUIRE WITHIN

This will be the first thing you ever do for just yourself, she told herself, pushing open the door. This will be the first place of your own.

At the sound of tinkling bells, a small man shot up from behind the counter, as if surprised to have a patron in the store. As she looked around, she saw it was overstuffed with brooms, shovels, ropes, cords, wires, fuses and all kinds of farming equipment. It seemed that one could buy anything they were looking for, although she'd be surprised if anyone knew precisely where to find it.

She paused in the doorway, watching as the man faced the mirror behind the counter, slipped on his suit coat, adjusted his tie, and plopped an old hat on his head.

"Howdy," he said, rushing over to greet her, "you must be Miss Gladinger. I'm Jim Hickens."

His voice was golden, melodious, befitting a store owner who was also the local land commissioner. When he lifted his hat in greeting, she saw the permanent impression it had made around his ears.

As she shook his hand, he yelled over his shoulder, "Iris, come see. You're not going to believe it. She's *here*."

A tall woman came from the back room, wearing a plaid shirt and dungarees. She lifted a pair of glasses from her nose and let them droop from their chain around her neck.

"My, my," she exclaimed, coming towards where she stood. "See Jim, I told you she'd make it."

Seeing Iris close up, with the same curly gray hair her grandmother had, made something in her give way. "Please, call me Francine," she managed, before a single tear slipped down her cheek.

Iris's smile faded. Jim quickly produced a folded handkerchief, and although he seemed concerned that she'd come all this way only to break down in his store, he smiled warmly as Francine pressed it to the corner of each eye.

"There now," Iris said, patting her hand. "Let's find you a seat."

They each took an arm and seated her by a cluttered desk, lowering her carefully into a chair.

"I'm so terribly sorry." Francine blotted her eyes with the handkerchief, careful not to smudge her makeup. "It's just that I'm so pleased to meet such nice people at the end of what's been a rather long journey."

"Honey," Iris said, sitting down behind the desk, "it must be absolutely exhausting being a young woman these days. I know I wouldn't have the energy for it." She laughed pleasantly. "To think of crossing half the country alone. You got the pioneer spirit, that's for certain."

"That's without question," Jim said, handing her some paperwork to sign. "I can't say in all my years I've ever had someone buy property sight unseen. What is it exactly you aim to do with it?"

"Why," Francine said playfully, "I'm not prepared to show anyone my cards just yet, Mister Hickens, if you don't mind."

"Well," he said, glancing at Iris, "just so you know there's going to be some people here that will be…suspicious. Especially concerning young women buying up their land. And the crown jewel of it at that."

"Folks are strange about this sort of thing. Possessive," Iris added, handing her a pen. "Jim's just warning you is all."

There seemed to be, in that moment, a sense that they too shared the towns' sentiments. That they'd rather be selling to someone a bit more, if not local, more…manly.

Francine paused, studying them, before dipping the pen in the inkwell. "This land has been for sale for several years, as I understand," she said. "If they liked it so much, I reason their qualm is not with me, when they had ample time to procure it. And besides, it's not their land and never was. Any more than it was mine." She snatched up the signed papers and handed them back over. "That is, until now."

Jim raised his hands, as if to say she was preaching to the choir. "Reason, my dear, is in short supply these days." He rummaged through the desk and found the keys, then held them out to her. "That was once one of the finest dude ranches in the valley. Nicest property in town if you ask me. Sitting just a stone's throw from Cutthroat Lake."

"Frankly, I'm just glad I got here before anyone else," Francine said, swapping the paperwork for the keys.

"Now," Jim said, a twinkle coming into his eye. "You ready to see what you've bought yourself?"

Two

Jessica Quick stood at the kitchen sink pressing a handful of ice cubes to her face, as long as she could stand them, before pulling them away. She half-groaned and half-sighed as she opened her eyes and looked out the window at her sister Lynn, who was playing with her two kids in the yard. Beyond them the snow-peaked Tetons Mountains loomed like a mirage. She squinted at the clock above the oven, then back out at the sun, which indeed was already halfway across the sky. Lynn noticed her standing there and put her hands on her hips, shaking her head.

Jessica looked down at the melting ice cubes and dropped them in the drain. Beside the sink stood the bottle of Old Crow she'd been drinking from the night before, and nearly gagging, she tucked it in the cupboard and went to bathe and dress.

When she came from the house, Lynn was sitting under the shade tree while the kids, Joey and Lee Ann, watched Jessica come and grab one of the limbs, tuck a strand of hair behind her ear and give a pained smile.

"Mama," Joey said, looking up from the pile of rocks he was playing with, "is something wrong with Aunt Jess?"

Lee Ann dropped a stick and gazed at her standing there. Above, a bird tweeted. Jessica was twenty-two; just home from the university the previous spring. She was, as near as anyone in town could figure, a woman now. College educated at that. She was of medium height and build, with chin length blonde hair. Her face was pleasant but unremarkable, except that—having spent most of her time out in the sun—she looked the same age as her sister, who was three years older.

"Yes, sweetheart, she is sick," Lynn said. "But that's why she's here with us. To get better." She shaded her eyes and glared at Jessica. "Ain't that right? Been months since you graduated, Jess. You done celebrating yet?"

"I gotta get to work," Jessica replied, digging in her jeans for her car keys. "I'll be back tomorrow evening probably."

"Ain't no way to live," Lynn said, as Jessica turned and walked away. "You should know that."

Jessica climbed in her old green Ford and shut the door, her hand shaking as she tried to fit the key in the ignition, before the key ring finally dropped to the floor. She sat there with her head on the wheel, steadying herself.

Lynn's husband's truck was long gone. Although it was a Saturday, Scott had left for Culver's Garage before sunup. Likely only a few hours after she'd come back from the Sundowner and stumbled down the hallway to bed. In public she usually paced herself, nursing beers so she was good enough to get home and finish the job with the hard stuff. But last night, when the feelings had got to be too much to handle, she'd drank straight whiskey all night, water back.

She'd returned to Braxton the previous spring from Laramie, leaving behind nearly all her things and a man she'd gone with for two years. He was a professor at the university, ten years her senior. In her way of thinking, he'd done everything a man could do to disappoint a woman. She'd given him everything: her virginity, her love, and her complete devotion.

He'd left her the previous fall when she got pregnant. Said it wasn't his, although of course it was. She ended up miscarrying early on anyway. If it was a hard bit of news she thought he'd like to know, she didn't give him the satisfaction. All that winter she watched him pass outside her apartment on his way to campus. Not once did he call or check in.

By then, she was used to men disappointing her. Three years before, her father—a heavy drinker himself—had died, after going south to Texas. By all accounts, he'd abandoned her twice then. He was the one who taught her how to hunt, fish, and trap. When people asked why she liked the outdoors so much, she'd usually just shrug, although the real answer was that nature didn't ever up and leave you.

Jessica leaned her head out the door at the end of the driveway and vomited. She sat back and wiped her lips, looking back at the house. Those who knew about what had happened in Laramie never said a word about her drinking. And as she drove on into town, the late March sky a brilliant blue, she told herself it was just a phase, and she'd be through it soon enough.

She'd have to if she intended to work for the Wyoming Forest Service. Already she'd sent in several applications, all of which had been returned. No woman had ever held the job, they told her, and the woods were—in their own words—no place for the fairer sex.

"No place for a drunk, neither," Lynn had told her, looking over the letters. "You don't watch out, you're gonna be one of those sour women at the end of the bar shacking up with any man who'll buy her drinks."

Lynn had reason for concern, of course. They both remembered the dark cloud that would fall upon the house when their father was at the bottle. And how he had a temper like tinder: any little thing they did could set him alight. Their mother should've packed them up and left him, but she didn't. That would've been unthinkable in those times. Where they were from, a woman prided herself on putting up with things, no matter how bad it got.

Jessica stopped in the café and forced down a warmed over hamburger and a cola, replenished her supplies in town, then began the twenty minute drive to the trailhead. She figured she'd be there earlier than her boss expected her, but the truth was she'd needed out of that house, and out of her sister's judging eye.

Ed McCann was already waiting by the trailhead, at the eastern edge of The Flying U Ranch. He was wearing one of his customary Pendleton shirts, and he walked down to meet her as she pulled up. He wasn't bad looking for an older guy, and still had the steely-eyed, bow-legged look of a cowboy. Must've been something to see in his prime, she thought. Besides the false bridge of upper teeth and a half missing thumb, both taken by who knows what, he'd made it through his line of work better than most. Probably a pack horse that got him, she figured, knowing how fast they could draw up a rope. That would account for the thumb. The teeth she didn't know, nor speculate, and she never asked.

He wore a bucket Stetson and a pair of silver-framed glasses. As he rested a leathery hand on the door jamb, he took off his hat to reveal a head of salt and pepper hair.

"I'd hoped you'd be here earlier," he said in his gravelly voice, picking the stub of a cigarette from his lips. "Park it and let's get moving."

He turned and walked towards his truck, an Army surplus Jeep with a trailer full of supplies in tow. As he did she cut the engine and reached in her glove box, pulled out a pint of gin and slipped it deep in her canvas duffel, then jumped out of the car.

It was only days before the first guests were to arrive at the Cutthroat Lake Lodge, and as they passed along the narrow trail in the Jeep, cleared in the twenties when the camp was built, Ed worked the gears quickly. It was the first year a vehicle had made it up to camp, but the going was still slow. Previous to that, a pack train of mules and horses made the supply trips along the four-mile long trail, which took all of a day. Jessica figured Ed was sixty-five or so, and had been making this trip for the twenty-five years he'd run the lodge. In that time his camp had grown in the esteem of the fishermen and hunters as the best of its kind in the country.

She looked down a hundred feet into the creek and saw the water was high, which would make fording it ahead difficult. Beyond the treetops, wilderness went as far as the eye could see. These mountains were full of wild game, which guaranteed success to the outdoors men who lined up to hunt there. Most came in the fall for elk, when vast herds roamed Six Mile Hole, which stood at the base of the Crooked Mountains. Hunting accounted for only a small percentage of animal kills. The long winters and violent predatory wildlife—which were returning after being hunted out in the past century—accounted for the rest.

The first guests of the season, however, would be coming to fish the high lakes and rivers. Those waters seldom saw fishermen, and as a result were positively brimming with trout. And while those coming the next week would undoubtedly be fishing in spitting snow or freezing rain, they'd be rewarded with fish hungry after the thaw.

Cutthroat Lake Lodge was, in all actuality, just an old western bungalow style camp overlooking a lake. The camp stood at the top of a ridge, just below the timberline. It consisted of two permanent wood buildings: The "Lodge" itself, and a makeshift barn. The lodge served as cafeteria, replete with kitchen and tables, and comfortably seated up to fifty men. The barn had a dozen horse stalls and room to store gear and tools. Between them stood a fire pit and an ancient

15

spring-fed well, a hundred feet deep, dug long before Ed set up camp there.

Surrounding the two buildings were eight, twelve-foot by twelve -foot wooden decks, upon which stood the "bungalows" —canvas tents that were erected every spring and taken down in the fall. Each bungalow was furnished with a wood stove and two bunk beds. The commodes were two pine outhouses, but no one considered these permanent, as the wind constantly blew them down, sometimes when they were occupied.

Although this was her first season on the job, and the season had not yet officially started, Jessica had already been up to camp several times. She'd made trips in the weeks before the thaw on horseback, making it passable by clearing fallen trees, so they could begin to stock Ed's little outpost.

Jessica was the only townie available for such piecemeal work, as it was weeks before Ed's usual crew assembled in town. Guides and able-bodied young men, Ed had told her, were in short supply after the war—especially in Braxton. She'd only narrowly avoided a desk job in a government office herself during the war because she was enrolled in college. While battles had raged overseas, the once bustling lodge and the nearby dude ranches all but shut down.

Any reservations Ed may have had about hiring her on had given way the week before when he'd gotten the Jeep stuck in the same creek they were about to ford. Per his instruction, she climbed in the Jeep and waited for him to attach the winch line to a tree on the other side of the creek. But when the line became hopelessly snarled, she put the Jeep in low gear and inched across the creek with the trailer in tow. Ed had stood on the opposite bank, watching as she passed over boulders that he always got caught up on, then pulled the entire assembly ashore, dripping rivulets of water.

Jessica had popped out of the driver's seat, retrieved the winch line, and fastened it to the bumper. All while he stood there rolling a cigarette, smiling at her.

She'd made herself indispensable to him those first weeks, cleaning up what had been strewn about camp by animals, mending holes in the tents, clearing the pathways between them, sweeping the cobwebs out of the kitchen and cafeteria, and stocking their gear. She never kicked, never grumbled. Never gave the impression that she was trying to prove herself, nor that she was one to shy away from tough work. No, she just seemed to operate the only way she knew how: at full throttle.

Without being told she seemed to know, or had built into her, the understanding that time was short, and there was no time like the present to get things done. Quick, hard-working, efficient—she'd quickly become an indispensable part of the crew. So much so that Ed had already inquired if she was available for the fall hunting season—and although it was unspoken, she knew the job would last indefinitely past that—or as long as he had paying guests.

Regardless, he already seemed concerned with losing her and had made it clear there'd be enough work to keep her employed, even in the off-season, on the little ranch he and his wife Esther operated just on the outskirts of town.

The hunting season was short for all species they pursued—grouse, black bear, mountain lion, whitetail and elk. September to December. Some years the weather didn't cooperate, although that usually wasn't enough to deter the die-hard hunters, who Ed never required to pay a deposit. Hunting was a rain or shine affair, and most of his clients knew and respected that. Those who didn't weren't invited back.

Ed once confided to Jessica that he felt lucky if he could enjoy the wilderness for a few months, pay off his employees, and clear a thousand dollars—while other seasons he was happy just to break even. She believed him when he said it. The job's main reward was just being outdoors. When she was up there, there was no concern for anything except the job in front of them.

When camp was operating, her job would be to help run the kitchen. His wife Esther would oversee it and attend to the camp housekeeping duties. But by and large Jessica's job was as a full-time cook, which Ed assured her was the toughest but most appreciated job in camp. If not the single most important. And while she felt competent in preparing the large, simple meals the job required, they both knew she'd be even more competent showing men where to find elk and trout there in her own backyard.

"You gonna let me guide a trip sometime?" she joked to Ed that morning as they worked their way up to camp. He glanced over the rim of his glasses at her and then back out the windshield.

But as they approached the creek her smile faded. She knew the answer as well as he did. Qualified or not, his clients wouldn't follow a woman into the woods. Not even Calamity Jane herself. And Ed, who'd seen how hard she worked, knew she'd come to deserve those tips rich guests gave the guides when they got them their trophy trout or bull elk. Right or wrong, there was an underlying belief in all such men that her duties lay elsewhere.

"Maybe next year," he replied finally, switching the Jeep's transfer case into low gear. He'd answered in such a way to make it clear the question was out of place. Even if she was only kidding. That there was as much chance of him putting on an apron to help in the kitchen as there was of her going out on a trip as a guide.

"Looks high today," he said, stopping near the bottom of the hill.

He was right: the creek was positively boiling over its banks. The weather had been warm lately, melting snow on the mountain peaks, filling the creeks that drained the valley. The water was now covering the boulders she'd been able to see just days before.

"You want me to drive it again?" she said, but immediately knew it was the wrong thing to say. Judging from the high water there was no way for him to wade across with the winch cable as he usually did, lashing it to their sacrificial tree on the opposite bank, which was already heavily scarred from use.

She stood in her seat and began to climb out to carry it over herself.

"No." He revved the engine. "It's too dangerous. We're going to have to go for it."

Ed backed up the hill and paused there, studying the rushing creek a minute. When he hit the throttle, Jessica sank back in her seat. He was in second gear when they reached the water, taking a diagonal line across and downstream. The engine chortled as the water grew deeper, the tires trying to find their bite, but by midstream they'd lost their momentum and stalled out. Before he even issued his first cuss word she was out of the truck, hip deep in ice cold water, trying to find traction on the slick rocks.

"Get the hell back in here!" Ed yelled over the rushing water, but she pretended not to hear.

The water was up to the fenders and already the truck and trailer

18

had slipped sideways. As Ed tried to restart the motor she grabbed the winch hook from the front bumper, and teeth chattering, uncoiled the cable and grabbed the winch bar, and began wading across the creek. It was a feat most men couldn't pull off, given the leg strength and balance required to offset the current. One slip sideways, and if she met the stream face first, she'd be pulled down and wouldn't come up.

With the next step, the creek suddenly grew two feet deeper. She gasped as the water went up to her armpits and the current became too great. The winch cable, hook and bar suddenly felt like lead, but she didn't let go. Her boots began to slide on the rocks—and the shoreline, only thirty feet away, began to blur. Her heart began to hammer against her ribs, her entire body went rigid. The feeling she had was that of someone who was about to fall off a cliff. Ed was standing up and shouting at her and she caught sight of him as she was turned around and pulled under.

A rush of noise. Biting cold. She felt herself tumbling. Twisting. Seconds, minutes, she didn't know. As she spun she saw light and dark, dark and light, until she banged against something hard—a boulder, she reckoned—and heard her own muffled cry as she struck it. Now the current was so strong she could only momentarily get her head above it for a sip of air before she was again pulled back down. And when she went down for the last time, everything went quiet. The strength in her legs was gone, and she lay wedged beneath the rock, still clutching the leaden winch bar.

She watched bubbles passing by in the blackness. How foolish, she thought, to die this way. And how easy it had been! The world became darker, and the impulse to breathe became strong; stronger than any hunger, fear, or pain she'd ever known.

And then there came a calming image—a face. Her father's, she thought at first. But no—it was someone else's face, one she didn't know but one that was somehow familiar. His face was ice blue and his beard was made of weeds. Around him there was a glowing light, and he was holding out a shining hand, coming to get her. As he did she just lay there, watching him come.

But in the next instant, she saw Ed appear, yanking the winch bar from her hands. He cast it aside and she felt his hands loop under her arms and lift her up.

"Stand up, woman!" he yelled over the rushing water, and when she stood and gasped, sucking in bucketfuls of air, she was filled with a joy she hadn't known until then. And after she'd caught her wind she saw it was indeed Ed. Soaking wet. He'd lost his hat and eyeglasses, but had seen well enough to grab the winch line and follow it to her.

"March!" he yelled, and pointed her towards shore. As her legs began to move weakly, he kept his arms locked around her, bracing them both. For the life of her, she didn't know how that man could be so strong, when the stream had beaten her down to nothing in seconds.

Soon he'd thrust her on the rocky shore and was kneeling beside her, heaving in giant breaths while wincing and grabbing at his chest. His face was contorted and screwed up, water dripping from his hair and his shirt, and when his eyes opened and he saw her breathing, he fell on his hands.

"Goddamn, you're alive." He grabbed his chest again and then slowly stood, looking down at her. "I thought you were drowned." He shook his head. "I thought you were dead."

"I'm sorry," she said between gasps, and he must've seen how scared and humiliated she was, sitting there shivering, because he didn't admonish her there.

"Well, come on then," he said, brushing back his hair, looking naked without his hat. "We're not dead. So let's get back to work."

She stood, dripping and dragging the winch cable behind her, which she then slowly lashed around the tree. Overhead, an eagle lit from a tree limb. She followed as it swooped over the stream bed, eying them. Ed pulled the cable tight and attached the ratchet and began pulling at the lever. As the slack was drawn up, she watched the Jeep and trailer begin to inch across the creek. The water was beating against the passenger footwell, and as the Jeep went down in the same hole she'd fallen in, water flooded the floorboards.

She came and took her turn at the ratchet. Ed reached for his cigarette makings in his breast pocket, and managing to find a dry paper, rolled and lit one and stood there smoking while the Jeep came close enough that he could safely wade out and restart it.

When the truck and trailer were safely ashore, the winch reattached to the bumper, she saw Ed's hat on the downstream bank and went and fetched it. Before he took it, she poured the water and gravel from it and straightened the brim. It was the only kind of thanks she could've managed, and as he put it back on his head, he simply nodded.

Jessica then retrieved her duffel from the floorboards. Its entire contents were wet, including her wool jacket. Without it, she knew, she'd freeze in her cot tonight. As she unzipped the duffel the pint bottle of gin spilled out onto the floor. Ed looked at it, then at her, but didn't say a word. He climbed in the rumbling truck and threw it in gear. She pushed her bag on the floor and swung up in the seat beside him.

Of course Ed couldn't stop paying hunters from drinking once the guns were put away, but she knew he certainly couldn't tolerate it of his employees, especially while they were on the job. And especially not this early in the season.

"I catch you drunk, I see you with a bottle," he said, pulling up the rise and switching back into high gear, "if any *guests* see you with a bottle, and it's on down the trail for you. Understood?" He glanced over at her. "Don't think I can't smell it on you right now. Some days I swear you're wearing it as perfume."

"Look, I'm not some drunk or something. I just like a little at night. Helps me sleep."

"I need to hear you say it." He halted the truck and sat there staring at her. "That stuff doesn't have any place out here. It screws up a man's judgment. Even when they aren't drunk. I know because I've been there myself."

She knew he was referring to her jumping in the raging creek. Without another word she reached in her wet bag, pulled out the bottle and emptied it on the ground, as much for him as for herself, because at the moment she wanted nothing more than a drink and was deathly afraid she might take it.

That night they sat around a fire eating beans from cans they'd leaned against it, poking holes in the top so they'd know when they were done by their bubbling. As they ate, sparks flew skyward, dancing among the stars that seemed so close and yet so far away. Before long Ed was asleep against the log and after a while she shook him awake and led him to his bungalow. She then retired to hers, eating chocolate she'd brought and drinking water from her canteen.

As she fell asleep, her bones still aching from the cold creek, she thought of how it had felt to be trapped underwater. She thought of other things too: Her father. Her old boyfriend. Her lost baby. Where was that gin when she needed it, she thought, tossing in her cot, the cries of wolves suddenly rising in the night, hollow and eerie sounding.

And as Jessica closed her eyes she saw that icy face from the creek. All blue and mossy looking. Maybe he'd been some kind of ghost—perhaps he was the man who once lived there. The one who'd drowned in Cutthroat Lake, back when it was called something else.

How did she know that, she wondered, as she drifted off to sleep? Before she did, she somehow also knew that Ed also had seen the man before, and was afraid of him too.

The following morning was cold and brilliantly sunny. She awoke and took inventory of the kitchen, and decided that at least here, all was done that needed to be done, and all was accounted for. While she didn't know much about cooking, she was glad that the job didn't require much real cooking skill.

The meals, she was told, were simple and unvaried—hoecakes, syrup, powered eggs and stewed tomatoes for breakfast—mashed potatoes, canned meat, beans, and gravy for supper. As long as there were good hoecakes, a salt shaker and bottle of ketchup on the table, she'd been assured, the guests would be happy. The lack of variety in their diet would be offset with wild game, Ed had told her, and she'd thus be expected to clean and prepare whatever the men had rustled up.

After testing the emergency telegraph line, which required constant mending as it was a thin wire strung between slender pines running down to the post office in town, Ed was reasonably assured with the return pulses. They then cleared out and headed on down the trail in the Jeep, where they forded the now calm stream and parked at the trailhead.

Ed squinted, stopping before they reached her Ford. "Hold on now. Don't get out just yet."

He slowly reached into the back seat and came up with his battered rifle. An old 45/70 caliber carbine that had been used, he'd proudly told her, at The Battle of the Little Bighorn. As for the veracity of this statement, she wasn't sure, but judging from the size of the bullets it took, she knew it was weapon enough to kill anything that moved.

Jessica looked out the windshield and saw what had caught his attention: a trail of large footprints led from her car and into the woods.

"They may still be hanging around."

"What?"

Ed eyed the prints. "Damn big wolf if it was one. Could be a bear."

There was no hunting of wolves or grizzlies permitted anymore, but hunters had a healthy amount of respect for such wildlife, and were always suitably armed to contend with them. The winter before a local hunter had his face chewed off by a young grizzly, which ripped out his tongue, nasal cavity, half his teeth, and one eye. It had been so cold the man had barely bled, and by the time his fellow hunters got to him, they found him sitting on a log singing a trail song, his bloody exposed teeth whistling in the breeze. He was in such a state of shock that he'd ridden home behind one of them on horseback, sitting upright with his parka hood pulled tight over his head, talking jovially, yet unaware that no woman would ever get in bed with him again, no matter the price.

Ed set the rifle across his lap, opened the trapdoor action to check there was a round in the chamber, and stepped out of the truck. She watched through the windshield as he crept towards her car, crouching to run his hand along the footprints. He waved her over while continuing to scan the woods.

"I'll follow you down the rest of the way," he whispered, opening her door.

She climbed in her car and started it, watching in her mirror as he returned to his Jeep. Both vehicles formed a procession as they drove back into the valley, where they stopped in parting beside the entry to The Flying U Ranch.

"No one's been hunting out there in near five years," Ed said, gazing off into the wilderness. "I've never seen as much sign as I have this spring. It'll be good hunting, but we've got to put eyes on the back of our heads."

There was a long pause. He looked up the trail and then back at her. "Be seeing you next Thursday then," he said finally. "You rest up now."

As she drove back to town ahead of him she reached in the glove box and pulled out a pint of whiskey, took a long swig and set it between her legs. She caught her reflection in her rear view mirror and turned it aside in disgust. Between sips she eyed the claw print on her hood and figured it was at least the size of her own face. Maybe bigger. In a way, she felt marked by it. But after a quarter of the bottle was in her, she began to forget the print. Or at least it didn't worry her that much. And she knew when half of the bottle was gone, nothing could touch her, and perhaps then she'd forget all the other bad things too, even if just for a little while.

Three

Jim Hickens' truck was lousy with papers. They were clipped to the sun shade with clothespins. Sprawled on the dashboard. Tucked between the seat back. His boot knocked over a thermos as he climbed in across from Francine. It was an old truck, from before the war, with a wooden framed bed. The seat was frayed, the windshield smeared with dust, and the motor grumbled as it reluctantly came to life. He threw his hat on the dash, lifted the thermos and poured coffee into the lid.

"Welcome to my mobile office," he said, offering the cup to her.

She shook her head at it and he shrugged and took a sip, breathing hard through his nose. The ashtray overflowed with cigarette butts. The floor was caked with dirt. An old cowboy style revolver lay in the open glove box. She wondered what he had in his battered truck, or on his person, that would possibly warrant its use.

A moment later, Iris opened the door and climbed in beside her. Francine scooted over until she was hip to hip with them both.

"Honey," Iris said in her western drawl, holding up her hands, "you're going to just *love* it here."

Jim lit a cigarette and put the truck in gear. "Probably not what you're used to traveling in," he said, laughing. "Out here, nothing stays clean for long. You'll see."

He turned out of the alleyway beside his store and headed north, past her DeSoto parked in the street with the top still down. The road heading out of town had been freshly oiled, and went off towards the horizon as far as she could see. A truck came up slowly from the distance, the bed filled with hay. Jim raised his hand to wave and the driver nodded back. The road was bordered by grassy banks —only just beginning to green—and lined by wooden posts strung with barbed wire. Every mile or so there was a perpendicular side road, marked only by numbers.

Beyond stood the Tetons, a silhouette in the late afternoon light. As the land flattened in the valley, the cool air blowing across her face, Jim shouted over the noise. He told her what had gone on here during the war, which seemed, as she suspected, almost nothing of note. Most of the able bodied men, he said, had been sent—not into battle—but to government livestock farms and slaughterhouses down south.

As the countryside passed, she felt blissfully removed from her old life on the New York socialite scene: the parties, the salons, the shopping trips. All the painstaking efforts made to project oneself as well-bred, successful, wealthy. The women she knew spent their time as freely and carelessly as they did their money. Shopping, dining, vacationing—even those with children left at home with a nanny—always managed to exclaim how exquisitely *exhausting* it all was.

One day that past fall, her feet soaking in a tub at a midtown salon, Francine had a strange feeling come over her. She climbed down from her perch and slipped on her shoes. She told her friends that she'd left the oven on. Her best friend Dottie yelled that she should call the housekeeper, but Francine was already out the door, her wet feet squeaking in her leather heels as she walked to her apartment on Fifth Avenue.

She passed the doorman, rode the elevator with an elderly couple who'd been in the building practically since it was built, and slipped in her apartment. An apartment she'd painstakingly decorated over the years, with velvet sofas, wall-to-wall carpeting, and billowing, heavy drapes. A place where everything had its place, even places for children, should Thomas ever want them. There were places for her too, of course, but everywhere she sat in her home, it seemed there was something poking her through the cushions, as if reminding her that she wasn't wanted.

She slipped off her wet shoes and walked down the hall to the bedroom. When she pushed open the door she saw something that she'd never be able to get out of her mind—her naked husband on his knees, doing something to another man that he'd never done to her. They were enjoying each other to such a degree that they didn't even notice her standing in the open doorway, watching them in horror.

Francine's heart felt as if it had been dropped out the window. All the blood seemed to go with it, and she had to grab the door to keep from falling down. When Thomas finally looked up and noticed her, his expression was that of surprise, and then, shame. At this, she shut the door and walked back down the hallway.

Everything went quiet. For a moment, the world was perfectly serene. The noises of traffic below seemed remote, and even the sound of Thomas calling after her, as he ran down the hall wrapped in only a towel, catching the elevator doors before they closed, seemed as if she was viewing it on movie screen.

"Frannie," he said to her then, "don't be such a cold fish."

"Thomas," she replied flatly, just before the elevator doors closed. "I could've been a lot of things for you. But I could *never* be your patsy."

The doorman stared at her bare feet as she passed him and walked out into the bustling street. It was only a few blocks to Dottie's place. She'd be home from the salon by now. She was the only person who she could tell, the only person who'd know what to do.

While New York law didn't bode well for women in such cases, her husband—after a long and drawn out legal entanglement—agreed to the divorce. Her attorney advised her, since her assets in New York—bank accounts, possessions, stocks, real estate holdings —would be frozen until the divorce was finalized, which could take a up to a year, that she take what money she could get her hands on and run.

"Do you have any close friends here, family?" he asked, sitting in his office overlooking Park Avenue. "Someone to hold the money for a year? To hide it, so to speak."

Dottie had proved to be her only close friend. An uptown, party throwing socialite—her exact opposite in every way. She was married to a rich older man, a photographer of some renown. Dottie didn't grow up in the socialite set, and in this they had common ground. But Francine found that she was a bit of a—well, she was no more faithful to her husband than Thomas had been to her.

Francine shook her head.

"Then take what money you have," he'd said, leaning over his desk, "and spend every last dime of it. On real estate. Or land."

"Where?" she asked.

"Hawaii. France. *Jupiter*. Anywhere but New York State."

As they drove, Jim Hickens talked about the man who'd owned the land before her, using it as a cattle ranch in the years since it had functioned as a dude ranch. He spoke of things she was not yet knowledgeable, but soon would be: its irrigation access, the size of the barn and livestock stalls, its well, its feeding equipment.

"We're at nearly seven thousand feet right now," he said. "Very few have ever done well raising cattle out here. Those who do, it's a matter of pride. I tell you," he said, looking out the window, "it hits twenty degrees below zero in the winter, and that tests a man's allegiance pretty quick. Some make it, and some don't."

Iris laughed. "There was a man come down here years ago from Idaho. Said he was going to show us all how to make good use of this land. Growing *potatoes*. Well, come harvest he pulled those potatoes out of the ground," she held up her index finger, "and they looked about like *that*."

The truck slowed as the road ended, a broad pasture land sprawled out to the east, a river flowing beside it that wound through a divide. Then he came to a stop and pointed to a wooden gate that crossed the road ahead.

"That there's the trail up to Cutthroat Lake. Only way in and out of those mountains. Don't be alarmed if you see folks coming and going. A part of it may be on your land, but it's been grandfathered in, so to speak. The Sioux used it for over a thousand years before us. Used to call it Jump Lake. Well, we renamed it. Sounds a little nicer for tourists."

Jim turned at a plain metal mailbox, drove across a cattle grate onto a pebble driveway. They stopped at the crest of the hill under a large wooden sign that read:

THE FLYING U RANCH

Francine gazed up the large scrawling wooden letters, the giant carved *U* with a lasso painted around it. The sign was sun bleached and weather beaten now, but just as she remembered it.

"There she is," Jim said, continuing down the driveway. "Your new home."

Straight ahead stood the main house. The lodge, Iris called it. Seemed to be what they called any sort of building that wasn't an outright shack here. It looked smaller and less impressive than it did in Francine's memory. Rough wood siding, patched roof, long sagging porch out front. Big faded red barn behind it with a rusting grain elevator. Surrounding it were seven cabins that also looked like they'd seen better days.

Inside there was a wide entryway—necessary, Iris said, for taking off dirty boots and clothes. Conveniently, there was a boot puller left behind, a boot bristle cleaner, and a black wrought iron coat rack mounted on the wall beside a mirror. All of these, Iris said, were remnants of when guests used to come inside the lodge for dinner at night.

"I remember," Francine said, looking at the large bearskin rug in the middle of the room.

"You've been here before?" Iris asked, smiling.

"Oh, about fifteen years ago. I was just a child then. Came out for a summer."

"Did you hear that, Jim?" Iris asked. "She's been here before."

"Well," Jim said, pulling some old sheets off the long leather sofas that sat in the middle of the room, sending a dust cloud into the air. "That would certainly explain things."

"It's just as I remember. A little run down. But it's," she said, spinning and looking at them, "perfect."

It was indeed a grand room. Francine ran her hand along the lodge pole pine furniture, the battered piano where she remembered guests gathering to sing songs after dinner. She looked up at the stone fireplace which went all the way up to the high, arched ceiling. There, a wall of windows faced the northern mountains, and beneath the windows stood a long table that could seat nearly forty guests. Beside it, through a split door, there was a large kitchen with two iceboxes, and a trapdoor that led down into a dry cellar. In the corner of the kitchen stood a winding back stairway that led up to three bedrooms and a large bathroom.

They then quickly toured the barn—which, unlike the house— was completely empty. It was amazingly dark inside even at that time

29

of day, and Jim had brought along a gas lantern, and held it high as he led her around. "They don't build them like this no more. You could hold a damn rodeo in here."

They had, Francine remembered. They had.

There were a dozen livestock stalls, now bare, as well as a large hayloft, a dozen milking stations and a large gated area that looked as if it could hold a hundred cattle in close proximity.

Jim drew the lantern over the thick dust and cobwebs covering the entire barn. There were places in the roof, nearly fifty feet above, where daylight peeked through.

"Best get someone to patch those holes up before they get any bigger. Come winter, the ice will start popping the other shingles off in a hurry."

"I'll make a note," Francine said, smiling.

Outside again, she squinted, and from the barn's back doors she saw the surrounding cabins. Jim had mailed her, in New York, a hand-drawn map of the property and buildings, and as they walked across the open field from the barn to the nearest cabin, she imagined herself walking across that same crude map.

Jim shoved on one of the cabin's rough pine doors a minute before it finally gave with a bang. Light spilled in through the windows on two rusty beds, an eaten up mattress, a small wood stove, and an oil lamp. It was a cabin just like this she'd stayed in years before, with her entire family. In the coming weeks, she might remember which one had been theirs, but as for now, they all looked about the same.

"Hard to believe Hollywood folk used to come all this way to sleep in a shack," Iris said, stepping inside. "But those were the times, I suppose." Her boots made a scraping noise as she turned on the gritty floor. "Shame really. Now it's all just—" she ran her fingers along the bed frame—"dust."

Iris leveled her eyes at Francine. "And is that what you believe?" she asked coldly. "That they're coming back?"

"Come now," Jim said, "there's more to see yet."

"I hope so. I certainly came back," Francine said, before turning towards the door. "And just in time. This place was about to rot into the ground."

"Everything will return to the earth eventually," Iris said, clapping the dust from her hands. "I believe the Bible says that."

"Something like that anyway," Jim said, taking Francine's arm and leading her outside. "Don't mind her," he whispered. "You'll see when you get older that the world never seemed as good as it was when you were young. Iris and I just remember this town when it was the jewel of Wyoming. There's nobody who wouldn't like to see it all come back, but I don't think she wants to get her hopes up."

"Well, I've got hope and money," she said, as they walked back to his truck. "You tell anyone who wants to be bought out that I'll pay the same per acre as I've paid here."

Jim nodded as Iris reached in the truck and pulled the revolver from the glove box. She turned and held it out to Francine.

"Just a little something I want you to have, for protection from bears," Iris said, winking. "Or anyone that comes around that you don't want around. You just point the business end of this at them and if that isn't enough to scare them off, fire one into the air."

"Careful, that's loaded now," Jim warned, as Iris handed the gun to Francine.

It felt heavy. Blunt and ugly. She'd never held a gun before and as she wrapped her hand around the grip and fingered the trigger, she felt a strange sense of power.

"Don't point that at anything you don't intend to kill," Jim said. "And if you pull that gun on someone, you better be prepared to use it. Understand?"

He walked to the bed of his truck and pulled out a rusty object, then leaned it against the nearby fence. A chipped and battered *Open Range* sign. He counted out ten paces and positioned her there, right where the grass met the driveway.

"Shoot the 'O' out of that," he said, folding his arms.

Francine looked at the sign, trembling in the wind. Whatever shrewd and malevolent part of her that existed, hidden deep inside all her life, came out of her as she gripped the gun and aimed down the sights. When she pulled the trigger, the gun bucked in her hands, rocking her back on her heels. A blast of smoke. The sign fluttered against the barbed wire, a fresh hole in it, nearly a foot off the mark.

She looked at Jim and grinned, brushing her hair behind her ear as she leveled the gun again. Standing there, her body rigid, handbag swinging on her arm in the breeze, her heels dug into the land that she now owned, she peered over the gun sights and it was no longer

31

a metal sign she was aiming at, but Thomas's heart.

The gun barked as she fired off three shots in quick succession, sending the sign spinning. When it came to rest she saw that she'd knocked the "O" right out of it.

"That'll teach 'em!" Iris hollered.

When she finally lowered the gun, the points of her eyes were like the tips of icicles, and for a moment no one spoke, as they all seemed to realize that this—all of this—was indeed deeply personal, and that it wasn't the end of something for Francine, but the beginning.

The sun had set by the time she'd filled her car with supplies from Jim's store—bed sheets, lanterns, matches, gloves, boots and clothing—and drove down the street to the grocery. The young cashier stood watching in the brightly lit windows, chomping absently on a piece of gum, as Francine dropped the groceries in her trunk, slipped behind the wheel, and sped away to her new home.

There, she lit a fire in the hearth and sat at the piano to play from a book of music she'd found, entitled: *Cowgirl Ballads and Trail Songs*. As she plunked out the melodies, wondering how long it had been since they'd been given life, she began to hear a strange overtone. High and piercing.

She paused, lifted her hands from the keys and looked out the window. Outside it had grown dark, and as the notes of the piano died away she heard the sound come again, this time louder and closer.

Francine raced to lock the front door. She then stood with her back to it, her heart racing in her chest as the sound came again, so close she could feel the vibrations against her back. She'd heard enough radio and seen enough movies to recognize the sound immediately:

Wolves.

Four

Francine grabbed the pistol and ran to the window and looked out. The wolves' braying had suddenly ceased. Moonlight spilled over the fields, blue and shadowy, and she scanned the barn and the cabins beyond for any sign of them. It was eerily quiet then, just the sound of her heartbeat in her temples. Perhaps the wolves were far away, she told herself, but kept the pistol cocked and at the ready anyway.

As she continued scanning her back field, she noticed something that made her freeze: the windows in one of the back cabins was alight. One of *her* cabins. She peered out more closely and saw that from inside it came the unmistakable flicker of a lantern.

"Well I'll be damned," she mouthed breathlessly, both frightened and indignant.

She grabbed her coat and her own lantern, pushed open the front door with the pistol in hand, and peered out. A cold wind beat against her face. She slipped her feet into her heels and stepped out on the porch. Already it was bitter cold, and she pulled her coat tightly against her and, waving the pistol around, stepped carefully down into the field. There was her new DeSoto, the top still down, and her eyes could make out the rocky driveway glittering in the moonlight.

When she was a hundred feet from the house the wind picked up, and the lantern went out. She stood stock still a moment, holding her breath. Moonlight, she told herself, as her eyes adjusted to the dark, was better than the lantern anyhow. She stood there until the mountains came into focus, indigo blue against the starlit sky.

She dropped the lantern and turned again, the pistol in both hands. The lighted cabin stood two hundred yards off, and as she crept past the open barn doors, something flew out over her head. She ducked, listening as its heavy wing beats faded into the night.

"Francine Evelyn Lilley," she said aloud, conjuring the voice of her mother, "what have you gotten yourself into?"

And at that, the light inside the cabin—not a hundred feet off
—suddenly went out. Francine had the chilling feeling, standing in
the great wide open, that she was now being watched.

The sound of the wolves resumed then, farther away now, to the
west. It was answered this time by wolves to the north and then to
the east, where her property abutted the trail up to Cutthroat Lake.

Francine realized she was, at the moment, surrounded by wolves.
She didn't move. Didn't swallow. For a long moment, she was afraid
she would stand there all night until she froze to death. Or was eaten.
Whichever came first.

And then suddenly came the sound of rifle shots. Three sharp
cracks that rolled and echoed in the hills. They came, as far as she
could tell, from the western edge of her own property, nearly a mile
away. She heard an animal squeal and then again it was quiet.

Francine sprang to life. Running past the barn and into the
house where she shut the door behind her and threw the bolt.

As she stood there breathing heavily, she saw the open cellar
door and she went and slammed it shut, then sat with the trembling
gun aimed at the front door, while her friend Dottie's voice came to
her in the dark: "Frannie, I dare say you've gotten yourself in over
your head here."

She awakened at sunrise, dressed in the clothes and boots she'd
bought the night before, and went outside, still clutching the gun.
She stood on her porch a moment, staring at her reflection in the
window and covered her mouth with her hand and laughed. They
were, unmistakably, the clothes of a dime store cowboy. She looked
at the pistol, as if deciding what to do with it, and finally tucked it in
her western style belt.

She then marched over to the same cabin she'd seen lit up the
night before and knocked loudly on the door.

"Hello," she said, and decided her voice sounded too apologetic,
as if she was afraid to disturb someone who was living on her land.
She lifted her chin and spoke louder. "Whoever is inside this cabin
needs to come out this very moment and explain themselves."

After a minute and no response, she pushed the door open and
looked inside. There was no one there, and the room was much

cleaner and nicer than the cabins she'd seen the day before. How Jim and Iris had missed showing her this one, she didn't quite know.

There was a coat hanging from a nail, a pair of old cowboy boots sitting beneath it. The bed was made neatly and on the stove, still warm, was a pot of coffee and half a hoecake. A shirt hung over the back of a chair and as she lifted it she saw, stitched on a tag on the inside, the name *SONNY*.

She held the shirt a moment, and as she did she looked down in a wastebasket and saw a velvet covered case. She looked around, and unable to help herself, reached down and picked it up. Opening it, she saw two medals. A Purple Heart and a Distinguished Service Cross. For the life of her, she couldn't understand why they were in the trash, but dropped them back in it when she heard a horse approaching.

When she stepped from the cabin and looked to the east, she saw a rider coming her way with a black dog in tow. He was sitting erect and dignified in his saddle, and judging by the beige riding pants, fine shirt and clean white hat he wore, he was not the man living in her cabin.

A hundred feet off, he lifted a hand, slowed, and came to a stop beside where she was standing in the middle of the field. His Appaloosa whinnied as he pulled tight on the reins. When she caught sight of his face, a wave of recognition came over her, and as surprised and happy as she was to see a familiar face after the night before, she could not manage a smile for him.

"Mister Heaton," she mustered, staring up at where he sat on his horse. It was, she was quite sure, the same man she'd been sitting next to at the Denver train station just the day before. Although she didn't believe in fate, the shock of the coincidence left her speechless, if not slightly suspicious—that she, who'd never been on the good side of chance—should have bumped into this man again.

"Why, it's you." He pushed back his hat and gave her the same quizzical, if not disappointed look she was wearing. "What are the chances here?"

"I'd say about a thousand to one."

"Well, I'd say your name in greeting but as I recall you did not give it."

"Miss Lilley," she managed. "Francine Lilley. I just bought this place."

"Is that right, Miss Lilley? Then I assume you spoke with one of our finest, Mister Hickens."

She looked at him a moment before she answered. He was trim-waisted, broad at the shoulder, and his gleaming eyes showed how pleased he was with his own presence, there atop his handsome horse. Fitted with the nicest saddlery she'd ever seen.

"That's right," she answered finally.

"And did your husband make it from Los Angeles okay?" He flashed a knowing smile, leaning back in his saddle. "Or has he gotten tied up?"

"No," she said, shading her eyes, "he hasn't. I mean he has." She shook her head, hating that she'd been flustered by him. "As it just so happens he won't be making it this time, Mister Heaton."

"Is that so?" He chuckled warmly, pressing his fist to his side.

"So I suppose my ruse wasn't very convincing then?"

"Well, let's just say I know costume jewelry when I see it, Miss Lilley." He lifted his hat off his head to reveal a neatly trimmed head of brown hair. "And if we're done with introductions, I'm afraid you'll be seeing more of me in the future. I'm your neighbor over to the east. I came over this way looking for a calf that's gone missing. There were some coyotes in the area last night. Perhaps you heard them."

"I thought they were wolves."

"Wolves!" He shook his head, laughing softly. "No. Wolves haven't been around here for nearly a hundred years. Hunted out a long time ago." He pointed down to the black dog. "Old Codger here and I went out shooting at those coyotes last night, trying to scare them away. I may have hit one and was hoping to find him out here."

"Looks like you may have hit your dog instead," she said, noting the blood crusted on the dog's ear. She looked closely at the dog a moment, into its wild eyes. It was no type of dog she'd ever seen, almost half wolf itself.

"No, he got into a tussle with one of them before they broke and ran." He ran his fingers over the brim of his hat. "I'm afraid that now these woods are now full of the creatures we thought we had eradicated. Anyway, they say it's bad luck to kill a coyote, but anyone living here for a time might change their minds when they remember the damage they can do."

He stared down at her with an amused expression, studying her outfit, the gun still shoved in her belt. "This new place of yours has seen better times for sure." He shook his head and grinned. "But I don't think the good old days are coming back."

"Well, I clearly believe they will. That's why I bought it. To turn it back into a dude ranch."

At this he laughed softly. "My dear Miss Lilley," he said, "no one buys a ranch to get into dude'ing. Especially not in these times. People got into dude ranches to scrape by when they couldn't pull a profit on the land." He laughed again. "And let me tell you, folks here are clearing out. War's over. Cattle game is over too. And no one," he said, shaking his head, "wants to play 'Cowboys and Indians' again. They're coming back here for something else, and I've got the lock on that in case you have any ideas."

He gazed off at the mountains around them, as if seeing something that wasn't there. "I own most of this valley, down to the Snake and beyond." He looked over her land and nodded. "If all goes by plan, I'll own all these mountains soon too."

Something about him made her blood boil—his self-possessed air, the way he seemed to know her and the town better than they knew themselves. Perhaps it was all bluster—a way to intimidate her or anyone else from trying to buy up the land. But now that she'd said it, she was even more determined to whip this place back into a working dude ranch, rather than look foolish in front of him.

He glanced at the shirt she was holding. "That yours?"

She'd forgotten she was holding it and nearly tried to hide it behind her back.

"It seems I have a guest on my ranch already. Although he was neither invited, nor is he paying."

He leaned back and chuckled again.

"You seem to find everything I do quite amusing don't you, Mister Heaton?"

"Please, call me Will."

"I think it's best we remain formal, Mister Heaton, if you don't mind."

"As you say," he said, bending over to take a better look. "But that shirt, judging by the look of it, is some cowboy's shirt. Did Jim put up some cowboy to watch over you?"

"No, he most certainly did not."

"Well, I'm sorry. I won't laugh at you any more, Miss Lilley. I admire your gumption. But I guess even old Jim, the tight wad, wasn't going to let some lady come out here to live alone. Not with men like me around." He winked. The dog stirred at his feet. Something about its crooked teeth. Its eyes. Burning. She didn't like it.

"I don't need any help out here," Francine said. "I can see to who I want to hire and who I don't." She stepped back and, as she did, tripped over a cow patty and fell flat on her fanny.

"Miss Lilley," Will said playfully, placing the hat back on his head, "most people go out of their way in life to avoid that sort of thing, but it looks like you have a tendency to step right in it."

Just then, as she was wiping off her hands, two horses approached from the direction of his ranch. Atop them were two young dark-haired boys who looked at her a moment, sitting there in the dirt, before they spoke.

"Mister Heaton," one said breathlessly. "We done found your calf. Well, what's left of it."

"Those must've been some coyotes, what they did…" the other said, glancing at her uncertainly. "Well, it's all tore up. Pretty bad."

"That's enough, thank you." Will looked at his two cowhands and shook his head. "Please excuse my intrusion here today, Miss Lilley," he said, turning to her. "It seems my calf has been found. We'll be on our way now." He tipped his hat and said good day, and rode off quickly with his cronies in tow.

Francine stood and dusted herself off, her face burning with embarrassment. Perhaps he was right, she thought, looking at the shirt she was holding and down at her silly cowgirl outfit. She was foolhardy, as was this entire idea of hers.

But perhaps he didn't know her as well as he thought he did. While there were things about men like Will Heaton that she didn't understand, there were plenty of things she did, as they were qualities all men shared. And yet she felt foolish to have shown him her cards, when he knew better than to show his own. That playful gleam in his eye suggested he held the winning hand, and defied anyone to call his bluff.

As she went and hung the old shirt back where she'd found it, she looked around the cabin some more. Whoever it was had spruced the place up nice. It looked much like the cabins had when she'd stayed here, and there was an optimism about what he'd done that she liked. But as she walked back out the door, she figured if he was going to stay here rent free, he better find it in himself to fix the rest of the cabins up too.

Five

Most of the fishermen and hunters who came to his camp, Ed had learned in his time operating it, were professional men on vacation from their jobs as lawyers, stockbrokers, doctors, and oil men; from places like California, New York, and Texas. They were men who'd grown up in the woods, as the world had been full of woods not fifty years before, and it was rapidly disappearing, along with the fish and wildlife. In his estimation they were attempting to reclaim their youth, back when outdoor pursuits were the best entertainment to be had in a small town. Especially when those woods and waters held plentiful wild game.

There were also blue collar types—tradesmen, carpenters, plumbers—who'd grown up in the region, moved away, and remembered how good the fishing and hunting had been there. Ed kept the camp modest and its accommodations sparse, so most anyone could afford to visit. But by and large it wasn't the price that had kept it exclusive. It was the endeavor of getting to Braxton itself, and then on to camp, that discouraged all but the hardiest of outdoors men.

Not once had he overheard guests discussing their professions in camp, nor pull rank on one another—even in the years leading up to the war. And during The Depression, when business was just steady enough to keep it afloat—no one would know by the look of the other or their gear, what they did for a living. If a guest was a politician or a garbage man, it never came up. Fishing and hunting were the only languages spoken, and most who came there spoke it fluently.

Some fished with bait—red worms, crickets, grasshoppers—with short rods and heavy reels. Some with wooden plugs or silver spoons; other with flies tied from feather and fur, and long fine rods made of split bamboo. Some, feigning the English aristocracy, fished only with floating dry flies, as a matter of principle. As a matter of principle too, these men also released the fish they caught, which

40

offended the sensibilities of nearly all the other fishermen, who liked to have their pictures taken beside stringers filled with their haul.

The only real disagreements in camp were over which was the best method to take trout, but in that, it was a sporting disagreement. Nonetheless, as days went by, it would invariably have the camp divided. An informal tally would be kept of fish caught per man on each method. Some attempted to goad others into joining their group. Some even went as far as changing tents, so as to sleep amongst their own. It always struck Ed as funny that men who never would've rubbed elbows in life left at the end of week as equals—all on account of their tackle preferences—and often with promises to meet in the off season for a drink.

And of course there were those who knew nothing of the outdoors or fishing at all. Men and women, young and old. The men he employed to guide these backcountry trips down to the rivers and high lakes were expected to teach these people how to fish, where to fish, and—at times—fill their stringers for them.

How these people ended up there, Ed would never know, and there were grumblings amongst the regulars—who'd visited without fail for a week or two every season since he'd opened camp—that Ed should instill the same referral policy that dude ranches required for guests. Ed wouldn't hear of it, as more often than not, these complaints only came when a newcomer was catching fish and the others were not.

He'd built the camp on the site of the homestead of an old hermit whose name no one remembered. How the man had survived there, living solely off the land, enduring those cruel winters, was anyone's guess. The homestead had been abandoned for twenty years when Ed came into it, and by then the roof was stove in and all type of critter and vermin had had their way with the place.

It was just an old log cabin, but well-built, and it was evident that some degree of thought had gone into it. The old pot bellied stove it housed, he reckoned, must've required great effort to get out there —enough that Ed had reused it when he turned the large cabin into what became the main lodge, along with the thick oak front door, which he always kept protected with a coat of red paint.

The use of the color red was an Indian way of warding off evil spirits, which may or may not have worked for the old hermit. Even the Sioux had found the region inhospitable. And as near as anyone could figure, judging from the note the hermit had curiously left nailed to that cabin door during the blizzard of 1903, stating he was out of food and the woodpile was frozen solid, he'd walked across the frozen lake with his dog, intending to shortcut the trail into town, carrying a box full of his gold.

When a trapper came by in the spring, before the thaw, the dog lay dead beside a thin section of ice. The trapper reasoned the old man had fallen in and, unwilling to let go of his box, sunk to the bottom of the lake. The dog, not wanting to leave his master, had frozen to death there, waiting for him to return.

Ed was there to greet the first guests of the season the following Saturday. He was standing on the edge of Cutthroat Lake, which was full of highly prized cutthroat trout, named so because of the distinctive red markings below their gills. The lake was a good sized, kidney shaped, and very deep, due to its glacial origins. Ed had once sat in a canoe and let out all the line on his bait casting reel—over three hundred feet—and his weight never touched bottom.

He stood there on the long dock that morning, smoking and looking out at a bank of dark rain clouds, fist pressed against his hip, studying them. He wore a red cravat around his neck, cowboy boots, hat, dungarees and a Pendleton shirt. As he turned at the sound of a whistle, he looked up to see Jessica standing there waving her arms at him.

She was dressed for the job of working in a hot kitchen, which left a lot of skin exposed. It was the first time he'd ever hired a woman cook, and he was concerned that she'd prove a distraction to his guests. And yet she'd given the impression, in the way she moved and talked in the weeks she prepped camp with him, that she was all business. She spoke plainly, and it was clear that she was used to being around men, and wasn't prone—either by her nature or as a self-protective measure—of getting close to them.

She was dressed in a pair of canvas short pants, leather boots, and wore her wool Henley with the sleeves rolled up. It was a man's outfit, and yet her shape was distinctly that of a woman. She wore no makeup or jewelry save for a pair of silver stud earrings and a ring that she said had belonged to her grandmother. She was ultimately fashion-less, which gave the overall effect of her having made no effort to draw attention herself, and it was precisely this which he feared might make her so attractive to his guests.

When he'd fished her out of the river the week before, reeking of booze, he knew that deep down she was troubled. One just coming to know herself and the hardships of life. It wasn't his business, he reasoned. And yet, like Esther—who he'd met forty years before— there was something about Jessica. He'd met only two women like her, and he'd married the first.

Esther respected him even when she didn't agree with him; she shared in his interests, even if she didn't need to participate in them. When he'd first come up to make this camp operational again after the war, when people said he should retire, Esther led the charge for him. When he told her he wanted one last season before he hung it up, she'd contacted every outfitter in the region, and to his surprise, people sent in their reservations, just as she said they would.

In his mind, men and women had their distinct roles, especially here. And if a woman expected equal pay, she should be willing to do equal work. And Jessica had done that, whether swinging an axe or hauling water. But Ed knew she'd taken the job without knowing how lonely it could be out here. By mid-season, when most employees began to itch for some freedom, maybe a little human companionship, he figured he'd find out then what she was made of.

And as he crested the hill to join her and saw the first tired horses making their way into camp and the guests atop them smiling at the sight of Jessica, he lifted a hand to wave. The pack train was led by his two guides, with fourteen guests trailing behind both on foot and horseback. He stood there with his thumbs in his belt, nodding and tipping his hat as they passed. Many of them were regulars, men he knew by name, and as they shouted out to him, he felt the thrill and satisfaction in having them in his camp again.

"Ed, you old coot," they yelled. "We're gonna really get them this year!"

The yelling and hooting went on a while, and Ed just stood back on his boot heels and laughed. The weariness he'd seen in their faces was gone as they seemed to realize their long trip had finally come to an end.

As the guides handled the horses, tying them up near the stables, the guests looked about the surroundings, some of them not having seen it since before the war. Other faces were entirely new to him, and as the group assembled, smiling and jabbering and shaking hands, a gentle but steady rain began to fall.

Ed raised his hands to quiet them, and dove into a speech which was as familiar to most of them as it was to him.

"Welcome gentlemen," he said, looking at all their faces. "I'm Ed. The boss here. Nice to have you all. I trust you all had a long ride up, so we'll get you settled in the lodge and then go over the rules. The guides will handle the horses. Just grab your gear and follow me over, and after we eat, we'll assign you to your bungalows."

The camp held twenty-eight guests, but as he counted off the role, there were—here in the early season when weather was often spotty—just fourteen men.

"Now, it's swell to see you all. Glad to have some of you back and to see some familiar faces. After yet another great war of ours has ended, if I can be solemn a moment…well, I realize there are some faces we will never see up this way again. Men who were brothers to these parts, men and boys that some of you all knew as well. To this we can do nothing but enjoy what they've fought for, as by all rights this wilderness here is as much yours as it is mine, as it was theirs. So as we enjoy it let's remember to give them thanks."

Assessing the group, they were for the most part experienced and capable men, fit, and in good health. There were a few younger men with them. Sons accompanying their fathers; often as a last chance to see where their fathers had liked to spend their time, before they were sent off into the world. While the gesture was respectable, Ed had often found these young men wholly unprepared and uninterested in the wilderness. They were smart enough not to ask if there was a radio on the premises, as there was nothing of the sort out here, or even true electricity, besides what came from a generator he ran for a few hours each day to keep the kitchen going. But often these young men would no sooner be unpacked than they'd be reaching for their comic books and a flashlight, and a place where they could lay down and sleep.

The rain became heavier and Ed waved his hands for them to all follow him inside. The men filed into the lodge, smearing

44

their muddy boots all over the clean floor—which would remain hopelessly dirty throughout the season—and as they apologized to Esther, having come from a world where floors were expected to be clean, Ed stood on a bench and addressed them.

"Now many of you have heard all this before, but bear with me. There are only two rules here at camp, and these rules are only meant to keep you safe, which will assure that places like this can operate. Never—and I repeat—never, has a man been killed here. And that's because we all respect nature, and follow a few simple rules."

Ed cleared his throat. "These rules are very clear—always listen to me, and always listen to your guides. At all times." He scanned the room, unblinking. "Understood? The weather is our worst enemy here. When he tells you it's time to come in, it's time to come in. I don't care if you have the biggest fish of your life on the line. Break him off and get back to camp. There will be other days. Your guide knows…he's had a lifetime of experience to know how fast things can go from bad to worse here. He's not jumpy, or skittish, or trying to save his own ass. If he says it's time to get a move on, he means it. You disobeying him could mean the difference between life and death. Got it?"

The men murmured and nodded.

"The second rule," he said, " is also a matter of life and death." He broke into a broad smile. "Stay out of Esther's and Jessica's kitchen here, and don't mess with their schedule. They've got lunch all laid out for us, but this is a special occasion as lunch is not usually served, as we'll all be out scaring up fish."

Ed looked at Jessica and Esther, both wearing aprons, hands behind their backs. "The lodge here opens at five a.m. sharp, closes at seven, and then opens for dinner at seven, and closes again at nine. Get in, get fed, and get out to where you need to be. In an effort to have this place clean and ready for you, it's off limits at all other times. Understood?" He scanned the rows of faces. "Life here revolves around the kitchen. It's a finely tuned machine. Don't mess with it."

He nodded at them and held out his upturned hands. "Now one last thing I want to settle before we eat. Some of you may have heard that this is to be our final season open up here, and I can tell you it's only with great reluctance that Esther and I have decided that's how things must be."

There were some groans among the group.

"Now, now." He lifted his hands again. "I assure you whatever happens, I'll do my damnedest to keep this place in the hands of folks like us if it's the last thing I do. I want, more than anything else, to have a place like this preserved so others can come and see it and use it just like we have. It just seems like the state has some other ideas for it." He looked at Esther. "Well, the taxes went up here during the war. Taxes they know damn well I can't pay by their deadline next year."

Ed paused as he looked over the group, a tear in the corner of his eye.

"Now I've said too much," Ed said. "Let's eat."

The men filed out into the main field after lunch, where there stood a large fire pit and wooden log bleachers surrounding it, for campfires and jamborees that happened whenever the weather was fine, or there was some reason to celebrate. But given the current weather it was a rather drab image, as all burned out campfires seem to be, especially when rain is falling on the white ashes of yesterday's good time.

After the men were shown to their bunks, and they were all settled in with their gear stowed, they heard the bray of a horse and watched as a lone straggler, food stores hastily lashed to his pack train, arrived. Ed went out to greet him. A kid name Jake—about twenty-three as near as he could figure—a yet untested guide who seemed about as cocky as they come, sitting smug up in the saddle of his sorrel, one side of his hat pinned up and a lever-action rifle laid across his lap.

"See any grizzlies?" someone shouted as several guests came out and gathered around him.

Jake didn't look at him and slid off the horse and stood there, seeming to enjoy being the center of attention.

"If I had, his hide would be draped over one of these here horses." He cocked the lever on his gun, expelling an unspent round and catching it in midair, before tucking it in his breast pocket.

Ed said to Esther, putting his arm around her as the guides helped un-strap the food: "And so it begins."

Ed overheard Jessica shooing men out of the cafeteria, who'd already come in from the rain to ask for coffee when they should've been in their bunks assembling their gear for an afternoon fishing trip out on the lake. And he figured it struck her then that men who'd come all that way to be in the great outdoors sure seemed to hate the idea of actually being out in it.

He watched as she handed them cups of coffee, brushed them away and resumed unpacking the newly arrived stores. All seemed to think this was a loose rule until they saw her at work first hand. Esther and Jessica were—at two in the afternoon—already preparing dinner, and didn't need these men in the way of having it ready for them. Meal prep was a full-time job, one which couldn't get done if they seemed to think the lodge was some sort of midday gathering place.

Finally, tired of handing out coffee, Jessica yelled: "You all get now. When I ring the supper bell you can all come on in but as for now, if you want a hot supper tonight, kitchen's closed."

Ed came and took these guests down to the lake, unlashed several boats, put three men in each, while the rest sat on the dock or on the shoreline. While the guides rowed the boats out onto the lake, one pair of guests—a father and a son—came down to the water carrying some new fangled spinning rods, which he and the others had only heard about, but had never seen in the flesh.

They were fine outfits—fiberglass rods, English made reels. They showed their function to those gathered there—the bail arm that gathered the line neatly while the spool moved up and down. The two guests were very proud of their modern tools, and asked the others there on the dock to stand back while they demonstrated their use.

"You can cast lighter lures on a lighter line," the father said, opening the bail and casting a tiny spoon shaped lure—no heavier than a pebble—nearly a hundred and fifty feet out into the lake. He snapped the bail closed and began to reel in the fine thread line. To the amazement of all there, he immediately hooked a fish.

The man stood there calmly, adjusting the drag and holding the rod steady as the fish began to take out line.

"Cross his eyes, Daddy," the boy said and the man lifted the rod tip, and with a confident jerk, set the hook in the fish's mouth. The man appeared in complete control until the fish seemingly grew larger as the battle continued, and then suddenly began swimming away at a pace that had the reel screaming.

The man looked down helplessly at his fancy new reel, displeased at being made the fool, while the others stood there laughing.

"The damn fish is running me out of line!" he yelled.

But soon those sitting on the dock stood, their smiles gone, as the reel began to screech and the rod bent until it looked like it would snap. Ed joined the growing crowd, lifting his hat as the fish ran far and deep into the lake.

"I'll be damned," someone muttered. "No fish that big in this lake."

"Someone cut my line before he breaks my rod!" The man shouted frantically, looking at the crowd. "Hurry!"

A man came forward with a pocket knife, but before he could open the blade, all the line paid off the reel until the knot securing it gave with a final and resounding *ping!* The group stood there in the ensuing silence, gazing out at the lake, then the rod—now returned to a straight position—as if trying to understand what had just happened.

A moment of silence followed, as it often did when a large fish was lost.

"I would've been able to land him on my old bait rod," one man offered smugly, breaking the silence. No one answered him. They just stared out at the water and then at the man who'd lost the fish, as he turned and walked dejectedly back up the hill with his son scurrying behind.

One guest tried to cast his bait rig out to where the fish had been hooked, but the bait flung off and the hook fell empty not fifty feet from the dock. As he muttered and reeled in his line, Ed tossed his cigarette into the water. Indeed there was nothing that big in Cutthroat Lake, and while those standing there believed it had only been a big fish, and the tackle not up to snuff, he had the unsettling feeling that it had been something more than that.

He'd once hooked a two hundred pound Marlin down in Florida and it had made a reel sing like that. But no cutthroat trout had taken out all of a man's line, new fangled rod or not. As the misting rain turned to a cold, steady drizzle, a chill passed through him; there beneath him in the silvery, stirring water, Ed had seen the reflection of an old man he didn't recognize staring back up at him. While the others headed back to camp, he stood on the edge of the dock, his shirt soaked through, until the gusting rain obscured any last sign of him.

Six

As Francine stepped into the Sundowner to meet Jim Hickens for a drink and to talk business, the twenty heads in the place turned. She was early. The room was lit mostly by neon, and the sunlight pouring in made the patrons squint at the figure standing in the doorway. She wore a blue dress, gold necklace, and heels—and must've appeared as if she'd walked into the wrong bar, all alone, there in a part of the country where women don't travel alone.

But she wasn't naïve. She wasn't lost. She was quite aware that her presence would attract attention, and that those in town who'd heard of her arrival would be curious about the New Yorker who'd bought The Flying U Ranch. And she also knew the heavy clunk her pocketbook made when she dropped it on the bar and ordered a whiskey, the pistol barrel sticking out, confirmed that she had protection from anyone who might try and take advantage.

The bar's exterior was a log cabin façade, to make it appear as if it was from pioneer times, thus striking a tourist's notion of what a proper western bar should be. Stepping further inside, Francine saw that the joke was on them, as the bar was not more than ten years old. The walls were pine board, the floors beige linoleum, except the area nearest the cigarette machine and the jukebox—the dance floor—covered in a green and white checkered tile. The Formica bar was lined with bare lights, turned down so low that their filaments glowed not unlike matches that had just been blown out.

There were several west facing windows, but long canvas shades were pulled tight to the window sills, assuring that not even a patch of light could sneak in. The ceiling glowed with neon beer signs, which shimmered on the mounted heads and bodies of various mammal and bird lining the wall.

A smoky haze filled the room, which consisted of the bar

and a few circular tables, and a small bandstand beside the dance floor. It was not being used when she walked in, but as the jukebox began to play a scratchy Texas Playboys song, a young man asked a woman to dance and they sauntered out onto the floor.

Francine felt a twinge of envy, watching them. She'd already reconciled that the best years of her romantic life were behind her, and before her now lay a life of practicality. She understood this as well as she understood anything. She was nearing thirty. Likely a decade older than the girl who was twirling and giggling on the dance floor.

She'd truly given her best years to her marriage. And although for months she and Dottie had pointed fingers at her husband, as she sat there at that bar, a dark and murky shadow cast over her, it seemed that the finger had now been turned to her.

And perhaps justly. Her courtship with Thomas had been so brief and matter of fact it had taken their parents' breath away. That here were two young people so sure of what they wanted from life. What sunny times those had seemed to her then— after all, marriage was something she'd always dreamt about. And her mother, of course, had been thrilled—her Frannie, a Gladinger? Francine had felt quite the prize then, as the best asset a young woman had, she'd been taught, was her purity.

And in many ways, it had escaped even her marriage unscathed. So, she'd ignored his cold kisses on her cheek. The frequent trips he took with his business partner, leaving her alone in their fancy home. Something was wrong from the start and she'd known it. And yet she hadn't done a thing about it, instead distracting herself with all the things that riches bought, convincing herself that the higher she was lifted in the world, the smaller her marital problems would become.

It had been a pact, she saw that now. Unspoken perhaps, but one she'd entered blindly. Perhaps willingly. Thomas had always been the savvy one and she the out of towner, perpetually breaking off a heel in a subway grate, much to his embarrassment. He'd taken advantage, plain and simple; cheated and lied and gotten everything he wanted. Of that, there was no doubt.

But she'd been duped; both by Thomas, and by herself. And

51

so if she carried herself coldly now, erect and dignified, it was simply because she had to. To compensate for all the years of having been made the fool.

Francine watched as her drink was placed in front of her. As she tried to pay, the bartender, a squat woman with a gold tooth, held up her hand.

"I'm Griff," she said, introducing herself. "You the one who bought the old ranch? Will Heaton said if you come in here everything is on the house."

"Mister Heaton?"

"Yeah, he owns the place. Owns most everything this side of town. He said if a fancy lady came in it would probably be you."

"Well he doesn't own *me*. So if it's just the same," she said, holding out a dollar bill, "I'd rather pay my own way."

Griff had already turned and left to answer a call for another drink. Sighing, Francine placed the bill on the bar. As she sipped from the smudged glass, the sour warmth of the whiskey spreading through her, she began to relax.

"So," Griff said when she returned to refill her glass, "you done bought the old place."

"Why yes," Francine said.

"Shame. That place was for a sale a long time and no one would touch it."

"I can't see why not. It's a beautiful place," Francine said, but when she looked up, the woman had turned again to fill more glasses.

She cautiously eyed the men lining the bar, some of them talking and laughing loudly to attract her attention. They wore woven straw hats with leather tassels, bright plaid shirts with pearl buttons; their faces were open and handsome, their eyes bright and clear. They were pleasant enough—good boys—but not for her.

For the few brave enough to approach, she did nothing more than look straight ahead, sipping from her drink, thanking them if they lit her cigarette, saying only that she was waiting for someone —a man—who'd be there any minute, which was enough for them to tip their hats before re-joining their friends with a mere shrug of their shoulders.

"I'm not supposed to say things like this," Jim said when he arrived, removing his hat and ordering a steak for them both, "but I heard through the grapevine that three hundred acres on your side of town might be coming up for sale. Cutthroat Lake and the surrounding mountains. Man who owns it is taxed up to his ears. Now I may be speaking too soon, but I'm saying this before Heaton gets wind of it, which he may already have. It won't be cheap. But if you're interested, I can get the papers drawn up. All I'll need is some kind of deposit."

"Yes, of course. I'm very interested."

"The thing about it is that it's almost all mountainside. Wilderness. It's not ranching land."

"Well, I don't know what I can do with that."

"Well, some are thinking Heaton's trying to turn this into some sort of winter resort town. Like they did all over Colorado. And that he's gonna buy up that land and carve that mountain into God knows what, and you'd have a bi-way and a goddamned ski lodge towering over your little ranch there."

His face was getting red as he spoke; spit flew from his mouth like sparks. He held up his hand. "Now I'm sorry, but folks getting upset about an outsider buying up their old places is one thing, but turning the side of our mountains into a winter playground is enough to get me razzed."

He sat there, catching his breath. "So you can see, once I got wind of this, I wanted to talk to you. The thing is, Francine, it's expensive. The kind of thing only a guy like Heaton could afford."

When the steaks came, Francine just stared at the blood pooling on her plate. Perhaps that's all there was to Heaton's cards, she thought, smiling; and how proud he'd seemed with his grand idea. *Skiing.*

"How expensive?" she asked.

"Twenty thousand dollars is what's owed in taxes, and that's all the owner wants. Then he and the misses are gonna head down to Texas and retire."

Francine nearly dropped her fork, and Jim didn't bother to look and see her reaction.

"That's big money for these parts, I know. But it's some of the most beautiful wilderness you'll ever see. There was word it was going to be bought up by the Rockefellers or some such thing, but that never came to pass. I suppose even to them, it wasn't worth the price." He picked up his own fork. "But how do you put a price on such a thing? Those mountains are Braxton. Without them, I'm not sure this town ever would've existed. Would be a real shame to see it get all carved up."

A dark cloud hung over the table. He pointed with his fork. "That's a T-Bone you got there. You're too skinny and you have a lot of work ahead of you. Eat up."

After he left, she stayed, finishing her drink. The meal had been paid for by Will Heaton. Nothing Jim or she said could get Griff to take their money.

As she sat there, she found herself staring at a figure that had just walked in and sat opposite her. He set his black hat on the bar top and ordered a bottle of beer. When it came he began absently lassoing it with a piece of string; drawing it tight, loosening it again. He looked up in her direction from time to time while ignoring the two young women who came and sat beside him, intent on catching his attention.

He looked about twenty-five. A quaff of jet black hair. As if to accentuate it, he wore a dark black shirt, black jeans, and black boots. He had high cheekbones, sharp sideburns, and dark, brooding eyes. To her, he looked like a gunslinger, even if the only gunslinger she'd ever seen was in a Hollywood film.

Her drink gone, she looped an arm through her pocketbook and headed out the door without looking back. She walked across the parking lot, turning when she reached the DeSoto. From there she saw the cowboy appear in the open doorway and place his hands on its upper frame, watching her closely.

Poor little fool she thought, watching as he sauntered out, boot heels dragging in the gravel. He may have thought himself some smoldering movie star, but he was no gunslinger. He was, like everything in this town, just a façade.

54

Before she drove off, she watched him climb in an old truck. As the lights of the Sundowner faded behind her, its headlights suddenly appeared in her rear view mirror. Her heart began to beat double-time, and when she accelerated, it stayed close behind, even as she turned and sped along the driveway to her place.

Her hand fumbled in her pocketbook as she pulled up to her dark house, and when she stepped from the car, dust spilling over her, the man was already out of the truck, its headlights aimed on her. She stood in the door jamb and with both hands raised the pistol into the blinding light.

The man didn't slow as he came and stood before the end of her gun. She was trembling as he reached out and snatched it away from her.

"I knew you wouldn't use it when the time came," he said, opening the cylinder gate and removing the bullets. "I'll be keeping these so you don't get hurt."

"What do you want?" she asked, backing up against her car, shading her eyes from the light.

"You don't belong here." His voice was deep and steady, his mouth hardly moving when he spoke. "No one wants you here. Not even me."

"And who the hell," she asked, "are you?"

"I'm Sonny. Jim hired me to spruce up the place before you came. He doesn't know I stayed on, but I wanted to make sure you got on okay." He handed her the empty gun. "But I decided tonight in the bar...I can't be liable for you."

"You followed me there?" She blushed. *That's* why he'd been watching her, because he was getting *paid* to.

"A woman out here all alone. Only a matter of time before something bad happens." He crossed his arms. "I don't understand what people like you have in mind when you come out here, but I can tell you this isn't New York City. There's no one to hear you when you yell for help. So I think it's best you go back home."

He tipped his hat as he turned to leave.

"You hold on there a minute," Francine said, springing off the car. "I never asked you to watch out for me. I never asked you to stay." She shook her head. "I'm here for business. *Money.* Is that something you can understand?"

"I don't know much about business," he said as he walked back to his truck, "but neither do you if you bought this old place."

"That's fine. You go on. You strike me as the type that likes to stay out of things anyway."

"Lady, what do you know?" he asked, turning.

"I know men like you. The kind who don't like to get involved in anything. Might explain why you're living out here behind my house."

"Well, I'll be on my way in the morning then if that suits you."

"Nothing would please me more," she said weakly, reaching for her pocketbook, which had fallen during all her fumbling.

"Good luck," Sonny said as he climbed back in his truck. "I'll be out of your way at first light."

"Shame," she said, stepping inside her house and locking the door behind her, "I kind of liked him."

That night she was again awakened by the sound of howling wolves and lay there in bed gripping the empty gun. At daybreak, she went and knocked on Sonny's door, hoping he hadn't left. She watched as the door swung open and he appeared, staring at her wearily. He was shirtless, lean and muscular. A bandage was wrapped around his left arm, spotted with blood.

"I'll be gone in a minute."

"Before you go," she said, trying to look away. "I'll be needing those bullets back."

He leaned on the door frame, brushing back his hair. "You can get a whole box of them in town. But I'm not giving those bullets back."

She sighed, pausing a moment, then looked at him dead on. "I've decided I want you to stay on here. That is, if you're free."

He looked back at her, squinting. Except she couldn't tell if he was squinting or if that was how he always looked.

"On one condition," she added. "You help me fix this place back up. Then I'll hire you on when it's a functioning ranch. You look like you know your way around a place like this."

"I have other obligations yet. To friends I still haven't seen, since the war." He looked down, and seeing he was still bare-chested, reached for his shirt.

"I realize this is all beneath you, and in your esteem maybe I am too. But for all your chivalry, I owe you some kind of debt."

He shook his head slowly as he buttoned the shirt, as if to apologize before he drove on out of there. Just as he said he would the night before.

"Maybe you're right about me." She stood up straight then, unable to keep a flood of emotion from her voice. "I'm no good at business. But I'm bound and determined to turn this place back into the best, whip-crack dude ranch this town has seen in a long time." She squinted back at him. "I'm going to work my fingers to the bone. Scrub this place until it shines like a new dime."

He smiled for the first time. "Why in God's name would you want to do such a thing?"

"I have my reasons."

"People are going to say you're crazy, you know."

"If I let what people say bother me, I'd still be in Manhattan, married to a scoundrel." She folded her arms "So what do you say?"

"Thing is, Miss…"

"Lilley."

"The truth is, Miss Lilley, I'm on the lam, as they say. My family doesn't know where I am and I haven't shown my face in town except for last night." He laughed softly. "And anyway, maybe you were right about me too. I was really in the thick of things over there, so I'm just laying low a while, to try and clear my head."

She looked at the worn pine boards on which she stood, then back up at him. "I understand."

"And I've got enough money saved to have bought this place outright. But," he added, "I surely don't have your gumption. Everyone says that my home town here has seen its day. To think that it could be something great again makes me feel…hopeful."

For a moment, he could've been talking about her. Or about himself. Or maybe he was just trying to let her down easy.

"If I stay on," he said, looking at her squarely, "I want a cut. I'll work with you for free, and when this place is up and going, I'll take twenty-five percent of the profit."

"Well, I'm sure there's a dozen men I could hire in town for a decent wage."

"Not like me, Miss Lilley," he said, crossing his arms, "not like me. I knew this ranch in its prime. And I know what it's going to take to get it back there. And I also know what it's like for people to call you crazy."

She bit her lip, considering his offer. "Can you work with your arm like that?"

"It's just a cut." He covered the bandage with his hand. "It's almost healed."

She stood there, studying him a long time. "Very good then, Mister…"

"Trace. Sonny Trace."

"Well, Mister Trace," she said, extending her hand. "A gentleman's agreement, so to speak?"

"Call me Sonny," he said, shaking her hand firmly.

She was about to say that she'd prefer to keep it formal, but stopped herself. "I'm Francine," she replied, breaking into a broad smile. "It will be nice working with you, Sonny."

Seven

Will Heaton stared at the mutilated carcass of his prized calf, lying there in the sun. It looked like a prune, the skin drawn so tight that he could see its ribs, the outline of its skull. Beyond, the pines grew thicker and thicker until the forest was pure blackness. He turned from where he was crouched beside the calf and looked towards the barn, where it had been safely secured the night before. He knew, because he'd bottle fed it himself, rubbing its head until it fell asleep in a pen he'd lined with fresh straw.

It had taken some breeding to get a calf like that. Pure Texas Longhorn. Its mother had died in birth and soon after he watched it shakily roaming the corral, looking for a teat, but each cow would brush it away, until at last, laughing, he took to tending it. It embarrassed him, and he acted like it was a burden. But he'd smile when it came gamboling up to him, and although he knew it foolish, he'd named the calf—the pride and future of his herd —Henry.

"Damn it." He looked down at the calf's bulging eyes and turned away. His line riders stood behind him, hands on their hips, one of them holding the reins of their horses. His dog Codger sat there growling uneasily at the woods.

"Looks like we've got a real problem on our hands, boys," Heaton said.

"I've never seen the likes of it," the one holding the horses replied. "They didn't even eat it. Just ham-stringed it."

"Hell, didn't even eat his ears or tongue," the other said, kneeling down beside it, lifting its head. "If it's wolves, they bit it in the neck. Dragged it out here. Shots must've scared them off before they had a chance."

"It done lost all its blood." The horse tender gathered the reins tightly and looked back towards the barn. "But there ain't no blood trail here."

Heaton looked back from the direction it had been dragged.

Nearly a quarter mile. But there was no sign of it ever having even touched the ground.

"Could a bear have done this?" he asked, showing the first sign of uncertainty he ever had in front of his employees. "Doesn't look like something coyotes could do."

They all stood there studying it, rubbing their heads.

"Hell," the horse tender said, "Codger here was the only one that got a look, and unless he starts talking, I'm not sure we'll really know."

"Whatever it was, it'll come back tonight, then we'll know." Heaton stood and removed his hat and scanned the forest. He then looked back down the hill to where his house stood. Even from a half-mile away it looked giant, looming like a black shadow as high as the distant mountains.

"Did you all see that Francine?" he asked, climbing on top of his horse. "Boy she doesn't like me."

"That'll change, sir," the horse tender said, handing him the reins. "She's just got her guard up now. She'll come around."

"I don't know if I want her to come around." He brushed back his hair and put his hat on his head. He looked off at her house, nearly a mile off. "That woman is trouble if I've ever seen it. Best we keep our distance."

He turned in his saddle and gathered the reins, pausing to look down at his calf lying there.

"You all clean this up," he said. "We'll keep watch here tonight."

The men just looked at the calf. "What do you want us to do with Henry, I mean *it*, sir?"

"Burn it," he said without looking, putting his spurs to the horse. The dog sat there a long moment, growling, before it turned and followed after his master, who, as he crested a hill and descended upon his homestead, brushed a sleeve across his eyes.

As he bathed and dressed, he watched from his bedroom window, the tendrils of black smoke rising into the clear blue sky. The windows were tall, lined by thick blue drapes, giving a wide view of the eastern mountains. A shortwave radio played in the corner, broadcasting the morning news from Los Angeles. He stood in front of a walnut dresser, running his fingers through the bristles of a brush, staring at himself in the mirror.

Despite the din of the radio, there was an interminable silence about the house. What liveliness there'd been years before, was filled now with the plodding footsteps and sour voices of his cronies, who were now coming back to the barn to tie up their horses and fetch his car.

After combing his hair, he slipped on a cream colored suit coat, adjusted his black tie, eying the photograph on his dresser. It was that of a young woman, dressed in white, sitting on a velvet sofa. His wife, Matilda. Childhood friend, adolescent sweetheart. Who'd known him when he was just a kid living in a dirt floor shack.

More often than not, he could forget what had happened to her, but today, the image of the calf reminded him of that weak, sallow look she'd had in her final days.

A knock sounded on the door frame, and when he turned, a young woman was standing there, wearing nothing but a paisley silk robe, untied, a long slit of creamy skin that went from her painted toes to her bottle blonde hair.

She leaned sleepily in the door jamb, paying no mind to him or the photograph, interested only at the scene outside the window.

Her voice was reedy and high when she spoke. "I thought I smelled smoke," she said, inspecting her fingernails. As she entered the room, reaching for the photograph on his dresser, he grabbed her wrist.

"Hey, what's the big deal?"

He buttoned his suit coat. "It's time for me to get to work."

There came a pause, her eyes scanning the room, filled with heavy furniture and a large brass framed bed. "When you gonna let me sleep in here with you?"

He grinned at her. "When I make an honest woman out of you."

"That'll be the day," she said, drawing her robe closed.

He released her and walked past her to the hat rack by the door.

"You're a piece of work, you know that? You keep me in that dingy hotel in town and call for me whenever you want me, and then you won't even let me in your room."

He selected a hat from the rack, gray with a black band, and ran the brim through his fingers.

The girl stood studying the photograph, before her eyes finally turned to him. "Are you still in love with her?"

A voice shouted from downstairs. "Mister Heaton, your car is ready out front."

"Get dressed," he said to the girl. "I'll give you a ride back into town."

Pulling up outside the hotel, engine idling, he produced a roll of cash from his pocket. He held it out to her. "Pay your bill and go on home. There's enough here for a train ticket, expenses, and a trunk full of mink coats."

She looked at the tremendous wad of cash. "You really know how to make a lady feel filthy don't you?"

People walking by on the boardwalks had stopped to admire his silver Duesenberg.

"And what does it make me if I take that?" She eyed at the cash a moment, then the kid who was standing there ogling the car. "What are you looking at buddy? Get moving."

Heaton chuckled. "I have a feeling you're going to be just fine."

"What do you care?" She grabbed the cash and without looking at it, slipped it in her purse. "There's nothing for me back in Cheyenne." She got out of the car and stood there with her arms crossed. "I had high hopes when I came here, William Heaton. High hopes."

"You should head for Hollywood. A face like that can take you far out there."

She blushed. "Do you really think so?"

"Have I ever been wrong about anything?"

"You're full of it." She smirked, dropping her arms "God help the woman who falls in love with you."

"I'm afraid that ship has already sailed for me. But you're young. There's still hope for you yet."

He tipped his hat, leaving her there as he drove out of town, looking at his watch.

He was late.

The bulldozers and steam shovels were already at work as he pulled up at his latest construction site, pushing and lifting dirt into a great pile. He watched the greasy machinery, the shaking earth beneath them, sending dust clouds into the wind. There were men in overalls and hard hats, yelling and pointing. He was employing half the town out here, he thought, stepping from the car.

The foreman greeted him, holding a roll of blueprints. He listed all that had been done: rock blasted and removed. Trees slashed and cleared. The ground had been leveled and the outline of the airstrip was already in place.

It looked, Heaton thought, admiring the torn landscape, much like a battlefield. To the northwest he could see the mountain where the resort would be, a string line already running from the base to the mountaintop—a chair lift that would soon be operational. The first of its kind in Wyoming.

Soon it would be a new section of town—Winter Park—he intended to call it. With a resort hotel, a heated indoor pool, a full service restaurant. There'd be entertainment, and if the paperwork got pushed through—from the many hands he'd greased—there'd be gambling too.

To the north and east, across the bowl-shaped impression in the valley, stood his own tract of land as well as the old dude ranch adjacent, and to the east of it a mountainside that rivaled the one he was building on in the west. Soon, he'd own that too, and connect the mountains, and then this dingy old cattle town would acquire a level of prosperity theretofore unseen.

The foreman flattened the blueprints on the car's coffin-shaped hood. The airport terminal drawings had come from Switzerland, as had most of the architectural designs he'd already incorporated into the development of Winter Park.

The terminal would be aluminum and glass—modern, clean, bright. From his airport they could be bussed to his resorts, a chalet, or one of his ski lodges. There'd be accommodations for any budget. And, he thought, looking at the airstrip where there would soon be daily flights arriving from California, he'd get a percentage of every ticket sold, for every plane that touched down here.

This was no business for the weak-hearted, he thought,

standing there and looking out over his work. And the next year would prove whether he'd make good or if this old hardscrabble town would break his back.

That night, back at the ranch, he and his cronies sat watch behind a bale of straw. The air was clear and cold, their breath coming out as steam. Staked to a chain out in the back field was a live calf, larger than Henry had been, and from where they lay in wait they could hear its soft bleating.

Around eleven, the three of them drifting in and out of sleep, the cattle in the barn began to stir. Will had settled down but a moment before he heard the distant and chilling howl of a wolf. The single note soon became a chorus.

"Ain't no coyote," one of his cowhands said, opening his eyes.

"No," Heaton said, putting his rifle up on the straw bales. It was a military surplus M3 Carbine, replete with an infrared telescopic sight. He flipped a switch and the giant scope began to hum, the reticle filling with a fuzzy light.

He scanned the rifle over the field, turning knobs, until he could make out the shape of the calf. It was resting now, lifting its head only when the wolves howled, to let out a trembling bleat.

Zooming out to the edge of the woods, he saw the rocks—a fainter shade of white—still warm from the sun, and the underside of leaves, warmed from the rising heat.

His cronies were staring off into the dark beside him when he first caught sight of a shape moving behind the trees. His heart began to knock perceptibly as he drew back the bolt and slid a round into the chamber. Finger steady on the trigger, he watched the figure moving through the woods towards him, growing larger and larger as it came, stopping occasionally to sniff the air, until at last it stood at the wood line, where it filled his gun sight.

"Mary, mother of God," he said. He pulled back from the scope, blinked, and saw that the world was incredibly dark. Putting his eye back to the scope, he zoomed in again, but the shape was gone. When he moved the rifle, he saw that the calf was gone too, the ground freckled with warm blood where it had been not a minute ago.

A chill passed through him. "Let's get back inside fast, boys," he said, standing and leveling the rifle out at the field. He was night blind, and in the grainy haze of blackness, the world held a supernatural possibility to him that it had not moments before. For that one second, he indulged the possibility what he'd seen bore no resemblance to any living creature he'd ever known, and had not been of this earth.

"What in hell was it?" his line riders yelled, as soon as they were inside with the door dead-bolted behind them. Heaton brushed at the air, trying to regain his cool, dignified composure while sitting there holding out his hands, blinking, until they came into focus.

He looked at them then, catching his breath, Codger hiding under his legs. He shook his head when they repeated their question, gazing up at their frightened faces, his own glistening with sweat.

"I don't know, but there's something big out there." He stared back out the window. "Something I've never seen the likes of before."

Eight

The task of feeding nearly thirty hungry mouths, Ed's wife Esther was to remind Jessica all that summer, was about keeping it simple, both in recipe and menu. Esther was in all measures a very exacting woman, as tightly bound as the bun on the back of her head. Her hands were sinewy, calloused, and yet she always wore a cotton dress. Although she was near sixty, her hair was still jet black and she showed no signs of slowing. Along with thrift and rock solid efficiency she had, in Jessica's mind, all the qualities of a pioneer woman, including the less desirable ones, like piousness.

Esther prided herself to Jessica on only needing twenty-five ingredients to make all their meals. The matter of quantity was another matter, upon which she relied on the weekly pack team that came up the mountain from town, to replenish her wares. She always ran out at the first sight of it to tear through the packs, and would cry out and nearly faint if something was forgotten. And yet, she was always sure that she had surplus staples in her inventory—flour, beans and salt—so they'd have enough to tide them through an extra week if need be.

Rice. Ten pounds. Flour, fifteen. Salt. Three pounds.

Beans. Fifty pounds a week. They ate them for breakfast and dinner. Lots of beans. Brown, black, white. With rice or without. Sunday nights they went all out—country fried steak, gravy, mashed potatoes, biscuits, with a side of buttered corn and a chocolate fudge sheet cake for afterwards. But the rest of the week, there were beans.

Drinks. Two percolators stood on a table at the entrance to the lodge—both filled with coffee. They ran constantly. Milk was always of the powdered variety, and drinks were the same, consisting of things that many of the guests wouldn't have thought of drinking otherwise—powdered lemon and orange juice. And yet all commented, with addition to the food, how damn good everything tasted out here. As cooks, Jessica knew they had this at their advantage, as when it was raw and wet out, a simple thing like a hot hoecake and coffee tasted like heaven.

The men often spent their evenings gathered in a bungalow, passing the time by telling stories or playing cards, while their wet gear dried by a wood stove. The very nature of this place, its isolation, removed the pressures placed upon them at home, as they were men who were depended on by their families, children, wives, and even their country. And it was here, Jessica noted, that life once again became simple. Winning the pot in a game of poker, landing the biggest trout of the day, brought a person a sense of satisfaction that was hard to find elsewhere in the world.

Of course there were men who took it more seriously. Who judged themselves based on their prowess as hunters and fisherman. They'd come there to try and best a state record in trout or elk, and had been pursuing such a goal their whole lives. To such men, this place was a testing ground of their manhood, and regardless of its merit, she found that their gung-ho enthusiasm was infectious to the others.

Esther and Jessica respected such men, and their care for them came not in wifely ways, but by way of feeding them, nurturing the inner fire that burned in all of them. While their physical presence was separated by a curtain that divided the kitchen from the dining room itself, their presence there as women was needed, and felt.

Behind this wall they themselves were functioning in every endeavor that was womanly, and this disparity was not lost to anyone who visited—although it may have been forgotten at times by those who winked or placed an unwanted hand upon Jessica's waist. But within the code of nature there was a set of rules, established and enforced in a tribe-like situation that existed in such a camp, and in this the errant hand would be smacked away with impunity, or otherwise removed by simply moving her body, which was in motion from the moment she rose until she went to bed.

Hers was still a young woman's body, unfamiliar with the aches and pains which Esther seemed to know so well, with the creams she applied to her joints every night after the dishes were dry, when she complained quietly how time had robbed her in many ways. With Esther's pretty, if not deeply lined face, came the subtle warning to Jessica that time was a swift lover, and if not careful, it could sneak up and ravish you.

And as much as Esther seemed to like her being there, Jessica also knew she felt the job belonged to someone older. More settled. That at Jessica's age, she felt women should be doing whatever it is young women were supposed to be doing. And any woman who thought it wise to fritter away her best years out in the woods was either foolish or running away from something, or both.

And so, Jessica felt the nagging sense that she needed to put her better qualities to work while she could. And yet the men who came here were, without fail, married. To a woman who saw the world in black and white, a married man was strictly off limits, and discredited from being any sort of romantic interest the moment she saw the ring.

While it remained unspoken, Esther seemed to think that love was, in the end, a practical matter, and the simpler one kept it the better. This showed in her marriage to Ed, which seemed not unlike a firm handshake. In this she may have seen herself in Jessica, or wanted to see herself.

And yet Jessica already knew that pain was temporary, as was pleasure. Pleasure, at least where love was concerned, always had a lingering to it that could cloud the mind. That had no use out here. Had no real use in her life as far as she could see.

Pain was swift and decisive, but she found that it dug furrows, deep and lingering. Those dark thoughts of the past year were there each night as she fell asleep, and followed her into her dreams, then snapped her awake each morning, like the echoing cries of a baby she'd never been able to hear.

Each night, the guests fed and nestled in their bunks, Jessica and Esther stood cleaning up while Ed made the rounds, to see that the men had everything they needed and that their gear was stowed for the morning. Were it hunting season, all rifles were cleaned and ready to be put into battery immediately upon leaving camp. A herd of elk could bolt up a hill and within minutes be two miles and several mountain ridges away from where a hunter had patiently stalked them for a day. And so, triggers and hammers need not fall on empty chambers. The safety of such weapons, according to a popular expression around camp, was between one's ears.

In the off chance a gun was to go off unexpectedly, Ed had warned the group, the hunter would be escorted back to camp—handling his own weapon the entire way, as no one disarmed another man out there—where he'd be left to wait on the next available exit from the camp. His refund for the remainder of his trip would be made available to him, but Jessica doubted a man would ever accept it, and would take it as his penance, counting themselves lucky that no one been killed by their negligence.

Each night, Jessica would bring in fresh water from the well while Esther wiped down the floors and tables. Percolators would be filled for the morning, whereupon at promptly four-thirty they'd throw the switches and the orange pilot lights would flicker and they'd wait there a breathless minute to hear the steaming and bubbling sound they made, pausing momentarily as they passed through the dining hall, setting out plates or lighting burners for the warming lanterns on the buffet table, to hear if they were still working.

Coffee was no joke out here—breakfast could be bad, but coffee had to be hot and on time to those waking up in the cold and wandering in there still half-asleep. Even those who professed to avoiding coffee at home drank it out here, and some even asked the type upon leaving, often surprised that it was just a cheap grocery brand, again proving to her that everything tastes better out in camp.

Jessica often looked out the little window while she worked and saw the guides busy at work. Ed allowed the guides half-hour meals, but they never seemed to take them. They'd come in and split a biscuit, toss some bacon and eggs in it, then walk out the door with a steaming cup of coffee in the other hand, and eat beside their horses.

The guides would often be up at midnight, while everyone else was snoring, checking and double checking packs, and were lucky to get four hours sleep. These were the men upon which the entire camp relied for successful fishing and hunting trips. They were required not only to find fish and elk, but to carry extra food rations and know how to make impromptu shelters, should hunters decide to stay in close proximity of game, or otherwise be prepared for whatever situation the unrelenting wilderness might require.

Each guide, at all times, per camp policy, was required to have on their person a high caliber revolver, large enough to penetrate the hide of a charging grizzly. They were each required to demonstrate to Ed that they could, at a moment's notice, draw upon and kill such a creature, by shooting at a dummy target he swung at them from an old clothesline that he'd tied to a high tree branch.

While an old laundry bag stuffed with leaves and a charging grizzly were two different things, it was an important skill to have, as bear often attacked when a man's back was turned. And while no one had been charged in about ten years, and few bears had actually been seen—and even then only at a distance—the rule remained in place.

The guides were a rotating crew of about three or four young men. Many were ranch hands in town who came out when work was slow, and Jessica didn't get much of a chance to know any of them. They were a clique to which she and the guests themselves were not entirely privy. Ed had confided to her that, being in short supply, he often had to hire men he hadn't worked with or otherwise knew anything about, being forced to take them at their word that they knew what they were doing.

As Jessica watched one evening that spring, she saw these large pistols strapped to the hips of the guides as they packed their gear for the morning fishing trip, gleaming in the moonlight, silver and blue. One of the newly hired on guides was a man named Jake— more of a kid really—short and loud mouthed. She'd heard him bragging of his exploits, his prowess with horse and cattle and even the vast wilderness itself. All talk, as far as she was concerned. He was handsome yet, with dark hair and piercing blue eyes, and damn if he didn't know it. One night, Jake had looked up and saw her watching from the window and grinned crudely, before resuming his work.

She never carried a pistol herself—couldn't afford one. She did carry an old beat-up 30/30 rifle in a scabbard across her horse. Although some said it wasn't strong enough, she knew that the bottleneck cartridge it fired had been around over fifty years, and wouldn't have been were it not enough to get the job done. As she stood there scrubbing pots and pans each night, the old rifle was leaned in one corner of the kitchen, cocked and loaded. If a bear smelled food and decided to push through the side door—or even a guy like Jake, drunk and with lust in his eyes—she'd be ready, and more than happy to pull the trigger.

Nine

During the night, someone had cut down The Flying U Ranch sign by the front gate. Neat as you please. Francine and Sonny sat atop their horses staring down at it, nearly twenty feet tall and thirty feet across. It had stood there over seventy years, she figured. Had seen all kinds of people pass under it during that time, herself included. And now it lay on the ground face up, its wooden lettering cracked in the sun, two stumps protruding from the earth, surrounded by piles of sawdust.

She was dressed in jeans and a plaid shirt, already broken in and filthy—in the past few weeks there didn't seem to be a day when she wasn't brushing dirt out from under her fingernails, until finally, she'd quit bothering. By now, The Flying U was well on its way to becoming a working ranch. She had no desire to let it be just some vacation home and let the land go to waste. By her reasoning, she could keep Sonny here operating it, employ some seasonal hands, and move on to other ventures in town.

But looking at the sign laying there, the letters shattered, the ends fresh where the posts had been cut, she definitely wasn't leaving this place now. Suddenly, she had an even more maternal feeling for it, and was amused that someone thought she could be scared off so easily. At least that's what she wanted Sonny to think, anyhow.

Over the past weeks, he'd taught her how to be a regular cowgirl. She could shoe a horse now. Mend a fence. Lasso and tie up a calf. And she even knew what those strange words meant in that book of cowgirl songs that rested permanently on the piano: good-mouthed, shorthorn, bottle brush, and most notably…greenhorn.

"Well, Francine. I hate to say I told you so, but I think people are trying to tell you something," Sonny said, turning to her.

"Not so subtle is it?"

He climbed from his horse and knelt by one of the stumps, running his hand over its white heart. "Bunch of vandals. Probably just some kids in town. Looks like they cut it with a double-handled saw. They leave dust just like that." He pulled off his hat, brushed back his hair. "I could ask Jim if anyone's come and bought a saw like that lately."

She looked at him and grinned. He was useful to no end, and seeing him there every day, ready and eager—well, it was hard not to grow attached. "I don't want to give them the satisfaction of knowing it bothered me," she said. "I'll have some new sign posts put in. And we might as well paint it while it's down."

"Well, if I find out who did this, they best look out." Sonny examined the fallen sign a moment before he tried to lift it, and as he did he grabbed at his arm, wincing. He let the sign drop and turned away from her. "I'll bring the truck down and tow it back up," he shouted.

She shaded her eyes, looking at his face, suddenly gone pale. "You alright?"

He looked up and nodded towards the road. "They're here."

Francine watched the trucks as they slowed and pulled into her driveway. Towing large silver trailers, filled with head of cattle. They rumbled right past the sign and through the gates without stopping.

Already there were eighty head of young cattle on the property, and with these next two truckloads the number would be nearing one hundred and twenty-five. It was a small operation, no doubt, but an operation no less. They were the best kind of cattle to buy— Hereford—Sonny had told her, and he knew cattle.

There'd been more work here than he signed on for, and payday for him was next spring, when the first guests would visit the ranch. She didn't know what kept him coming back. Each day she awoke and expected him to be gone. She'd hold her breath while looking out her kitchen window, exhaling only when he came from his cabin and stretched in the sunshine.

As he smiled at her from atop his chestnut horse, waving as he herded the cattle towards the troughs by the barn, he was twirling and doing all he could to get her attention, more giddy than the calves that sprang around beside their mothers, and she couldn't help but feel a little giddy too.

As the trucks dragged away the empty and stinking trailers, banging away as they went down the road, she felt very sure of things for the first time. "No one can scare me off," she muttered, and when she turned to lead her horse to the barn, she saw that Sonny had put all the cattle away in the pen, but he was missing. She thought little of it until she came from the barn and saw his horse dragging its reins and grazing in the field with an empty saddle.

"Sonny," she called as she rounded the side of the barn and saw him laying there, unmoving.

"Sonny!" she yelled, as she ran and knelt beside him. Were it not for the weak moans emanating from him, she'd have thought him stone dead. She rolled him over and he let out a loud groan, holding his arm.

"Damn horse spooked and threw me." His face was screwed up tightly and beaded with sweat. "Help me up."

She looped his good arm over her shoulder and together they walked unsteadily to his cabin, where she helped him up the steps, nudged open the door and lay him on the bed.

"I'll be right as rain here in a bit," he managed, closing his eyes tightly. "I just need to rest."

But as he lay there, she saw blood dripping off his shirt onto the sheets.

"Jesus," she muttered, ignoring his murmurs of protest as she unbuttoned his shirt, trying to avoid looking in his eyes while slipping his arm from the sleeve. The arm had been bandaged, badly, and was soaked through with blood. As she began to unwrap the gauze, more blood began to flow down his arm.

"What is this?" she asked, looking at him. "Tell me now, Sonny. You're bleeding too much. I need to get you to a hospital."

He shook his head. "It's too far."

Francine sat looking down at his pale face and realized that if she didn't do something, and fast, he was going to bleed to death on this bed, today, right in front of her.

She tried to tell herself not to panic, but her body suddenly felt as if it was filled with ice and lava at the same time, and her eyes seemed to have retreated from her body and were now peering over her shoulder, as if curious what she'd do next. She knelt beside the bed, unbuckled her belt and slipped it from its loops in one long pull.

"Knife," she said. "I need a knife."

He nodded towards the bedside where there sat a paring knife. She quickly drew her belt around his upper arm, pulled it tight, then poked a hole in the leather and latched the belt closed.

As she began to remove the gauze, she saw the area around the wound was freshly bruised and beginning to swell.

"It's shrapnel," Sonny offered. "Pieces from a German mortar. I brought them home, Air Mail Express."

"No time for jokes."

"They didn't get it all out. It was too deep in places." He shook his head, looking out the window. "Blew up ten yards away from me in Bastogne. The three guys in my foxhole blocked most of the blast. Lucky me, I got pulled from action and was given a medal."

He looked up at the ceiling, then at her. "I've been thinking of writing their families, but what good would that do?"

The way he looked at her, she knew that they had died and he had lived. Because of them. She sat there a moment before she unwound the rest of the bandage.

"It looks like it's hit an artery or something. So we need to get the rest of it out. And now." As she looked at the wound, she could see a black fragment that had slowly begun to break the skin's surface.

Before he answered, she was out the door, running as fast as she could across the field to the house, where she rummaged through its cabinets for clean cloths, alcohol, thread and needle, a sharp knife and tweezers. Then, carrying the bundle in her arms, she burst back into the cabin and dropped them on the bed beside him.

"Now, lay still," she said, and set to work.

She examined the wound more closely: three pieces of shrapnel were now poking through. Each flex of his arm muscle had pushed them outward. And all that time on the ranch, mending fences, bending, lifting, pulling things for her—he'd never once complained.

Damn *cowboys*, she thought, as she liberally doused the wound with alcohol. He began to grumble, but she quieted him and told him to be steady while she pulled out the fragments with the tweezers.

He bit his lip and closed his eyes as she dug in and pulled, depositing the pieces on a white cloth. They were, in the end, no more than pebble sized chunks. Burnt, twisted metal. What ugly devices men could come up with to murder each other, she thought, as she threaded the needle to sew him up.

"War's a strange thing," he said, as if reading her thoughts. He looked sleepy, relaxed, and didn't wince even as she drew the needle through the skin, and pulled the wound closed with ten box shaped patterns, just as if it was a seam of fabric.

When she had the wound cleaned and dressed, he began nodding off.

"Go on and rest," she said, gathering up the tools and cloths and opening the door. "I'll come and check on you at dinner."

Sonny closed his eyes and muttered his thanks, and after she tied up his horse, she went back into the house and fell on the floor and began to cry, in great heaving sobs.

She was interrupted by the sound of a ringing phone, a sound so unusual out here that she shot to her feet and hurried across the room to answer it.

"Hello?" she said, wiping away a tear with her sleeve.

"Frannie? It's me, doll!"

The voice on the line was familiar, with a heavy New York accent, and sounded disconcertingly clear for a long distance call.

"You know, your dear friend Dottie. Would you believe that I'm in town?" There was laughter in the background. "*We*, that is. Fred is on assignment to capture the wild west or some such thing. With his whole entourage of course. He thought, what better place to stop off than Braxton on this grand expedition of ours?"

Francine's mouth hung wide open. She looked about the room, out the tall windows and over the mountains, bracing herself against the table on which the telephone stood. No, she thought, pressing the receiver back to her ear, she was not asleep and this was not a dream.

"I assure you everyone in New York is gossiping of your Western exploits. To hear them talk, it's like you're a regular John Wayne now. Which I simply know is not true. Not *my* Frannie. Not the girl who files her nails every chance she gets."

There was something strange in Dottie's ensuing laughter. She sounded unusually frantic and scattered, even for her.

"Dottie…" Francine managed after a long pause.

"Fred says he is simply *dying* to see you. I'm so sorry we didn't get in touch sooner, but you're one hard girl to track down. Finally had to have the…concierge here…cough up your number and address. Anyway, here we are at a hotel in town, and we've decided these accommodations simply will not do. We're going to make other arrangements, but in the meantime, we have to get our bearings, and have a real honest to goodness drink." Another peal of nervous laughter followed.

"And well, I'm sorry to surprise you like this. It's just that this endeavor has been a bit pell mell from the start, I'm afraid. OK, Fred is calling for me from the car. We'll be seeing you shortly, doll."

The phone went dead and Francine set it in its cradle and wandered out of the house. She stood on the porch and looked down at her filthy clothes, reached up and felt her hair, then stood there gazing at the blood on her hands.

Not thirty minutes later a car pulled in the driveway, and after some quick hellos, the visitors from New York spilled into her front yard, reeking of liquor. Indeed it was a whole entourage. Walking the grounds, wandering through her house, as if it was all some kind of playground; but of course, she thought, the whole world was a playground for people like this.

Frederick stood there in her driveway, cravat around his neck, pipe tucked between his teeth, taking pictures of his model, a rather extreme looking young woman named Lana who was wearing a cowboy getup that looked fresh from the display window at Rafters.

He was a famous photographer, older than Dottie by nearly thirty years. Frederick Grosbeck. Francine didn't know his work: it was mostly commercial things, magazine and ad copy, and it wasn't until he turned his camera lens on the lodge, with the mountains in the background, that she realized this impromptu visit might be good for business, should they ever find their way into a magazine.

"Move aside a little, Dorothy," Frederick said in an equally thick New York accent, tilting back his hat. "I want to get a picture of our cowgirl Francine here. I must say she looks like the real thing, doesn't she?"

Dottie crossed her arms and stepped back. She too was dressed in cowboy gear, no doubt with the intention of catching the interest of Frederick's lens, which she hadn't been able to do since their courtship. Francine knew it was a sore subject. Dottie had married the man thinking she was his muse. But now she stood there looking down at Lana and even Francine with a twinge of envy.

77

Frederick took his pictures, came and kissed her cheek, and then they moved on, following after the two young men who were already lost somewhere in the house.

"I tell you, it's like I don't exist sometimes, Francine." Dottie shaded her eyes, looking out over the mountains. "What's a girl got to do?"

Dottie was indeed pretty, with black hair and full lips, even if she was past what some may have considered prime modeling age. She crossed her arms and dug her boot heel into the ground. "I think he's in love with that girl."

"Don't be silly," Francine said. "She's just a kid, Dot."

"Follows her around like a puppy. At dinner the other night, in Denver—big fancy steakhouse—he tucked her napkin into her blouse so as not to ruin it."

Dottie walked the length of the porch, looking down at her balled hands. Then she suddenly turned and perked up, eyes wild and bright.

"Oh, it is so very nice to see you Francine. You can't imagine what it's been like not having you around. I must say I've been hoping this whole adventure of yours would be short-lived. Life just isn't the same without you back home."

Francine looked out over the ranch, listening to the murmur of voices inside. The two men who'd gone in were using her phone, and she could vaguely hear them now making travel arrangements. She just hoped she could keep them all away from Sonny, so he could get some much needed rest.

At the thought of him, she suddenly wished it was just the two of them, so she could tend to him. This sudden instinct felt odd, and although she couldn't yet understand why, seeing him on the ground that morning, unmoving...well, she'd realized then that she wouldn't be here were it not for him. She likely would've gone back home. Right back to New York with the same strained smile Dottie was wearing now.

"Who's helping you out here?" Dottie asked, looking out at the barn. "Certainly you aren't doing it alone?"

"I have a help. A ranch hand."

"I'll bet you do," Dottie said, winking.

Francine crossed her arms and smirked.

"Well, I'd just give anything to have a man around. I mean a real man. The strong and sturdy type. I'm afraid, my dear, I know all too well how you felt living with Thomas all those years." Dottie turned and looked at her. "It was a shame that you didn't find out about him sooner. Seems you were the last to know. All the girls started telling stories after you left. They all knew Thomas years before us."

Francine felt herself beginning to boil.

"No one blames you for going crazy," Dottie said, patting her hand. "That's all I mean."

"Well thank you," Francine said. "Your words fill me with such solace."

"I'm sorry," Dottie threw an arm around her. "Here I am, stirring up all of this. I didn't mean it. It's good to see you doing so well."

Just then the two young men came out of the house. They were blonde, of the same height and build; they even dressed the same, only in two different shades. Pleated pants, wingtip shoes, checkered sport sweaters. They stood there on the porch, striking a pose, doing their best to look the part of debonair Western gentlemen.

Just that morning, Francine had awakened feeling as if Manhattan was far behind her. A week ago she'd sent a lone postcard to Dottie, a letter to her family, but with no return address. As if to assure the past would become a distant memory, certain to fade into nothing.

But here it was now in her new home. And as she watched Dottie pace along the porch while her husband snapped more pictures of Lana, she realized that her friend's presence here was, in a way, a plea for help.

Francine could read her friend quite well by now. Dottie had always worn her heart on her sleeve, but when it came to saying how she felt, she hid her true feelings behind a smile, as if to project the idea that everything in her life was perpetually sunny.

Francine knew better. Years before, Dottie had passed through the same doors of society that she had, held open for her by others, going through one and then the next until what came out on the other side was someone no one recognized. She also recalled the parties Dottie threw back home, in which the spotlight would remain on her until the very end of the evening when she would grasp each guest's hand as they left, squishing her face up in a wad of emotion, before drawing herself to them in a tight embrace.

Such displays, Francine knew, were desperate performances. And yet Dottie had, as a result of always being center stage, amassed a legion of friends. Francine considered herself one of them. Even if Dottie's advice had been misguided, or if whatever perspective she possessed was hidden behind a mascara stained empathy, Dottie had been there after the divorce, while everyone else receded into their bright and cheerful apartment houses and shut the door on her.

As Francine watched the entourage assemble on her porch, she wanted to pull Dottie aside and talk to her. But already the two young men had exclaimed that they'd made their bookings for new accommodations, and to get to them, they'd made special travel arrangements for the group.

And at that, the visit was over and she felt Dottie begin to pull away. She saw the group's grinning white smiles as they piled in the car, so pleased with themselves for venturing so far, while around them lay the protective caul of their beauty, success and wealth.

Dottie came back and embraced her tightly before she climbed in the car after the others.

"Take care of yourself, Dottie," Francine said softly.

"You know I will," Dottie whispered. "And I'll stop back on our way out of town."

As the car circled and headed back down the driveway, she waved, feeling much as she had after one of Dottie's parties, a bit exasperated and breathless. The visit hadn't been thirty minutes but it had felt like days.

Sonny. At the moment she thought of him, he came wandering around the side of the barn as the car vanished over the hill. As he neared she could see the fine lines on his face, filled with grit. His smile, as he rubbed the bandage on his arm, seemed to suggest that he was feeling better.

"What are you doing up?" Francine said, spinning on her heels. "I told you to stay in bed."

Giving instruction to him seemed out of place, and his posture seemed to suggest he was still, in his deteriorated condition, unwilling to relinquish the upper hand to her.

"I saw you had company and came out to say hello." He looked at her a long time, until finally she turned towards him, her hands on her hips. He shook his head and looked down at his hands. "Those were your friends from back home. That's what you come from?"

"Why yes, they were."

"Strange folks." He stood watching the dust trail left by their car. Perhaps in seeing them, he'd understood her better. And perhaps forgiven her so many things, and only there and then realized there'd been nothing to forgive. Their differences and sameness were obscured merely by the fact that her surroundings were new to her, and she new to them. And that her time there had been filled with honest and genuine purpose, as had his.

"Well, you're not like them," he said, looking down at his boots. "I might even go so far as to say you're a real cowgirl now." At that, he pulled a red silk kerchief from his pocket and opened it up for her to see. Inside it was a long red feather.

"Red has always been good luck out here." He took the feather by the stem, and holding her shoulder, pushed it into her hat band. Then he neatly folded the kerchief lengthwise, looped it around her neck, and slipped a knot into it.

"Where did you get these?" She touched the silk handkerchief and then the feather, looking at him.

"Oh, I've had them. Been carrying them around a long time. Never knew quite why." Sonny toed the ground with his boot. "Maybe I was just waiting for someone to give them to."

Francine stood there a moment, not quite sure how to respond to this unexpected gesture. "Well, thank you. These are very nice." She looked at his bandage, eager to change the subject. "Your arm. Is it feeling better?"

"Good as new." He moved his arm around while looking out over the house and cabins with a sense of satisfaction. "Well," he said, clearing his throat, "I believe you're all set up here. I expect I'll be back next spring."

Her smile faded as quickly as it had come. "You're leaving?"

"I owe a favor to a good friend." He tipped his hat and winked. "I'll be back though. You can count on that."

And as she went inside, she watched him begin to pack to leave, which he did that afternoon in his truck. He returned at dusk and her spirits lifted, thinking he may have changed his mind. But when she went to his cabin in the morning and knocked, he was gone. Pushing inside, the bed was empty and the stove cold, and he, his horse, his truck, and any trace of him were gone, save the two war medals he'd left in the trashcan, and six bullets lined up neatly on the windowsill.

"Just like that," she said, thinking of how he'd left her life as suddenly as he'd come into it. She smiled as she swept up the bullets and closed his door behind her, not quite sure if she was ready to face the day alone.

Ten

Jessica was packing her dirty laundry in a canvas duffel as dawn broke over Cutthroat Lake. It was a Saturday, and all the guests had departed after a quick breakfast. The guides who had not drawn the short straw to lead guests back down into town were still asleep, the sounds of their snoring audible as she passed their tent, bag slung over her shoulder. She dropped it by the stables then walked back up to the tent she shared with Esther, who was readying for her own swift departure into town as well.

The preparations had begun the night before—time off was slim, and usually amounted to one night every two weeks. Some opted to stick around, but both she and Esther longed for the comfort of a hot bath. Had anticipated it so badly that after their pre-dawn breakfast, they'd primed the percolators, laid out all the measuring cups, set the tables, cleaned up, so that all that would need to be done upon their return was stoke the oven and fire up the coffee machines, so dinner would be ready for the next group of incoming guests on Sunday afternoon.

The sun had just begun to peek over the ridge, making the lake sparkle, and it now spilled in the doorway where Jessica stood. "If you won't be needing me this morning, I think I'll head on back to town and get cleaned up."

Esther looked up from where she was tucking the sheets back into her bed. "If you can wait, Ed and I will drive you down and pick you up early tomorrow if you'd like."

"Thanks, but I need to get a move on if I'm to get done all that needs doing. Want to see the family while I'm in town and I figure if I get there soon enough my sister will have a big lunch ready for me, and I wouldn't have had to make it."

Esther smiled at this as she fluffed her pillows. "You know we don't like you riding into town all by yourself. Wait for one of the guides to go with you."

Jessica bit her lip, and in the silence, the snores of one of the

83

guides could still clearly be heard. She canted her head at Esther. Not only did she resent the motherly treatment, especially on what was her day off, she didn't like being treated as if she was some helpless girl, especially by her.

"My horse needs re-shoed while I'm there anyway. I'll be fine." While there was truth in that, Jessica also hoped to get to the post office to mail yet another application she'd been working on, under the glow of a lantern that week, for the Wyoming Forest Service. She'd sealed the enveloped and snuck it in her bag just that morning.

Esther came to the doorway as Jessica began to walk away, dragging the duffel behind her. "You send a telegraph when you get to town, let me know you made it safe."

Jessica swung the bag over her shoulder and spun around. The morning was cold and her breath came out in a foggy vapor. "I'm not someone you need to look out for. I'm not your responsibility." She smiled and put a hand on her hip. "What if you don't hear from me? Are you going to be the one to come after me?"

Esther shook her head and resumed making the bed. "I just like to look out for you is all. Doesn't seem like anyone else is."

"I love that about you Esther, but sometimes I need to do things alone."

Jessica walked over to the stables. The tin roofing sheets were eight feet long, and here in the high, arid mountains, showed barely any sign of rust. Ed was always saying he'd replace it someday with shingle, and yet it was the driest and most protected part of the camp. No grizzly was getting in there, and besides, she knew that when Ed considered the amount of work it took him to haul that metal up there, he seemed less apt to tell those who laid eyes on the ugly structure that he intended to replace it. And, besides, as far as Jessica was concerned, "soon" in Ed-speak meant as soon as it fell down.

She untethered and mounted her horse, Jack, lashed her laundry to the back, and with her father's old 30/30 rifle in its scabbard, she was off, breaking into a trot as soon as she was immediately out of camp.

Ed was just coming up from the lake pulling a cart with supplies in it, and he paused when she passed by and lifted a hand to wave.

"You be back early tomorrow," he yelled jubilantly. He was

happy, she knew, because there was a group of last minute guests coming to the lodge, when the coming week had only been half-booked not the day before.

Jessica nodded and headed on down the narrow trail, the thin poles and telegraph line running along it, and soon she and the horse had settled into a slow lope.

It wasn't long before her thoughts turned back to what had happened in Laramie, and she quickly tried to think of other things. Beyond a bath and bouncing her niece Lee Ann on her knee, somewhere in the pit of her stomach came something stronger than the need for food or rest: that familiar but unwelcome urge for a drink.

She hadn't had one since she was last in town. Hadn't had any when guests were drinking the other night, afraid that unlike those who drank whiskey like she did her morning coffee—a cup or two at most—that even a sip would fill her with such a pleasurable warmth that she'd only want more.

She smacked her lips as she loped along those first two miles, growing thirstier as the sun began to beat down on her. With each step she was planning her day down to the hour, and already she saw herself parked at the Sundowner by three, and had even decided her order—a shot of Old Crow, Coors chaser.

Hopefully she could talk Lynn into going with her, to help keep the cowboys at bay. They weren't out-and-out pushy there, but the pool of decent men in town was so small that it could easily be polluted by having the wrong one latch onto you, take possession, even if just for the night.

Romance was merely a theory to her now anyway. Love a sentimental dross. And sex seemed—the longer she went without it—like something she'd just have to do without. For the rest of her life, even. Especially if things continued at their present rate.

Jessica paused beside the creek where she and Ed had hauled the Jeep across only a week before, near the spot where she'd nearly drowned. The memory of the blue man under the water came to her, making her shiver as she dismounted and began to cross, leading Jack by the reins.

85

Unable to tolerate her thirst any longer, she scooped up a handful of water, but drinking a sip did nothing to diminish her true thirst, and she threw the rest of it away. Even more than she needed a good drink, she reasoned, she needed a good man. One like Ed. She laughed aloud at the thought. There she was, and the only truly good man she knew was married and old as sin.

Truth was, she found those macho cowboy types distasteful, with all their swaggering and bravado. Besides, her heart was now stored high up on some shelf—no cowpoke could reach it, let alone herself. Perhaps someday she'd feel less like a desolate valley inside, but given her luck, the first man she let climb up and grab it would send it shattering on the floor.

The creek was ice cold and when it reached her waist she let out a shriek. Wincing, she pulled at the reins and Jack stubbornly followed. When she reached the opposite bank, dripping wet, she suddenly fell to her knees and couldn't bring herself to stand back up.

Jack snorted, but she couldn't move. It was as if something inside her had just snapped. Anyone happening by would see her there, face pressed in the sandy bank, but she was helpless to do anything about it.

Suddenly she heard loud, bellowing moans, and was surprised to find they came from her. She didn't feel particularly sad, and yet her sobs were coming out of her like someone was pulling at some rope, deep in her belly. And it just kept paying off some great spool, spinning faster and faster until at last, there was nothing left.

At last she sat up and wiped her face. Jack lowered his head, dangling the reins in front of her. She grabbed them and he pulled her to her feet, where she stood brushing the sand from her knees.

As she led him up the bank towards the trail, she stopped. Listening over the sound of the coursing water. Turning her ear, she heard something in the pines to her right. Something shifty and large. Something that perhaps had heard her cries and mistook them for a wounded animal. When she looked, the bushes rustled and something behind them moved.

Her heart dropped like a bucket in a well.

Further behind, she heard the footfalls and grunts of something even larger. A pair of mountain lions. A pack of wolves. A grizzly and her cubs. Whatever it was, she knew sure as hell if it caught sight of her and the horse that the animals would charge. And not a false charge, but the kind that would pull the horse from her hands, the rifle with it, leaving her standing there for dead.

She stood stock still while the bushes continued to move. For a moment she hoped that whatever it was would pass by without noticing her. It seemed unlikely, but she stood there gripping the reins, praying.

The bushes parted and a few bear cubs climbed over a dead log and into the pine boughs, not seeming to notice her standing there, until she leapt atop Jack—which caused him to whinny, alerting the cubs to their presence.

They were three in number. Shaggy, weak, and dusty looking. While she drew the rifle from the scabbard, lifting it to her ear and cocking it, the adult grizzly popped from the bushes and looked around, lifting its giant head to sniff the air. She knew damn well it could smell her, because she could smell it, foul and rank, thick with the scent of rot and scat.

Its muzzle was the size of the pine stump that stood beside it, and from what she could judge of the rest of the bear, it was the biggest animal she'd ever seen. She sat there, mouth hanging open, taking in its sheer size. When the grizzly stood on its hind legs, growling, she had to lean back to take in its massive silhouette.

The thunder of its roar, the shadow it cast down upon her, made the horse rear up, nearly throwing her from the saddle. There was little time to get Jack under control. The bear took one good look at them, fell back on all fours, and began its charge.

There was less than twenty feet between them at the outset. She dug her heels into the horse's flanks. Jack—God bless him— surged forward as the bear raced at them, and as he did, she pulled the trigger on the rifle which was, by some chance, level with the bear. She saw the fur on its hindquarters bristle with the impact, but it didn't slow. Feet lay between them and she ducked down as Jack shot up the trail, expecting the bear's jaws to close around her leg at any moment.

A minute passed. Maybe five. She and Jack were soaked in sweat, and her heart was beating in time with his footfalls. Finally she pulled back on the reins but he was reluctant to slow, until at last, with a hard yank and a yell, Jack halted as quickly as he'd sprung to life. Never would she have guessed he had it in him to stay that cool, and after she glanced back and saw the empty trail behind them, she prodded him on, patting his neck.

A drink, she thought, eying the canyon below, where beyond the treetops she could make out the vague shape of Braxton. A goddamn drink would be nice. As she continued along, looking behind her now and then, she realized that she'd narrowly escaped death twice in just a week. But there was little time to reconcile this fact there on the mountain, and as she neared the comfort and safety of town, she knew she should telegraph up to Esther and Ed, to warn them.

But they were probably already on the trail, and Ed knew to look out for bear anyway, having seen the signs by her car. And, she reasoned, if she did tell them about it, they'd reward her by never letting her out of their sight again. Besides, the bear was already long gone, with a bullet in its hip no less—and she sure as hell wasn't about to head back up the trail to see how it felt about that.

The bear. She could still see its crazed eyes. Its oily, matted fur. It had seemed nearly iridescent, standing in the shade of the pines. Something about it hadn't looked quite right. In some strange way, it had appeared almost...*ghostly*. When she snapped the reins Jack eagerly forged ahead, as if he too had not forgotten the sight—and smell—of that beast.

"You're losing it, Jessica," she muttered, unable to keep her hands from shaking as they reached the trailhead at last, there by The Flying U, its sign laying curiously in a pile on the ground.

Lynn and her kids were in the yard when Jessica rode up, just where she'd left them the week before. She dismounted to greet them, but they stopped short as they ran up to her. When she looked down she saw the rifle was still in her grip, her knuckles white, as they'd likely been since her encounter with the bear. She turned and hung the rifle in its scabbard as handily as she hung a soup ladle above the stove at camp.

"You little rascals," she said, scooping them up and kissing their cheeks. Lynn stood and, hands in her back pockets, appraised Jessica with the same concerned look that Esther had that morning.

"You look like you could use a bath."

"Yeah," Lee Ann said, "you stink Aunt Jess."

Jessica laughed, and only when she was stripped down and stepping into a hot bath, did the image of the bear's face popping out of the pines seem to fade. It was replaced by the thought of heading into town, clean, and coming home for a good night's rest in a real bed.

She came from the bathroom wrapped in only a towel, and found Scott waiting in the hallway. He was short, a bit round, and perpetually greasy from his work at the garage.

"Re-shoed Jack for you," he said, leaning against the wall with his arms folded.

"Thanks," she said, trying to squeeze by him.

He moved, blocking her path. "We sure do a lot for you around here. I sure do a lot for you, that is." He scratched at his cheek. "Thing is, I wouldn't have known you from Eve when you came back here. Left a little girl and came back a real woman."

She looked at the floor, hoping he'd step aside.

"Flash me," he said, grinning. "Right quick."

She shot him a look like he'd lost his mind. In no way had she ever done anything to remotely flirt with her sister's husband—the father of her niece and nephew.

"C'mon," he said, lifting his chin, "let's see what you've got."

She stuck up her middle finger, pulling the towel tighter around her body. "There's your flash," she said, pushing by him, the smile having left his lips.

"Oh come on now, have a sense of humor, Jess. Throw an old married guy a bone now and then. Ain't you staying here rent free, after all?"

As she slipped on her clothes, she thought of Lynn. Had she witnessed that little scene in the hall, she would've assumed she'd done something to bring it on. But Jessica never deserved the seedy attention she got from men. There was simply something in her nature that suggested she was one of the guys, but with a woman's body. That she understood them, and could— "throw them a bone" —as easily as she could a hot biscuit.

Fully dressed, she sat on the bed and placed her hands over her face and once again began to cry. Because in truth, she was almost lonely enough to have flashed Scott. Maybe it would've made it a little easier with her staying here. Maybe she would've even enjoyed the attention, gotten herself even more leeway.

She stifled her sobs as she put on her boots, still damp from the creek, and straightened her hair in the mirror. Sometimes things had a way of letting you know when they were at an end. She knew she needed out of her sister's house, to find her own place. She'd been living on pity for too long.

When she came from her room they were in the kitchen having lunch. Scott didn't look up from the table; Lynn sat there absently chewing her sandwich. She didn't seem at all surprised when Jessica kissed each of the children and told Lynn to come join her at the bar if she could. But even before there came the vague reply that she'd try, Jessica was out the door and heading down the drive in her Ford, a trail of dust swirling behind her.

Eleven

Francine awakened to the sound of machinery and men yelling down by the road. It was late—nearly eight—when she finally climbed from bed to see what all the racket was. She'd lain awake half the night with her now loaded revolver at her bedside, expecting to hear the customary howls, but none had come. For the first time since she'd arrived, it wasn't wolves that had kept her up and staring out at the moonlit sky. It was Sonny's absence.

As she opened a window and looked down at his empty cabin, she heard the cows lowing in the barn. She swore, dressing quickly in what had become a well-worn uniform: jeans, leather belt with silver buckle, buffalo check shirt and her dusty boots. Lastly, she slipped the red kerchief around her neck and donned her hat with the red feather in the band, then hurried down the stairs.

The cows fed, she jumped in her car and sped to the end of the driveway, where six men stood beside a truck with a crane on the back. They didn't pay her any mind as she stepped out and waved her arms, instead intent on placing a large steel pole in the ground.

"What in God's name are you all doing?" she yelled, but their upturned faces didn't waver as the pole was set and balanced. It was only then that she looked up and saw the sign attached to it, *Flying U Ranch* written across it in bright colors. Twice the size of the old wooden one that had been mysteriously cut down the week before. And this sign, judging from the cord running down the metal pole, was electric.

As a concrete truck backed in to fill the base around the pole, Francine jumped back in her car and, revving the engine, sailed past the workers and out onto the road. Three miles later she turned into a driveway paved with white gravel. Heaton's place soon appeared, a dark stained wooden mansion with black shutters, rising high into the sky. She climbed its steps and clacked loudly on the door with the heavy brass knocker.

One of his line riders answered and she stormed in without

invitation, unsure which way to go. She stood frozen while his dog barked at her, blushing with both anger and embarrassment. Above her hung a chandelier made from hundreds of elk horns, and wrapped around it was a marble tiled stairway; as grand and ostentatious as an entryway in a Western home could be.

She'd known houses like this all her life, even if only from a distance. A house like this could swallow a person right up; suck in a wealthy young man and spit out an old mad man. And then it would be left to wither and decay—just an old house on the hill that kids came to throw rocks at.

Will Heaton turned from where he sat on a cowhide sofa beside a large crackling fire. He was wearing a pair of riding boots that looked never to have been used, and he grinned, as if expecting her.

"Why," he said, "if it isn't Miss Thomas Gladinger of New York."

Francine listened as his voice echoed through the house. She hated how he knew such things about her. The way he could see right through her, when what she wanted most of all was to be left alone and not be seen at all. But even in this, he seemed to think he knew better.

"Why do you say such things?" she asked.

"Well, that's who you are, is it not?"

"It's who I was, yes."

"Very well." He stuck his hands in his vest pockets, seemingly amused.

There came a long pause. A silver coffee tray sat before him, two cups and a steaming pot. She wondered if there was someone in the house he was expecting.

"And what do I owe the pleasure of this visit?"

She stood there, looking at him, then around at his house some more. The log rafters, the way the stone fireplace seemed to go on forever.

"That sign," she said finally, leveling her eyes at him.

He let out a haughty chuckle. "What sign do you mean?"

"The one in my front yard."

"Oh," he said, lifting his chin, "I thought you cut it down? At least that's what I'd heard from our boys here."

"Someone cut it down for me." She crossed her arms and looked at him a long time. "Someone who doesn't like my being here."

"If you're here to imply that I had anything to do with it, I assure you that I did not. Now, if you'll excuse me, my coffee is getting cold."

She stepped forward. "So you don't know who cut it down then?"

He filled a cup with coffee and looked at her without saying a word.

"Well, it's a terrible thing to do."

"It was," he said, taking a sip. "But I certainly can't go around feeling bad for people. If I did I wouldn't be able to sleep."

"Well, I don't want pity from anyone, least of all you."

"That's good, because I'm afraid I've none to spare, Miss Gladinger."

"Will you stop using that name? That's not who I am anymore."

He looked at her closely. "Then who are you?"

It was as good a question as anyone had ever asked. And it left her, to her utter frustration, speechless.

"Coffee?" he asked, pouring some into the empty cup, where it sat, steaming.

When she didn't move from where she was standing—not quite in the room, and not quite out of it—he stood and held up his hand in invitation.

"Thank you," she said, sitting in a chair beside the fire, "Mister Heaton."

"Call me Will, please," he said, handing her the coffee.

"Francine."

He smiled agreeably. "All I really do know about you for certain, Francine, is that you love the idea of turning that old place back into a guest ranch." He seated himself on the sofa again. "I say that makes you one of the last true romantics."

"Why's that?"

"Because this isn't 1846. It's 1946. I'm afraid all that cowboy stuff is in the past. This is a new world now and people are seeking a new kind of adventure…and I intend to bring it to them. Ski lodges, chairlifts, an airstrip."

"Seems like you're making a pretty good wager."

"I'm all in, as they say," he said.

93

"And so am I, nearly."

He set down his coffee and leaned back. "Well, it sounds like we're both in the same business. Some may say that makes us competitors of sorts."

"Perhaps we are."

"But then, you must know that the way people spend their money is a form of democracy. Their vote. And already there are more tourists coming to ski than there are coming to play cowboy." He looked at her knowingly. "You've come and revived something they left for dead, I'm sorry to say."

Francine felt a tear welling in the corner of her eye, because she knew, in many ways, that he was right.

"But," he offered, seeing that he'd upset her, "it's damn admirable, I must say. The place is looking mighty sharp, or so I hear."

Francine set her untouched coffee down. "I suppose this is all a ruse then? You cut down and replace my sign, knowing I'll come over and say something about it. And when I do you dress me down, try and demoralize me."

He smiled. "That's the spirit. You are a business woman after all. See, it doesn't hurt to talk to the enemy, so to speak. See what he's thinking. Or what she's thinking, I should say. But…I'll say it again…I had nothing to do with your sign one way or the other."

He sat there grinning at her as he had once before, as if daring her again to call his bluff.

"Very well then," she said, before narrowing her eyes at him. "And perhaps I don't see things the same way you do. There's more than one way to do business, and I'm not intimidated by your grand ideas. I like my ranch. I'm proud of it. And anyway, I didn't fix it up all alone, so I can't take all the credit. I had help from the man who'd been living there. He…"

"What man?" Heaton asked, sitting up straight. "There was a man on your property when you came here?"

The conversation suddenly seemed to have aroused the interest of his line riders—who moved a bit closer.

"Why yes," she added. "He was living in one of the cabins. Sonny Trace. Do you know him?"

Heaton looked at his cronies and then at her. "Did he bother you?"

"Why no, of course not. He *helped* me. I wouldn't have been able to do it without him." As she spoke, she placed a hand on her kerchief, but quickly let it drop.

"I want to meet this man. You must introduce me."

Francine felt perplexed by the sudden shift in direction the conversation had taken. "Why, I can't. He's gone. And I tell you he will be missed. I'm in over my head with the amount of work I have to do."

"Well, maybe *he* cut down your sign. I must say there have been strange goings on here as of late. Very strange." His mind seemed to wander off, and he suddenly looked very tired. She wondered if anyone would or could ever get through to a man like that again.

"Well, I suppose it's no concern of mine, if he's truly gone as you say." He picked up a newspaper, folded neatly beside his coffee. "And anyway, I don't know of anyone by that name."

Whatever she had said, a darkness seemed to have fallen on the room, and his cordial nature had exited along with the light.

"You have a good day now," he said, and opened his newspaper.

One of the cronies came and, without speaking, led her out and shut the heavy doors behind her. She stood on the grand steps looking down at her car, and then the mountains on the opposite side of the valley.

What a strange visit, she thought. Here she figured she had a handle on things, but now they seemed more confused than ever, and the question of her sign had still not been answered. Strange goings on here indeed...

As she stood there she saw a gardener moving around the plants, humming a tune as he snipped at them. He was an old withered man, who looked at her and nodded, as if in recognition. He then continued moving between the shrubbery like a crane. His cuts were neat, perfect, and he paused before each one as if saying a prayer, then drew the shears closed. As if nothing mattered so much in the world as the cuts his blades made upon the branches and leaves of each tree and bush that lined that dark and empty house.

Francine climbed back in her car and slammed the door. She had to go see Jim Hickens, and now. Finally put down that deposit

95

for the land he'd offered her for sale at the Sundowner. Even if that meant she had to write a bad check. Anything to stall things. Anything to keep that land out of Heaton's hands.

Twelve

Jessica seated herself on a barstool at the Sundowner, as her shot of Old Crow and Coors were unceremoniously dropped before her by the bartender. Griff was indeed a fixture there, beefy and androgynous, of whom no one seemed to know much—not her real name or her age, nor where she came from—as she never said much to anyone, least of all to her. She lived upstairs, alone, and had a shapeless face like a wad of chewing gum, a bowl cut of graying hair, and wore long-sleeved flannel shirts, even in summer.

She was a bartender of the old Western variety, who wasn't there to talk about your problems or keep you company. She'd throw you out if you weren't drinking, and she didn't get in the way of fights, and instead leaned back against the gantry when they broke out, yelled at the fighters to take it outside, where they always did anyway. Perhaps she'd learned that men only had an interest in fighting when folks could gather around, and that fights without spectators had a way of fizzling out.

And although these tussles were always relegated to fisticuffs, it was said Griff kept a sawed off shotgun behind the bar if things got too wild. In such cases, it was good to have her around if one of the fighters broke the neck off a beer bottle and came at his assailant with the jagged end of it.

There simply weren't enough men around, Jessica reasoned, that they could kill each other with abandon. The life expectancy of a man out there—or so she'd heard—was twenty years less than average. Accidents, poor diet, hard drinking, not to mention the way influenza could go through a town like fire, had a strong effect on the way men lived. Those who had made it to forty were lucky, but they still worked and played on the edge, as life was just too short to do otherwise.

Some of the younger men and women couldn't afford to drink inside, and so they congregated in the parking lot. This was usually when the weather was warm, which was often only during summer.

For such occasions, Griff's shotgun served double-duty. Once a night she'd walk outside, sweep it around the parking lot. Anyone not fast enough to hide at the sight of her was treated to a blast from the business end of it.

As the bird shot tore harmlessly through the outcropping of trees surrounding the place, she'd always yell the choice words: "You all *SCREW!*"

The place was still mostly empty. Dusty sunlight filtered in through the blinds, giving off enough light that the overhanging neon signs only faintly glowed. Jessica looked at her wristwatch, saw that it was not yet two, and then at her sweating beer. While she figured she could wait until it reached the hour, she lifted her shot glass, and without pause, tossed it back.

An old man from across the bar was looking at her, grinning toothlessly. Such men were permanent fixtures there, but she didn't feel friendly enough today, so she tipped her beer at him, took a sip, and set it back down on the rough bar top.

A radio—hidden somewhere behind the bar—was broadcasting a baseball game in some hick town she'd never heard of. She listened until her beer was gone, her mind lost on the events of the past week, the wild stink of the bear still in her nose.

Jessica had often heard of bears charging guides, and it felt like a rite of passage to her, sitting there as Griff came and delivered the next round, which she nursed while lost in the ball game of which she didn't know the teams, or the score. Such contests no longer mattered to her. They were mere games. The stakes out where she worked—and hoped to spend her life—were, in many ways, much higher.

The jukebox sprang to life at three, and the ghostly voice of Jimmie Rodgers came through the worn speakers singing, "Women Make a Fool Out of Me." Griff had some kind of switch behind the bar, so whenever someone wasn't putting nickels in the machine, playing whatever recent tune was popular—it would play the music she liked: Ernest Tubb, Bob Wills, and The Carter Family.

Just after three, a familiar face walked in the door. It was the young guide, Jake, strolling in with his thumbs in his belt like he owned the place. He'd come in with a group of townies she didn't recognize; he was laughing, telling them lies about his exploits as a guide up at camp. His smile faded when he finally noticed her; he merely tipped his hat before vanishing into the smoky haze with a girl in tow.

Jessica stood to put a song on the jukebox and had to throw an arm against it to steady herself. Returning to her barstool, she saw the place had begun to fill. Several seats down from hers a man in an oiled duster now sat, his black hat tossed on the bar. He was looking straight down at his coffee, hands circled around the mug, watching the steam rise.

She paid him no mind at first, but then found herself watching. He was young—perhaps a few years older than her—and had the look, unlike most of the ranch hands who came in here, with their boots and belt buckles polished, wearing their best hats and crispest shirts, of a genuine cowpuncher.

Ordinarily she wouldn't have paid him any mind, but there was a particular way he sat so contentedly, like nothing else in the world, let alone the growing commotion in the bar, mattered. Beside his mug stood a shot of whiskey, which sat on a slim stack of bills. Each was yet untouched, and she stole glances at him as he slowly sipped the coffee, never lifting his head.

Other men were beginning to gather nearby, talking boisterously, looking at him curiously as they shouted their orders to Griff. Some of the men taunted the rather serious looking cowboy sitting there in his dirty clothes.

The man never looked up. If he heard them, he gave no sign, although she had the particular impression, as the men grew agitated at not being answered, that he truly hadn't heard them. Even they could see he was simply a man who'd stopped off on his way somewhere, consumed only with thoughts about the remainder of his journey.

After a few minutes she watched him stand, remove his coat, walk down into the dark tabled area by the dance floor, and slip his arm around a pretty blonde's waist. She smiled when she looked up at him in recognition, his lean figure, his black hair and bright smile. He spoke and she laughed, and then they began to move about the floor, turning and swinging slowly to the music, as naturally as if they'd rehearsed it a hundred times.

Jessica glanced down at herself, dressed more like a cowboy, and wished she'd put on a better outfit, a little makeup. When she looked over she saw he was still dancing with the blonde, who gazed up at him intently as they moved. When the song ended, he kissed her hand and she sat down with a pleased expression, watching as he walked back in her direction, clearly sorry to see him go.

The other men in the bar hadn't failed to notice his dancing with the prettiest girl in the place, and they stood with their arms crossed as he came back to his barstool. There he began peeling dollars from his stack, counting them out, before at last he threw them all back down, put on his hat, leaving his untouched whiskey on the bar.

"Just coffee?" Jessica said to him, smiling.

"Gotta be up early," he replied without looking at her.

"On a Sunday?" she asked, leaning over and pressing her hand down on his. As she did, she leaned a little too far and nearly fell on him.

He looked at her hand, then at her. He pushed back his hat, revealing a pair of dark brown eyes that seemed to cut right through her.

"Yes, on a Sunday," he said patiently. He then slowly slipped his hand from hers, and began walking towards the door, a few men watching with their arms still crossed.

"You a preacher," she drawled, spinning around at him, "or something?"

He didn't turn to acknowledge her, just placed his hand on the door and shoved.

She was on her feet, a bit unsteadily, faster than she would like to remember later. Outside it was dusk, a bitterness to the wind that hadn't been there earlier in the day.

He was walking across the gravel lot towards an old black pickup. She traced his steps until he reached the truck and yanked its door open. It groaned on its hinges.

"You driving that to the crusher?" she asked, gazing along its rusty rocker panels.

He pushed back his hat again, rested the sleeve of his work jacket on the open window. "You live around here?"

She bit her lip and smiled at him, "Sure do."

"Well," he said as he climbed in and shut his door. "Get in."

She pushed aside some papers and jumped up in the cab beside him. The floors were dirty, as was the metal dash—it was a work truck, after all—and yet all about it was a sense of purpose. There was a work belt filled with fence mending tools, lashed to the transmission tunnel. The seats were covered in a canvas cloth, waterproof by the look of it, and before he shoved back the sun visor she saw a neat stack of documents, ordered by size, smallest first, held in place with clothespins.

"I haven't seen you around here before," he said, flipping on the headlights as they pulled out of the parking lot.

"Been here about six months. Living with my sister Lynn until I get settled myself."

He turned right, heading east, the truck shuddering as it accelerated, before settling into a smooth and steady rumble. She looked back at her own car, sitting where she'd parked it, now surrounded by trucks. It was locked, she hoped.

He said nothing else as the road divided, and she, for the first time since leaving the bar, felt nervous. She'd never gone home with a guy like this. Never would've dreamt of such a thing a year ago. But life was too short, she knew that now; and so what if everyone in town was talking tomorrow? At least they wouldn't be talking about her being killed by some bear. Tonight she was still alive, and she was going to act it.

"Got anything to drink in here?" she asked, looking at him, the nervousness replaced now by a slow burning in the pit of her belly. She was imagining the warmth of him. His body next to hers. Those dark eyes staring down at her as they coupled, as smoothly and confidently as he'd led that blonde around the dance floor.

He reached over, brushing her leg, and dropped open the glove box: neatly ordered papers, some maps, a Colt 1911 pistol in its leather holster, and a half-pint of whiskey, still sealed.

"Help yourself."

She picked it up and offered it to him but he shook his head. She twisted off the cap and took a swig—real lady like—or so she thought, until she realized she'd drank the neck and shoulders off the bottle. As she recapped it, she saw from the road they were on that he lived out her way, and in anticipation of what was coming, a blush washed through her.

Lynn would kill her for doing this sort of thing, and sober, Jessica wouldn't think of it. But as she glanced over at his handsome face, double checking that his fingers didn't have any rings, she decided that she deserved this.

But she sat bolt upright in the seat as he slowed by familiar markings in the road: the particular fence posts, the old chipped red mailbox, a shot up Open Range sign.

"Where the hell are you going?" she yelled, gripping the door, as he made a sharp turn up the driveway towards Lynn's house.

He didn't answer, didn't slow, and yet across his lips came a faint smile.

"This is my sister's place." She tossed the bottle back in the glove compartment, eying his decidedly non-cowboy firearm of choice. "You a cop or something?"

At this, for the first time, he showed some sign of life and laughed, revealing a gleaming mouthful of straight teeth. God damn him. He was enjoying this.

He pulled up outside the house where her family was having their usual late dinner, and he was out of the truck in a heartbeat while she sank down helplessly in the seat, watching over the door jamb as he rapped on the kitchen door. Her sister nearly tore the door off the hinges, crying out when she saw him, hand to her heart.

"I'm sure sorry," Jessica heard him say, "but I ran into your little sister tonight. Boy she's all grown up now." He nodded towards the truck. A moment later Lynn's smile vanished and her hand dropped when she saw Jessica sitting there. A look of embarrassment and shame washed over Lynn's face.

"I didn't think she should be left out there in that condition," he added, "let alone drive home."

Jessica sat there boiling. If there was an abandoned well she could fall in at that exact moment, she'd gladly make the leap. She went back and forth between wanting to sink down and cry herself into a wet slobbery mess, or try and act innocent and retain what little dignity she had left.

She finally forced herself from the safety of the truck, passing him as she walked unsteadily towards the house; she didn't even look at him, or he at her.

Of all the low down dirty things a man had ever done to her, this was the golden nugget. And it was only as she was in the stark white light of her sister's kitchen, standing there feeling naked above a family of straight sober people seated at their dinner, the bang of his truck door and then the rumble as it pulled down the drive, leaving her there, did she realize that she was, just as she had intended to be, *very* drunk.

And yet it must've appeared as if that man had poured an ice cold bucket of water on her, the way she stood there frozen, her hands covering her body. For a long moment then, it was only the sound of dinnerware, of food being chewed. The freshly polished oak table. Bright salad bowl. An array of dressings. Steak and potatoes. Saturday night dinner. Their family feast after a long and tiring week.

All except for Lynn, who sat there over her plate, head bowed, seemingly more embarrassed than she. "What Mother would say if she could see you now," she said, glaring at her.

Scott grabbed her wrist to stop her, but glanced up at Jessica with the same sort of embarrassed expression Lynn wore, perhaps because of what he'd said in the hallway that afternoon, to someone who was—if not morally corrupt—assuredly not in control of all her faculties.

"What's wrong with Aunt Jess?" Lee Ann asked shyly. "Is she sick again?"

Worse than her sister not looking up at her, or her husband's shame, was the obedient expressions his children wore as he told them to eat their dinner; the way they finally looked away from her, like they did when they may have seen someone on the street with no arm, or an abscess on their face.

And so there they all were, trying not to look at anyone, until at last Jessica turned and stumbled down the hall, the sound of their eating resuming only after she'd shut her bedroom door— still littered with Lee Ann's toys, who she'd displaced in staying there with Lynn—whose goodwill she knew she was testing, if not exhausting.

Jessica stripped off her clothes and fell face first on the sheets, drifting into a deep sleep, interrupted only by the crack of light that came when Lynn walked in to sit beside her, to brush back her hair and whisper things she could not understand, before slipping back into a dream where she was making love furiously to that silent stranger.

Thirteen

Jessica awakened with the sun beating on her face. She raised a hand to block it before rolling out of bed, groaning. The room wobbled and she stared at a knot on the floor until at last it stopped. She then grabbed her bags and snuck down the hall. The fear of riding the trail alone again was not as frightening as being reprimanded by her sister, who, from the whiff of coffee Jessica caught as she neared the kitchen, had also risen early, intent on catching her before she slipped out.

Lynn was leaning against the counter as Jessica came in, set down her bags and brushed back a few strands of loose hair.

"Morning," Jessica managed, her voice dry and cracked. She squatted on the floor in her socks and began rummaging through her bags, more for something to do than for something she was trying to find.

Lynn turned to flip an egg in the frying pan. A moment later two pieces of bread popped up in the toaster, and she pulled them out quickly, blowing on her fingers after setting them on the plate.

"Sit down, Sis," Lynn said, adding a dollop of ketchup to the eggs. "I'm making fried egg sandwiches. Just like Mother used to do."

"I'm not hungry, and I'm expected up there before lunch. Actually getting a bit of a late start."

"Sit down," Lynn ordered, handing her the plate. Jessica looked down at the sandwich—it could've been a cow patty for how appealing it looked, her head banging and her stomach threatening to empty its contents without provocation. But she knew food was a necessity; and before she took a bite she reached in the fridge and found a bottle of soda pop, and cracked it open as she sat down, expecting it to be a chaser if the first bite made her gag, which it did.

But she swallowed it down as Lynn sat beside her with her coffee, took a bite of her own sandwich, the yolk dripping over her fingers and onto her plate.

Jessica knew better than to speak. Her sister was up early for a Sunday. These were precious moments before her kids came stumbling down the hall, rubbing their eyes and saying they were hungry.

Lynn was indeed the picture of motherliness, sitting across from her in a pink cotton robe. Soft and shapely, with nearly translucent, creamy skin that hadn't seen much sun or wind. Her voice was etched, not with tension, but with soothing melodic notes. A warmth radiated from her, suggesting that she could heal any living creature, simply by stroking and speaking softly to it.

Jessica herself had grown lean and taut since winter. Her shoulders, arms, and backside showed it. Her cheeks were pink and softly freckled, her hair gone a dirty blonde from the sun. She was wearing a blue wool shirt, a crisp white Henley beneath it, and a pair of faded Levi's. Even if her shape was distinctly womanly, there was in her demeanor something tough; and that hardness was a weapon that she was reluctant to set down this morning, even after what had happened last night.

"You're a grown woman now, Jess," Lynn said, pushing aside her plate. "I'm not going to lecture you. I know you work hard and play hard and all that cowboy shit." Lynn paused, as if surprised she'd sworn. "Sure, you need to blow off steam, but you're not one of the boys. Can't drink like them either. A few drinks and you're…" she flitted a hand in the air, "gone. To somewhere I don't know. Somewhere I don't like."

Jessica took another bite and washed it down with the soda pop. She didn't speak. A warm flush had crossed over her face and she dug the ball of her foot into the table leg, as if to brace herself.

"We all know what happened back in Laramie. And there's not a person here that doesn't sympathize. But you act like it didn't happen and just bottle it all up. Walk around here like a hard ass. But I know you, Jess." She leaned across the table. "And I'm not talking about last night. It's your life, and it's not over yet. You're still alive."

They sat there in silence a moment, the sun still beating on her through the window.

"Are you feeling any better?" Lynn asked finally, looking at her.

Jessica didn't know how to answer, because in truth, it should've been as clear as spring water how she felt. She mustered another bite of sandwich, wiped her mouth and stood.

Lynn placed her hand on hers. "You have a place here as long as you need. But you came here from a bad place and you're in danger of making this a bad place too. You just need to see the sunshine again. After all, those things happen to other women too. Maybe in the end it was just a sign."

"A sign of what?"

"That you weren't ready. Heck, you weren't even married."

Jessica stood there, fuming.

"Look, I'm just saying you'll have your chance again. When things are right."

She wasn't so sure. She wasn't like other women. Sure as hell wasn't like Lynn, who seemed to have no problems in that area. At times Jessica felt like there was some cord deep inside her that she could never grasp, could never quite pull tight.

"And I'm surprised you didn't recognize Sonny," Lynn added. "He graduated with me. Hadn't seen him since. He just seemed to light off for somewhere. By the look of him, I'd say he went off to war. But I guess he's back now. Funny, I hadn't heard. I usually hear everything about the old gang."

Lynn shook her head, staring at the door where he'd stood last night. "He sure is a dreamboat. Can't say I didn't wish there was something else on his mind when he came knocking."

"Lynn," Jessica said, grinning.

"Well, I'm alive too you know."

"Yes," Jessica said, seeing the blush that now covered Lynn's face and neck, "you most certainly are."

Jessica grabbed her bags and the 30/30 hanging above the door.

"Why don't you take something better than that? Scott has a rifle with a telescopic sight. I'm sure he wouldn't mind."

"No," Jessica said. "It's been my good luck charm so far." She was tempted to tell Lynn about the bear. But like Ed and Esther, she'd never let her leave if she spoke of it.

"Thank you," Jessica said, pushing open the door and looking back at Lynn.

"For what?"

She shrugged. "For everything."

Jessica saddled Jack and loped down the driveway. As she did, her latest application for the Wyoming Forest Service worked its way from her pocket and blew away in the wind. She stopped and watched it tumble across the driveway until it hit the fence, where it snagged on a piece of barbed wire. The horse whinnied as she sat there watching its fluttering, until at last she pressed her hat on her head and turned onto the dirt road.

She was several miles up the trail to camp before her head began to clear and her hands steadied. It was late morning, and judging the route in front of her, scarred with fresh horse and vehicle tracks, she was one of the last making their way up the trail that day.

Holding the 30/30 across her lap, its stock chipped and the bluing worn to bare steel, she remembered the first time her father took her hunting with it. Although the memory wasn't entirely sunny, and the rifle not quite the good luck charm she always said it was, it represented something that was important to her: loyalty.

He was towering over her bed that morning, drunk, trying to find the string to turn on her light. Swatting at it in the darkness, he looked like an angry monster—one made more frightening by the way it always came in the shape of her father—a man who was never there, and yet would never really go away.

She'd been afraid then. Always afraid. Her greatest fear of all was that someone would discover that she didn't love him, not in the way a daughter should love a father. And so, as he staggered out into the cold, coatless, the rifle dragging a furrow in the snow behind him, she followed.

Jessica wanted to touch the gray morning light, the empty trees scattered on the distant hillside, limbs reaching into the silvery sky. Her father was waving at her from a snowy ridge line. A black silhouette. He'd have frozen in that bitter wind had she left him then. But she ran up and took up the rifle, and he looked at her as if surprised to see her there, and she followed behind him clutching it until he collapsed against a tree, where, as the sun rose, he promptly fell asleep.

The slanted shadows the trees made in the snowy woods made it hard to see, but somewhere in front of them, not far away, a deer suddenly stood from its bed and wandered her way. Breath steamed from the buck's nose as she raised the gun, her heart beating double time. When it noticed her it waved its tail, and despite her instincts to yell and frighten the deer off, send it bounding to safety, far away from her father, she pulled the trigger, and the deer fell where it stood.

Smoke twirled in the wind. The hard metal butt plate had bucked against her shoulder and she rubbed at it as she looked off into the woods. Her father started and yelled at her until he saw the crippled deer, pushing along in the bloody snow, over a hundred yards off, and he looked at her closely, and then the gun.

Snatching it from her, he studied the situation a moment before deciding that she couldn't have made the shot, and so claimed the kill for himself, which she didn't refute even as he came in the kitchen where Lynn and her mother sat, wind and snow swirling around his boots. Proclaiming it was the biggest buck he'd ever shot. Jessica had stood beside him until the very end, holding him up as he told the story of his kill.

Jessica heard a noise on her way up the trail and instinctively drew the rifle to her shoulder. She stopped and listened closely, sweeping the gun over the woods until the sound came again; a wild yelp, not unlike a squeaking bugle.

Elk. As she rode on, she saw a tell-tale path beside the trail where a herd had recently crossed. Her elk hunting tag was in her wallet, and had been since she'd bought it the month before. She wasn't as much a hunter as she was a fisherman, but she hoped in the coming season she'd get a chance to shoot one—as with over two hundred pounds of meat, one elk would be enough to stock Lynn's freezer through to next summer. Not to mention the credit it would be to her name, especially if she was to kill it alone.

Of course she'd be crazy to shoot an elk this morning, gut it and quarter it while there were grizzlies present. And besides, elk season had not yet officially opened, and while she was many things, she was no poacher. But with the sounds of their braying growing louder, she slipped off the saddle with the rifle in hand, lashed Jack to the nearest tree, and went to have a closer look.

Halfway down the mountain, she leaned against an outcropping which gave a good view of the valley below. She'd always had a fear of heights, and her hands shook as she clung to the rocks like a magnet. From her perch she had a clear line of sight between the aspens and ponderosa that grew on the cliff. As she knelt there, glancing over her shoulder to make sure the horse was okay and nothing was following her, she felt the rocks shift beneath her, and nearly cried out.

As she gathered herself, raising the rifle and looking through the sights, she wondered how many hunters in the past thousand years had stopped in that exact spot, whether it was to sight game, or just get their bearings. It was a naturally prime lookout; any passing hunter or traveler would instinctively be drawn to it. From there, they could scan the valley below and peer between the nearby mountains. The game trails that wound through them had been there as long a time, changing as did the flora and fauna, but by and large remaining the same, as she found that animals flowed much like water, always choosing the easiest path.

Not wanting to damage the rifle stock further, she removed her hat and tried to use it as a rest, but found the position too low for her to see through the sights. She cussed, the braying in the valley beginning to fade. She looked at her boot, considered throwing it up on the rocks and setting the gun on it, but realized if the grizzly suddenly appeared, she'd be in a real fix.

She finally gathered a bundle of sticks, threw them on the rocks, and set the rifle on them. Drawing back the hammer, she began to scan the valley. Her heart sank. The braying had ceased, and the herd that had crossed the trail had likely moved on. But just as she was about to stand, a bull elk appeared from a stand of aspen. It paused before continuing from its hiding place, moving steadily towards her, not breaking its stride.

An elk that size, she thought, hadn't gotten that way by being so brazen. Even when in heat. As he came into a clearing, she saw his long, muscular legs, his heaving chest, and a rack of antlers the likes of which she'd never seen.

"Jesus," she muttered, leveling her sights on it. The elk was still a hundred and fifty yards off, a long shot by any measure, and she placed the front bead a few inches high to account for drop.

The bull stood frozen, unmoving. There were no obstructions in the bullet's path. There was no wind. It would be a clean kill. Already she could hear the chiding she'd get if she told anyone in camp she didn't take the shot, poaching or not. And of course, no one would believe her about the sheer size of it unless she had proof.

She closed her hand around the rifle's comb, placed her finger on the trigger. Her breathing steadied as she leveled the sights just behind the elk's shoulder. Right on his heart. It was perfect, she told herself; a once in a lifetime shot.

But it was also a long shot. One movement and she'd maim the animal, if not miss entirely. She was stalling, second guessing too much, and yet the elk was miraculously still standing there, as if hypnotized. Very soon, he'd slip into the trees just a few feet ahead, ending her chances at a shot.

You've already waited too long, she muttered, as she held her breath and squeezed the trigger.

CLICK.

Jessica cussed and opened the chamber, revealing the spent shell she'd fired at the bear the day before. Racking the lever, the shell went spinning in the air, and a fresh bullet slid into battery.

Her heart beat perceptibly faster as she peered through the sights, but the elk was gone. As she frantically scanned the woods for it, she noticed something else moving through the trees: a lone man, creeping from the aspens into the clearing where the elk had stood moments before. As far as she could tell, he was unarmed.

Jessica squinted as the man cupped his hands to his mouth and began making noises that sounded much like an elk. To her surprise, the same elk appeared from the adjacent timber moments later. Steam rose from its nose as it looked curiously at the man. The two could plainly see one another, and she figured that the elk would bolt, but instead it lowered its head and spread its front legs in an aggressive stance.

The man didn't flinch. As Jessica shifted to get a better view, the rock beneath her gave way, and she grasped at a nearby root to keep from going over with it. As the rock tumbled noisily down the mountain, she looked in the clearing and saw sunlight flash off a pair of binoculars as the man scanned the ridge to see what had caused the rockslide.

Minutes later she heard horse and rider tearing up the mountain, just as she was untying Jack, preparing to make a quick escape up to camp. A hot blush flooded her cheeks. Not only had she missed her shot, but she'd failed to notice the other hunter, and had ruined both their chances. If she'd intended to prove her prowess in the wild then she'd failed undeniably, if not shaken her sense of purpose in being there at all.

The way the rider was pushing his horse, as it huffed and whinnied, tearing up through the trees, she knew he was really going to lay into her. The pair popped out of the trees a hundred yards up the trail, turned and came galloping towards her. She could see the whites of the horses' eyes, its flared nostrils, as the rider pulled back on the reins and slowed. She was prepared to apologize profusely until he came closer.

He halted just feet from where she stood holding Jack. "You!" he exclaimed, steadying his horse.

"You!" she shouted nearly in unison.

Sitting before her, unmistakably, was the man from the night before. Sonny, or whatever his damn name was. Dressed just the same as he had been, except for a checkered wool jacket.

"What the hell are you doing up here?" they both replied in chorus, and then spent the next moments flustered as to who would answer next.

"I work at the camp up the hill," she mustered. "I'm on my way there now."

He looked off into the trees and smiled, as if she'd made a joke.

"I'm the cook there," she added.

"You, a *cook*?" He laughed and shook his head. "From what I've seen of you I'd be surprised if you could boil an egg."

To this she had no reply, but smacked the butt of the rifle until it fell in place in the scabbard.

He pointed at it, gripping the reins in his hands. "Were you planning on killing that bull? What were you, two hundred yards out? And don't you know elk season isn't even open yet?" He tipped back his hat and looked down in the valley. "Hardly what I call sporting."

She blushed again.

"And who do you think called a bull that size in?" He sat back in his saddle. "You think he just walked out of hiding into clear view, going against all his better judgment?"

"So you weren't hunting him?"

He shook his head. "Didn't even have my gun on me. Was just practicing my calls for September."

"Don't tell me you're one of those guys. Act like you can kill any damn wild thing with your bare hands." She put a foot in the stirrup and lifted herself into the saddle. "Hell, some of you act like you could scare one to death just with your prowess. Well I've seen enough of men and their prowess to last me a lifetime. I think you had your gun and just waited too long. Seems like some men just don't know how to take a shot when they have a chance."

He just sat there staring at her, the reference clearly not lost on him. "My, you sure do talk a lot," he replied, as if chewing something distasteful. "Rude and easy. Nice combination."

He tipped his hat forward. "And maybe some men like a challenge. Maybe I don't savor an easy kill, unlike most guys."

She shook her head, trying to seem like he'd missed the mark, but could barely keep her cheeks from continuing to burn.

"Smug and cocky ain't a very good way to go through life. Doesn't seem like it got you too far in life anyhow." She turned her horse, pointing up the trail. "And you didn't get your kill anyway. Even if he was standing there broadside. Hypnotized or whatever."

As she slapped the reins and Jack began to move, he rode up along side her.

"Well, he was there because I trailed him, called him out of hiding. He could see my eyes as well as I could his. I was *that* close." He held up his thumb and forefinger an inch apart. "And I was that close from reaching out and touching the bull of a lifetime before you showed up."

"I had every right to be there," she said, looking straight ahead. "I saw him come out of the woods and stand there. It's just bad luck that you were there or I would've taken him."

"Would that be before or after the rock slide you caused? Or you going to blame that on luck too?"

"I can't help when a rock decides to give way. And besides, it may have saved you from getting a mouthful of his horns. But as far as I'm concerned this conversation is over. I have to be at work and I'm not going to waste another minute here talking to you."

"After you then," he held out a hand. "I'll escort you. But I'll stay a sporting distance away. Two hundred yards sound fair to you?"

"I don't need an escort," she muttered, snapping the reins and tearing past him.

A quarter mile ahead she turned to see if he was still there. Sure enough he was, trailing just far enough behind to exert his unwanted, if not cruel, sense of chivalry. She might've enjoyed this treatment had she an upper hand. That is, if she'd done something to impress him, and he was following after her for other reasons; but as they continued up the trail, he was acting no different than if he was seeing an old lady across the street.

Back at camp, she watched Sonny dismount and tie up his horse. Within seconds someone shouted his name; and then like a swarm of bees they came, and he was suddenly surrounded by the guides and even Ed himself, who stood there beaming like it was his own son who'd just returned home from war. She shook her head as she realized Ed and the whole group had been anticipating his arrival all morning, if not all season.

"Sonny, my boy!" Ed yelled, shaking his hand. "I didn't know if you'd gotten my letters or not. Last I heard from you, you were over in a place called Bastogne."

"Well," Sonny said, tucking his thumbs in his pockets, "I'm back now. Just thought I'd come say hello while I was up this way."

"Well," Esther said, wringing her hands in a dish towel, "we had hoped you'd stay a while. We could sure use the help. We're fixing to get busy here shortly."

"Now, he doesn't have to stay if he doesn't want to." Ed rocked back on his heels, his face aglow like she'd never seen before. "Say, did you hear any elk on your way up?" Ed asked, before confiding to the others that Sonny was one of the best hunters he'd ever met. "Used to come up here every season and beat out all the old-timers. Been asking him for years to guide for me."

"No," Sonny said, glancing at Jessica quickly, "didn't hear a thing."

Jessica continued to eye Sonny after she slipped away into the kitchen. Esther was already in there, making hoecakes for that night's dinner, and within minutes everything had fallen into a familiar rhythm again.

An older guide named Dale was eating a quick lunch when Sonny walked in the lodge with Jake in tow. Dale jumped up at the sight of him, then turned to Jake and exclaimed that he'd hunted with Sonny and his father in the Crazy Mountains when Sonny was a boy, and added, slapping his back, "if he's half the hunter he was then, we're gonna be on some serious game right soon."

Dale threw an arm over his shoulder. "Come and eat with me. Plenty of room."

Sonny glanced at Jessica, who was watching the scene from the kitchen doorway. He waved his hands in protest until Jake kicked out a chair and Sonny finally relented. Dale waved to her and Jessica came with a plate, and although she was more of a mind to dump the contents of it—hoecakes and beans—on Sonny's lap, she gently placed it before him. Sonny took off his hat and threw it in the chair beside him, brushing his fingers through his hair.

She stood there a moment, watching the men fawn over him, as they usually did with her. They were nearly tripping over each other, peppering him with questions, asking how he'd been, how he'd done in the war.

"Oh, I saw some action all right, in Germany," he replied, and his tone of voice seemed to suggest he didn't want to add anything more.

"I was down in Florida myself," Dale said. "Working in a government slaughterhouse to feed guys like you. Wasn't glamorous work but it was my little contribution to the war effort."

Jake just sat there, running his fork through his gluey beans and looking at Sonny, who was visibly embarrassed with all the attention. While she'd often overheard Jake telling tall tales of the war, here he remained unusually quiet. With a real soldier beside him, he must've known his stories wouldn't hold water. More than likely, he'd weaseled his way out of service like so many others; she wouldn't have put it past a guy like that.

As others came in the hall to eat, Esther brought Sonny a second cup of coffee after he'd drained his first. Sonny took a sip, mopping up the last of his beans with a hoecake, giving Jessica the satisfaction that at least he liked their cooking. And perhaps, she thought, returning to the kitchen, maybe all the attention on Sonny was deserved. Most men would've taken advantage of her the night before, and been more than eager to tell about the little rockslide she'd caused as well.

She shook her head as she set to scrubbing a pot. If nothing else, the man had integrity. And he was handsome to boot.

"Don't even think about it, Jess," she whispered to herself, dropping her head. "He'll never love you back."

"Did you say something?" Esther asked, standing in the doorway, an eyebrow raised.

"Nothing," Jessica replied, scrubbing furiously now. "Nothing at all."

Book Two:

The Clover and the Bee

Fourteen

The drone of a plane engine came just after ten. A faint whine, scarcely audible over the wind, growing to a roar as it dropped beneath the clouds and entered the valley. Jessica had just returned from the well with water for the morning dishes and she paused near the kitchen to look up. Esther looked up too, cocking her ear, pushing open the screen door. The way the sound bounced off the mountains made it appear as if they were trying to locate a bee that was buzzing around their heads.

The guides were gathered beside the smoldering camp fire, hands shading their eyes as they also scanned the sky for the plane. Ed was the first to point it out, a small T-shape appearing below a silver bellied cloud. As the shape grew larger, the thunderous sound of the radial engine filled the valley; soon she saw the DeHaviland Beaver, floats suspended beneath it, as it descended towards Cutthroat Lake.

The weather that morning had changed suddenly and the chill of winter was in the air. The lake's surface was the color of gun metal and bristled with the northern wind blowing down from Canada. Ed sat on a picnic table and lit a cigarette as the plane lowered its flaps and began its approach.

Cutthroat Lake was indeed modest in size, not unlike the hundreds of glacial lakes that dotted the Wyoming high country, which were often named by the Indians who first encountered them. Some old timers Jessica knew still referred to it as Jump Lake. As legend had it, a band of Sioux had once been cornered by white trappers on a cliff, and escaped only after jumping a hundred feet into the lake and swimming to safety.

While there were allegedly cliffs on a part of the lake she'd never seen, the rest of the story seemed merely an old tale. Besides its history, there was little to distinguish it from the other lakes except for its kidney shape and unusual depth. But one thing was for sure: the way it was enclosed tightly by mountains made it entirely impractical for landing aircraft there.

As she watched the approaching plane, her palms grew damp. It nearly slid down the south face of a mountain before leveling off just feet above the trees. A strong gust blew it eastward, the rudder and engine compensating for the crosswind. The lake was bordered by tall pines, and those onboard must've been well aware that engine trouble here would mean they'd be pitched into them. Such a thing was a common occurrence: not the year before, word came that a plane full of sightseers had blown a piston on take-off near Yellowstone Park, killing all on board.

The plane made a final, sweeping turn and then quickly plunged, grazing the treetops before finally setting down on the water. The plane cut a wake across the lake and then came to a rest a hundred feet offshore. After a moment, it slowly began to taxi towards the dock, where Ed stood waving.

As it neared, the pilot throttled down and the plane coasted in, its aluminum skin glimmering in the light. Ed reached out and grabbed the plane with a long wooden gaff and eased it towards the dock. Finally the engine cut, blowing a swirl of black exhaust around those waiting by the dock.

All was quiet again. Jake and Dale stood side by side, she and Esther behind them, higher up on the hill. Sonny was off under a tree, hat pushed over his head as if taking a nap, but she noticed him stealing glances at the scene playing out before him.

The passengers busily exited through the small door while those on the ground tried to appear to be doing something more useful than just standing around watching. But as Jessica found, grinding her boot heel into the escarpment, there wasn't much for them to do until their luggage appeared.

When she heard it would be New Yorkers visiting, she'd expected the flashy and quick talking type, who looked down their noses at dowdy Westerners. And while she didn't know much else about the passengers, one was a famous photographer for some big glossy magazine. LOOK or LIFE; one of those. The rest, she assumed, were merely along to help.

The first two passengers that stepped off the plane looked more out of place than she could've imagined. Standing there, they seemed as unsure of what to do with themselves as the guides with them, and so they turned and began helping the others from the plane.

Watching them exit in their colorful clothes, still perfectly clean, she felt that this was somehow fitting. That here in the camp's final season, a group would come photograph the wilderness before it was gone.

The two men who'd stepped out first were brothers by the look of them. Similar height and build. Mid-twenties, she guessed. Pretty boys. Sandy blonde hair, held in place by some sort of cream that made it impervious to the wind. They wore bright chambray shirts and pleated gabardine slacks. Matching white canvas tennis shoes. While one held open the plane's door, the other stood hunched over, hands on his knees, as if happy to have landed.

The next off was a raven haired woman of about thirty. One of the models, Jessica figured. She was wearing, of all things, navy blue slacks and a red blouse, with heels, no less. She struck her as a Elizabeth Taylor look alike. Feline face. Firm, voluptuous figure. She gave a strained smile and waved at her audience.

"Hi boys," she said, placing her hand on her hip and cocking it to the side, "I'm Dottie."

Such a woman had never visited before, and the guides were tongue tied as they introduced themselves. Dottie paid them no mind, her eyes trained on Jessica.

"Well, look at you," Dottie said, looking her up and down. "A real cowgirl. Frederick is just going to eat you up."

She turned as an older man with wild hair and a goatee climbed from the plane. Frederick, Jessica presumed. He wore a plush, collared sweater, horned-rimmed glasses, and had a Meerschaum pipe clamped between his teeth. A wool cap sat atop his head, at nothing less than a rakish angle.

He looked very much the artist to Jessica, who'd never seen one in Braxton. In college, she'd known the exhausting collegiate types, but here, it seemed, was someone of note. There was, in his voice, as he called to the last occupant of the plane, the blasé tone of success, wealth, and power.

"Lana," he called again, as if to a petulant child, and after a moment a young blonde girl of about twenty appeared in the doorway. At first, Jessica thought she may have slept through the entire flight, given her laconic appearance. But as she stepped onto the dock wearing a white blouse and khaki riding pants, her perfect chin lifted in the air, it was clear that she was simply a girl who knew how to make an entrance.

The guides sucked in their breath at the sight of her and puffed out their chests. The girl assayed them with bored, opaque eyes, tamping a cigarette against a gold case. One of the brothers eagerly lit her smoke, and she stood with her arms folded, taking small, delicate puffs.

The entrance only lasted a moment before the pilot, dressed in oily coveralls, stomped down the steps and began tossing their matching sets of luggage on the dock. He brushed by the passengers and, hopping on the floats, opened the plane's rear hatch and pulled out tripods and camera cases and tossed them to Ed, who did his best to make sure they didn't drop into the water.

The pilot then climbed back into the plane and shut his door. The New Yorkers watched him nervously, as if uncertain whether he'd deposited them at the right camp. Jessica grinned, knowing how disappointed they were going to be with the accommodations. By the end of the week, she figured, these city folk would truly know what roughing it meant.

The guides stepped back as the entourage started up the hill. Lana led the pack, although it was clear she didn't know where she was going. She finally spun around at the top of the hill and said, gazing at the camp in a disgusted tone: "Is this the *lodge*?"

"Yep," Jessica replied, turning to the guides and winking, "that's it."

A minute later, the Beaver's engine whined and clattered as it started. When they turned, the pilot signaled and Ed pushed him off with the gaff. As they stood there in the blowing propeller wash, the plane turned and added power, once again filling the air with a thunderous noise.

But as it accelerated across the lake, it didn't look like it would clear the trees on the opposite shore. It slapped against the water repeatedly until the pilot dropped the flaps another notch. After several breathless seconds the plane finally lifted, its floats dripping water, skimming the pines as it rose and began making its way across the valley.

"You need more lake," Frederick said to Ed, and the group laughed uneasily as they continued to watch the plane until it was just a dot. They all must've understood that out here, there were no phone calls made to know that people made it safely. They'd know whether the pilot made it or not when he did or didn't show up at the scheduled time next week.

Dottie then turned and began the formal introductions, first stating that she was one of Frederick's models, as well as his wife.

"These are the Devine brothers, Stephen and Harold." She pointed a painted fingernail at each of them. "They are our staff, so to speak, and they also do some modeling for Freddie. Now, only *I* get to call him that. To the rest of you he is Frederick."

She winked at Jake, who stood there grinning at her so long that Lana practically had to clear her throat.

"Oh and this, as you may or may not know," Dottie added, "is Lana Lord."

Lana did her best to smolder, having perked up at the sight of Sonny, who'd just appeared from under his tree. As he approached, she held out her hand. Sonny looked at it a moment, then picked up her luggage and threw it over his shoulder.

"Miss Lord," he said, tipping his hat before heading towards the nearest tent, "I sure hope you have something in here warmer to wear than that."

Jessica hoped the woman had brought a brassiere as well, as no one—least of all Esther—had failed to notice her pale breasts, clearly visible through her silk blouse.

Lana lowered her hand, but her smile didn't fade as she watched Sonny go. While she stood gazing at him, the group headed towards the lodge, their own luggage and camera cases banging against their knees. Everyone in the entourage was smiling, perhaps thinking of the week of adventure they had ahead of them.

The guides couldn't keep from smiling too; they'd merely have to entertain the group, show them some picturesque spots to set up their cameras, maybe catch some cutthroat for them to pose with. Even Ed was in unusually high spirits, no doubt due to Sonny's presence, who seemed the closest thing he and Esther had to family.

But Jessica paused as the group filed into the lodge, then slipped into her tent and pulled out a canteen full of Old Crow. Peeking out the door, she took several long, burning gulps and let out a pleasurable gasp. She then tucked the whiskey away, popped in a stick of chewing gum, and went to wait on them all.

After breakfast, Jessica fetched a sack of flour from the lock box —a large wooden container behind the lodge—built to keep their stores dry and safe from wildlife. The lock box was made from the same knotty pine as the main lodge, leading her to believe it had been built by the same hardy individual who first settled here. The lodge was crude but sturdy, the work of a logical and industrious mind. Since Ed had bought the camp, it had been tweaked into a finely tuned machine. Ed always said he intended to build permanent cabins in place of the tents, but lamented that winter was quick to come and slow to leave, making it hard to make improvements.

Jessica was carrying the flour back to the kitchen when she saw Sonny by the stables, fussing with Jack. It was a cardinal sin to handle another person's animal, especially out there where people relied on their horses, and their horses on them.

"What are you doing?" she yelled.

He looked up at her, grimacing, as he tried to dig something out of Jack's foot with the end of a file. "This shoe was put on wrong. He's been limping."

"I would've noticed if my horse was limping."

"Well, he's not your horse, he's Scott's. And he *is* limping, and you didn't notice when you should have." He sat back in disgust. "Remind me to not let Scott near any horse of mine."

"He gentled this horse himself. Was just some old scruffy tailed pony when he found him. I'd trust Scott more than I'd trust you with him. Anyway, last I checked you only had a rusty old truck to your name."

"I got more than that," he said.

"I'm sure you're a regular Daddy Warbucks." She looked off at the lake. "All you soldiers bought a couple war bonds and you act like you struck gold."

Sonny picked up the file and resumed his work. "For a person who doesn't know me well, you sure seem to have some strong opinions."

"No," she said, scratching at the ground with her boot, "I

suppose I don't know much about you. But I wish you'd leave Jack alone and let Scott handle it when I get back to town."

"Can't. Sorry. This horse is in pain and I'm not going to let you ride him down like this."

She crossed her arms and sighed. "Have you come into my life to mess it all up? By God, before yesterday everything was going just fine and now everywhere I turn, there you are."

"No, I'm not here to mess your life up," he said without looking at her. "It seems to me like you're doing a pretty good job of that on your own."

"Well, you don't know a thing about me either then."

"Let me give you some friendly advice." He stopped and looked at her. "Don't be so hateful towards people who are trying to help."

"I don't need any help. And God knows why I'd take it from you."

He set back to work. "You don't believe in God, you don't believe in caring for your horse…just what do you believe in?"

"You know, I liked you better when you didn't talk so much."

"That's a shame," he said softly. "Because I happen to like you very much."

She turned her face to keep from blushing in front of him. "You've gone girl crazy after being in camp only an hour. Just like every other cowpunch up here."

"I just mean you're a swell gal, that's all." He tipped back his hat and sighed. "I'll walk him down next time I go to town. You can go down with Ed in his Jeep. You shouldn't be riding up and down alone anyway."

Jessica dropped the flour sack on a fence post. "You've got some nerve. I'll be damned if some…shiftless drifter…is going to tell me what do to."

"I'm just looking out for you," he said, rather earnestly.

"Everyone around here is always looking out for me. Always watching after me. Always in my damn way. I wish everyone would just leave me alone and treat me no different than anyone else. And I thought maybe you would. But you're just like all of them. You wouldn't treat anyone else here like you have me. It's like you want to embarrass and humiliate me just for sport."

She shook her head when he just sat there looking at her. "Maybe you're the strong, silent type," she said, turning back towards the kitchen. "Or maybe you don't say much because you have nothing nice to say."

"Forgetting something?" he asked, after she was a dozen paces away.

She turned and saw the flour sack sitting on the fence post. "Thanks," she mumbled as she grabbed it and stormed back to the kitchen, letting the screen door slam behind her. *Swell gal, my foot,* she thought as she went back to work.

Fifteen

Ed held a little bacchanal that night, after everyone was settled in. There was something in the air, hard to define, that had everyone in unusually good spirits. Even the guests themselves, although reluctant at first, seemed to have been won over by the charm of the old camp and the company. They sat around a blazing campfire after supper, passing a bottle one of the Devine brothers had produced from his luggage. While Ed himself was abstemious and held fast to a no drinking policy, they weren't hunters, and so he watched them drink freely and did nothing to discourage it. He figured that if a guest could pack the liquor in, they were free to do with it as they pleased.

The guides slipped off now and then, he presumed, to have a snort in private. While he wasn't the fool, he did nothing to stop it. Perhaps he'd come to regret this later, but because this was his final season, and there was no pressure for the guides to find game in the coming week, he didn't wish to put a damper on the festive spirit. Especially with Sonny there.

Sonny had written that past winter, saying he expected to be up at camp in early spring; what had taken him so long to make it up here was beyond Ed. But it was clear tonight, from the way Sonny refused the bottle when offered, and kept his distance from the female guests, that he was a professional guide, unlike the rest of them. A man like that could take over a camp like this, Ed thought, stirring the fire with a long stick. If he was of a mind to.

As sparks rose high into the night air, the sky clear and starlit, Frederick stood and rubbed his back. "Well, I ought to be turning in," he said. "All you young people. I can't keep up."

They watched him stumble through the dark, arms spread open and his lips mimicking the sound of a propeller, until he came in for a landing in his tent. Within minutes, those around the fire heard him snoring.

Dale followed suit a few minutes later and then it was just the young folks and Ed, who watched the two Devine brothers polish off the bottle and start to sing some cowboy song Esther had taught them earlier.

Jake sat there across the fire gazing at Dottie, and she back at him. Ed would come to regret not breaking this dalliance up when he first caught wind of it. While he never interfered in a guest's business, his guides were another matter, at least while in camp. He hired them solely on their word and references from places they'd worked. As for their true character, only time revealed if they were the good sort or not.

The Lana girl and Jessica sat in the corner, talking about where they were from and how they'd come to be there. They were of great interest to one another; two completely different women from two completely different places. They seemed glad to let their guard down for the night and engage in some genuine conversation.

"When Frederick got this assignment, he called me straight away," Lana said, now that he was asleep and she wouldn't embarrass him. "He's a wonderful man. He found me on the street. Quite literally. Said he wanted to take my picture. I thought it was just some kind of line." She shook her head. "He took me in and gave me this life. I owe so much to him. He's the closest thing to a father I ever had."

Sonny sat there in the shadows, listening. There was something comforting to his presence, but something unsettling too. He seemed lost, distracted; as were many such men returning from war, understandably.

Ed left Sonny out there after Jessica and Lana had turned in, to keep an eye on things. But as Ed looked out after changing for bed, Sonny was asleep with his hat over his face. As he watched, Dottie snuck out of her tent and crossed by the fire. He then saw Jake, crouched by the stables with a bedroll tucked under his arm. In the moonlight, he could see him lift a finger to his mouth to shush her, before he grabbed her hand and they ran off, giggling into the night.

The group assembled beside the smoldering campfire the following morning for their hike into Six Mile Hole. This would be the best place to get their pictures, Ed assured them, and while everyone had been enthusiastic the night before, they all looked a bit rough around the edges in the daylight.

The Devine brothers were still half asleep and Lana looked as if she'd just been shaken awake. Frederick appeared from his tent with his supplies, appearing as if he'd slept on a rock. Only Dottie and Jake looked alert, and were positively beaming, stealing glances at each other whenever they could.

Ed shook his head. He had other things to concern himself with, and besides, at least half of it wasn't his concern. The other half he'd deal with later.

With a shout, Dale brought out the pack horse.

"Where's Sonny?" Ed asked, grabbing the reins.

Dale shrugged. "No telling."

Ed looked over the pack, checking Dale's diamond hitches, and assured it was well supplied if the weather turned and they had to stay an extra night. After three straight weeks at camp, Dale was then relieved of duty for a few days rest in town. Within moments, he'd climbed atop his own horse, waved and headed on down the trail.

Ed then turned and waved the group forward. "We'll ride from here to the falls and then camp down in the valley tonight."

Jessica and Esther came out and saw them off, wiping their hands on their aprons, wearing concerned expressions. And as the group began a slow procession into the valley, they found Sonny waiting patiently atop a rock, and at the sight of Ed he waved, and led the group down the mountain.

Ed knew then, without asking, that Sonny was staying on as long as he needed him. It may have been the presence of a pretty blonde that had tipped the scales in his favor, but that was okay by him. Looking at Jake, swaggering beside Dottie, he needed all the help he could get.

As the group began their descent into the divide, the sun crested the ridge line, and for a moment, Sonny's silhouette was rimmed with sunlight. He burned white hot, not unlike a signal flare, until all the world that Ed could see before him was a burst of light. It was as unexpected as it was beautiful. He stopped his horse and watched the scene, so he would never forget the majesty of nature, and of life. Within seconds the sun had welded Sonny to the ridge, and just as quickly, he was gone. One by one the group followed, tall mirages walking blindly into the sun, until they too vanished. Ed prodded his horse and followed, and were he able, he would've seen the ridge itself disappear, and he atop his horse, walking a stream of light, down into the shadowy parts of the valley where God's hand had never truly reached.

They arrived at base camp at nine a.m., according to Ed's watch. The horse was watered and the group sat to rest. It was still quite dark in the canyon, and would remain so until about noon.

Jake unpacked the horse and began setting up the lone tent and stoking the wood stove that remained there year round. While Ed usually stayed on by the makeshift camp and tended the horse, with Harold crippled with a hangover, he was given the use of a bedroll and charged with Ed's usual job.

There was a bustle of activity in making camp. Everything had a rhythm to it, and the entourage seemed to understand this, and stayed out of the crew's way. While Frederick checked on his camera equipment, Ed assured that they'd taken the fishing gear and rifle off the pack horse and stowed them among their gear.

Ed felt sorry for Frederick, after what he'd seen last night, and as the group started off down to the river, he let Jake lead and offered to bring up the aft so he could keep an eye on things.

Jake knew the area well enough, and guided them in a westerly direction along a game trail. Within a half hour they were on a butte, glassing the sunlit valley for elk. Here, Frederick reminded Jake that he'd need to be within fifty yards to get a good picture of the herd.

Ed bit his tongue. Had Jake informed him of the photographer's wishes, he would've suggested they cut north to the first ridge, where the herd would likely still be bedded down at this hour. They certainly weren't going to be bathing in the sunlight below them, especially when the leaves were already beginning to fall.

"I see them," Jake said, pointing.

Frederick shot Ed a concerned look. Jake handed over the binoculars so Ed could scan the valley himself. He took them and focused in on a few small elk, which he hoped were part of a herd that was hidden in the nearby timber.

When the group was geared up, Jake threw his scoped carbine

over his shoulder and told Ed that he'd take the lead further into the valley. Ed nodded, hoping that Jake knew something he didn't—as wild game was unpredictable and would often do just the opposite of what was expected. As Ed fell in, he reminded Jake it was a mistake to give animals too much credit, or for a hunter to give themselves the same.

"Luck's on my side today. We may be dressing an elk within an hour if anyone's of a mind to take a shot," Jake said, bounding on ahead of them, Dottie hurrying close behind.

Ed watched them go on ahead, hoping Jake was right.

As if reading his mind, Sonny fell back beside him. "I can call them in if he gets us anywhere near a bull. They'll get the pictures they want."

Ed nodded and rubbed his chin. "There's not much about this Jake kid I trust."

"It's not your concern what happened last night. None of our business. And it's certainly not your problem."

Ed looked at him. "You saw it too?"

Sonny shook his head. "I saw it the second she stepped off that plane. She was trouble from the start, as they say. All we can do is let them get their photographs and get them out of here safe."

"I can't say it's not entirely my business. I hired him. And I'd have sent him on down the trail this morning, but I don't have anyone to replace him. Not many young men want to come out here nowadays. And this isn't an old man's game anymore."

"You're the last of your breed, I'm afraid," Sonny said. "No one wants to cowboy much more these days either. Too much work, too little pay. Too many other things a man can do now."

"And that women can do now," Ed said. "Times are changing there too."

They stopped and watched the group walk deeper into the valley. They looked upon them without speaking, as if understanding that this was the end of something, an era, if not more. Finally, Ed nodded and continued on down, following the group not by sight, but by the noise they made.

It took nearly an hour to reach the spot Jake had seen through the binoculars. They found themselves standing in a clearing of tramped down grass, where the elk had bedded the night before. The herd, however, was long gone. There'd be no pictures of elk today, let alone a shot at one. And so Ed decided on a place where they'd lay in wait the following morning, there in a crop of cottonwood upon which the elk had apparently been feeding just an hour before. Here, the group was instructed to leave no sign—they wouldn't touch anything, they wouldn't sneeze, wouldn't spit.

Ed tore a red handkerchief in half. "We'll be able to spot that from a mile away," he said, tying a piece of it to a cottonwood branch.

They followed the sign of rutting further up the trail. It was a small herd by the looks of it, but there was at least one bull elk among it, judging from the fresh sign he left high on the trees.

Ed stopped beside one of the markings and held up his hand to measure.

"That's some elk," Sonny said, as the others continued ahead. "That's nearly twelve foot high."

"That's no elk," Ed said grimly. "It's a bear. Big one."

They stood studying the markings. Large claws had neatly sheared off the bark.

"Which means we're following him," Sonny said.

"I don't want to alarm any of them yet." Ed turned and watched the group proceeding deeper into the woods. "Let's keep our eyes peeled."

Soon they were entering the bottom of the hole—the river canyon—where the light turned misty and the sight of red volcanic rocks, glittering in the sunlight, seemed to fill Frederick with inspiration. The guides sat back and watched as their team quickly set to work, setting up the camera, dressing up in fishing outfits. Stephen and Lana then waded ankle deep into the stream, holding fishing rods that they clearly didn't know how to use.

"Hurry," Frederick announced as he set up his camera's tripod, "the light is perfect."

Ed knew that within minutes the sun would pass over them, and they'd again be covered in shadow. But at that moment, the waterfall glowed and its spray filled the air with millions of gold flakes, before dropping into an icy pool. The two models stood mid-stream in their crisp designer clothing, their teeth already beginning to chatter.

Frederick stood snapping pictures behind his twin lens camera, stopping only to change rolls, until the light at last faded and he called them in, Lana's lips nearly blue.

He wore a solemn, pensive expression, and the smiles on his models' faces dimmed.

"It's no good," he said finally. "Good enough for my editor, maybe. But to me, it didn't look real. Looked more like," he shook his head, "like some kind of hootenanny."

The models went to change, and once dry, sat under a pine tree smoking cigarettes and looking glum.

"Dorothy hasn't even asked once for me to take her picture, as she usually does," Frederick said as he was packing up his gear. He turned and faced Ed, cleaning the camera lens with a piece of chamois.

"This was foolish of me. I thought I could get away. Make her happy again." He looked over at Dottie, talking to Jake beside the stream. "But even old men can be given to desperate notions. I suppose there's a price an old man pays for marrying a woman less than half his age. It's not the first time she's done this. Don't you worry." He sighed, tucking the lens away. "I may be old, but I'm not blind. She's gotten even bolder, doesn't even hide it anymore. I don't know who she thinks she's making a fool of. And I suppose I should hate a man like that, but I was a man like that once. I've had my day too."

Ed didn't speak, didn't want to lie and say he hadn't seen it all too. And for a moment he was thankful he'd married a woman like Esther, who never once gave him reason to worry.

"Well, my friend," Frederick said, closing up his duffel bag, "soon enough there will be no time left. For last chances. For my marriage, for my work. Or for adventures like this." Frederick turned and looked out into the shadowy canyon.

"I'm afraid it's the last chance for this place too."

"How do you mean?"

"Government's got me taxed up to my neck. Only way to pay is to sell it off, but the only man who can afford it is going to turn this all into a skiing resort."

Frederick shook his head and took off his hat, to get a better view of the surrounding mountains. "Would I be asking too much," he whispered, looking up, as if in prayer, "if nothing else, I get one last honest photograph of your place while I'm here? For the both of us?"

The group slogged quietly back to base camp, where the sickly Devine brother was still asleep in his bedroll. It was only past four but already it was growing dark and Ed stoked the fire and everyone gathered around for a supper of beans, flapjacks, and coffee with condensed milk. Sonny didn't join them, and even after dinner he made his bed beneath a tree by the horse, which did not deter Jake and Dottie sneaking out after everyone was asleep. Ed opened one eye as the tent flap opened, and there in the glimmering light of the moon, he saw Frederick lift his head and then let it slowly back down again.

The following morning, Ed awakened to find Jake dressed and ready to go. He was standing outside the tent doing gunfighter tricks with his pistol. Twirling it while Dottie and Lana watched.

Hollywood, Ed thought as he passed by. That would be a good nickname for a guy like old Jake.

"Isn't he marvelous?" Dottie asked, and even Lana seemed to understand the gleam in Dottie's eyes as she watched him.

"No bullets in it, Ed, don't you worry," Jake said, twirling it around some more before putting it back in his holster. Dottie clapped and Ed turned to see Sonny tying up his bedroll as Lana came and stood beside him, looking up with what seemed like genuine admiration.

Ed stayed behind at the base camp with the horse as the group hiked back into the valley, headed towards the field where they'd seen the bedding elk the day before. They traveled northwest, through the divide, and Ed watched them until they disappeared into the aspen.

He sat there on the wooden platform on which the canvas tent stood. He listened a moment, the noises of their movements fading until at last he was alone, with nothing but the quiet of the valley, the rustling trees, and the wind sweeping down the mountains like a big hand, waving a few errant golden leaves to the ground.

Were it not for the stove it would have been mercilessly cold. Soon there'd be snow, which made the tracking of the animals easier, but somehow everything was harder in winter; wetness permeated everything, from one's socks up to one's undershirt, and the icy sheet that would soon cover the landscape would make everything feel grim, and would bring danger to those who hunted there.

Ed was happy to rest. There was never a moment when he wasn't loading or unloading, hiking here or riding there. Life was a constant state of packing, unpacking, folding, unfolding, tying and untying, bending and standing, opening and closing, and it wasn't until that moment that he realized how tired he truly was.

Even that morning, he'd awakened at four, before anyone else. Sleep was never deep when one's mind was busy planning for the following day. And while he had good people working for him, he always had to make sure they were working together for the same aim. And in that, his job was often tough, especially with loose ends like Jake.

While he could've crawled into the tent for an hour's sleep, he instead went and checked on the little camp, and when all looked good he stood back as he sometimes did, and thought with a sense of pride what a fine operation this was. The horse they'd brought down with them, meticulously cared for and maintained. The thick leather bridle, their gear packed neatly to it, and even the canvas tent behind him, the inevitable holes patched carefully by Esther that past winter, in their own home.

He was glad Sonny was there, who knew this wilderness. Jake, he wasn't so sure. Hunters who packed in and hunted there alone were not only unsuccessful, they were sometimes never heard from again. The Crooked Mountains had a way of spinning a man around, making him lose his senses. Those who didn't respect the conditions that had given these mountains their name were often discovered only after their steps were re-traced in the snow. Their bodies frozen where they'd last sat down to rest. Having walked in giant circles, as if frightened by something, their maps and compass still stowed in their packs.

As Ed stood there, his thoughts were interrupted by the muted but unmistakable sound of a gun shot. A single sharp crack. He turned quickly as the sound of the report echoed and rippled through the valley.

As near as he could figure, it came from about a mile away. He looked over at his horse, the rifle still in its scabbard. No one else out here but Jake had a gun and he wouldn't use it unless the group was in danger. Such a noise, as any hunter knew, would send any herds in the area scattering.

Perhaps it had been a distress call, he thought, but as he waited for a follow up shot, none came. He scanned the ridge line with his binoculars for signs of other hunters in the area. While it was public land, the likelihood of anyone having come to this exact spot was improbable. Or maybe, Ed thought, Jake had fired at something else out there.

Grizzly, Ed thought, untying and mounting his horse. He dug his heels into its flanks and they shot off into the woods. As they galloped along he pulled his 45/70 from his scabbard and opened the breech to assure it was loaded. The brass casing sat there, the size of his thumb, and as he closed it and rested the rifle across his lap, he pressed into the woods, following the trail Jake's group had taken not an hour before.

He ducked overhanging branches, working through the woods, until he came upon them a few minutes later, sitting in a circle with their backs against the trees. Ed's eyes hurriedly scanned the group to see what had happened.

Jake rose slowly at the sight of Ed, his head hanging low. Sonny stood beside him, holding Jake's pistol, his holster and belt laying on the ground. Jake shoved his hands in his pockets as Ed dismounted and threw the reins over a nearby branch.

Jake, to his credit, was the first to speak. "My belt buckle broke, dumped my pistol on a rock. Damn thing just went off. Scared us all pretty good."

For the first time Ed had ever witnessed, he looked meek, apologetic.

"He was carrying it cocked," Sonny said. "Or he had the hammer set so light that it got pulled back on something. I heard the bullet whistle right by us. It's a miracle none of us was killed."

Ed stood there, looking at them, letting the weight of Sonny's words hang in the air.

It was still barely daylight, nearing six. The group was just a mile from where they intended to photograph the herd they'd scouted out the previous day. But their dejected faces showed that even they knew they weren't going to find the herd today either.

"Jake," Ed said, before turning and walking to the horse, "come over here."

Everyone seemed to know what was to happen next. Ed knew better than to have a conversation there, where not only the clients could overhear, but where Jake might have some kind of fit. But Jake must've known, like everyone else, that the moment that gun went off, he would be lucky to only lose his job.

"The damn cheap belt buckle I had, Ed. It just twisted," Jake said.

Ed stood there looking at the ground. "You know my rules on this. Now you ride on back to base camp on my horse and stay there until we return. I'm going to lead this team the rest of the day. You watch over camp and the horse and we'll talk when we get back."

Ed walked back to the group, leaving Jake standing by the horse. He collected the pistol from Sonny and turned to Jake.

"I'll give this back to you tonight." He nodded towards his rifle in the scabbard. "You hold onto that. It's too heavy for us to carry." He then reached up and unlashed his own pack from the horse. "You ride her on back and we'll see you tonight."

The horse looked at Ed as Jake mounted him, and without a word, he swung it around and headed back down the trail. Ed and the group stood there watching them go.

Dottie's lips trembled, as if she was about speak up. To go with him. But instead she stood there by Frederick and the rest of the group, fighting back tears.

"I tell you Ed," Stephen said, "I didn't like that boy from the start. I wouldn't think a man like you would hire someone like that."

Ed nodded and toed the ground with his boot. "I'm sorry everyone. These things happen. He came highly recommended from folks in town. He's young. And a man deserves a chance to prove himself. But what happened here, there's no excuse. Sonny here will take the lead and I'll follow. With a little luck, the shot didn't scare off the herd and you can get your photographs, Mister Grosbeck."

The group gathered themselves and continued on their intended course. An hour later they came upon the cottonwood with the red handkerchief tied to it. Ed glassed the spot and then handed the binoculars to Frederick.

"I don't see anything," Frederick said, working its levers and dials.

"Damn." Ed stared off at the bowl like impression in the valley. If the herd had rushed down into it, they'd be cornered there by two adjacent ridges. But today, it seemed as if the elk had simply vanished.

"Wait," Frederick said, pressing the binoculars closer to his eyes. "I see them. They're deep in those trees down there."

Dottie stayed behind with Harold while the rest of the group walked quietly down the game trail until they came to a bluff.

"Jesus, Mary and Joseph," Stephen muttered, and Lana placed her hand over his mouth as well as her own.

The four of them stood there looking down at the valley floor, which was crawling with elk. They could see hundreds of straw colored bodies, their dark heads and branch like horns, several feet high and wide. There was a sense of majesty to the scene before them and they stood there rapt and unmoving, watching the herd feed.

Stephen slowly took the tripod from his shoulder and carefully set it up on a rock. Frederick attached his camera to it and began adjusting its aperture and lens, lifting his head occasionally from the viewfinder to check the light.

"This is color slide film," he whispered, "I need more light than this."

"Wait a few minutes," Ed replied, looking up at the sky. "You'll get your light. But be quick. The herd will begin to move when the sun hits them."

Soon the valley indeed filled with light and Frederick quickly set to work. He was changing out a roll of film when they heard the thunderous drumming of a thousand hoofs, and when they looked below the herd was fleeing in a swirling mass. Within moments, the valley had emptied of elk, as quickly as water runs down a drain.

"Damn," Frederick muttered, snapping the fresh film roll into his camera.

Ed stood glassing the valley and saw the reason for the sudden departure—and it wasn't sunlight. It was a bear, lumbering through the field after the herd.

"There it is," he said, lifting his eyes from the binoculars and handing them to Sonny.

"I see him," Frederick said, looking through his viewfinder. "My, he's quite big."

"She," Sonny said. "It's a girl by the looks of it."

"Well, she stopped," Frederick said. The camera shutter snapped and he leaned back and smiled. "That one should turn out nice."

"She's looking right up at us," Sonny said, handing Ed the binoculars.

Sure enough the bear was standing in the middle of the field, lifting its nose to pick up their scent. Ed's heart began to thump in his chest. This might've been the bear leaving tracks all over the camp trail. She certainly was big, one of the biggest he'd ever seen. A bear like that would be hungry this time of year. Hungry enough to think of them as an easy meal.

Frederick continued to snap his pictures. "Magnificent," he whispered.

"How far would you say she is?" Ed said, turning to Sonny, who was already beginning to assemble their gear.

"Half a mile if it's a foot," he said, throwing a pack over his shoulder. "Too close for me."

"Yeah," Ed said, looking at Frederick, Lana and Stephen, "let's move."

As they hurried to rejoin Dottie and Harold, who they found huddled together and nodding off against one another, Ed decided that they wouldn't be spending another night in the valley. They'd hurry back to collect Jake and the horse, then make their way back up to main camp.

"Bear," Stephen said to the dozing pair. "Big grizzly. Frederick got some great pictures of it."

The two were slow to rouse and Sonny went and jerked them to their feet.

"What's the big idea," Dottie said, pulling her arm away from him.

"Fun's over," Sonny said, looking back at her with what Ed took for complete loathing. "It's time to get moving."

As the others assembled and started off, Dottie stood there with her arms folded. "Some day this has been. I want to go have a look at it myself," she said, and began heading down the trail towards the bluff.

Sonny came and grabbed her arm again. "If you don't fall in right now, we're going to leave you behind."

She glared at him, then at Frederick. "Freddie, are you going to let him talk to me like this?"

"Leave her," Frederick said to Sonny, then turned and headed back towards camp with the others.

Dottie tore away and huffed after them. As Sonny and Ed fell in behind them, Ed's mind was on the talk he'd have to have with Jake when they reached camp, where he'd be instructed to pack up his gear and head on down the trail.

But when they arrived an hour later, it appeared that Jake had anticipated such a talk himself—the tent flap was open and blowing leisurely in the wind, and both Ed's horse and Jake were gone.

"Well, I'll be a sunumbitch," Ed muttered, removing his hat and smacking it against his knee. "Damn it."

"He left?" Dottie said, turning frantically. "Jake *left* us?"

"Sure as hell did," Sonny said, examining what little had been left behind. "Without a horse or a real gun."

"Well," Ed said, as the others spun around in the clearing, looking for any sign of him, "I'm sorry again. I never thought in a million years a man would let us down like this." He sighed. "It's too late for us to make our way up to main camp tonight. Too dangerous in the dark. We'll have to stay the night here and head back in the morning."

"What about the bear?" Lana said, moving closer to Sonny.

"This'll have to do." Ed drew the pistol from his belt and held it up. Even to the New Yorkers, it mustn't have looked like much defense against the animal they'd seen. He opened the loading gate, and after assuring it had several rounds left in it, snapped it closed and shoved it back in his belt.

After a supper of stale hoecakes and water, the seven of them huddled around the stove. The mood was dark and grim until Ed lit their lone lantern and produced a deck of cards. All except for the Devine brothers, who were already fast asleep in their cots, agreed on a game of stud poker, eager to get the bear off their minds.

Ed cursed Jake under his breath as he dealt the cards. Frederick sat to his left, thoughtfully smoking his pipe. For all that had taken place between his wife and Jake, he seemed in fine spirits, perhaps feeling vindicated that Jake had proved to be the bad sort after all. He paid little mind to Dottie, who seemed distracted with Jake's absence and so picked up her hand only half-heartedly.

Lana sat nuzzled up to Sonny, who Ed was beginning to suspect was made of steel. While he disapproved of Jake's actions and would've eventually fired him anyway, Sonny and Lana were young and unwed. He saw no harm in them hitching up. And yet it seemed peculiar that a girl like Lana would take an interest in Sonny, although he supposed she saw something in him that she herself lacked.

As the players picked up their cards, a tree branch cracked loudly, not fifty feet outside. The tent went quiet. The Devine brothers, deep in their sleep, shot up in their cots as if on springs.

"What was that?" they shouted in unison.

"Maybe it's Jake," Dottie said hopefully, her eyes flashing towards the tent flap.

Ed dropped his cards and slipped the revolver from where it hung in its holster beside his cot. He held up his finger to silence the group, but they all nearly jumped when the noise came again. Closer this time. Suddenly more branches began to snap as something crashed into the clearing and snorted loudly.

Ed's blood went frost cold. It was foolish to have camped there overnight, he realized then. The possibility of the bear following after the group, and not the elk herd, had seemed quite remote up until that very moment. As he pondered their situation, more dire than he'd dare let on, there came a putrid smell. *Oh my,* he remembered then—just how bad a grizzly smelled—of scat, mud and rot.

The group of New Yorkers, by the time the smell hit their noses, must've understood the situation quite well too: there was an animal outside that could bat their tent down with one swat of its claw, then kill each of them with no greater effort, one after the other, until it was satisfied.

141

Ed blew out the lantern and drew back the pistol's hammer as the bear circled the tent, grunting and breathing wetly. Finally it stopped and let out a roar just feet from the open doorway, where he could clearly see its massive shape framed by starlight.

Still, no one moved. Nobody screamed. They were all, without question, paralyzed. It had all happened faster than he ever would've guessed. He'd read of Sioux women strangling crying babies when the U.S. Cavalry marched by their hiding places during the Indian Wars, to keep the tribe from being discovered. He now understood the necessity of such an act, of sacrificing one life for the sake of the others.

Ed stood and walked towards the open tent flap. He couldn't see the bear's face. Just the shadow of it, the faint moonlight shining off its bristling coat. It was waiting, he thought. Waiting to see what they would do. The others sat watching the gun barrel as if nothing else in the world had ever been so interesting to them. To see what would happen if he squeezed the trigger.

At best, Ed figured, the bullet would glance off its skull, if he was so lucky to hit it there. If he hit it in the shoulder, it would sink no deeper than the fat layer, becoming something akin to a wasp sting for a human, and would only enrage the animal.

Now they could hear it grunting, could smell the hot stench of its breath. The bear could've barged right in and had her way with them, but she was hesitating for some reason. As Ed stood there holding the gun, ready to fire at its charge, he looked down at Frederick's smoldering pipe, still clenched between his teeth. Ribbons of smoke were being drawn out the open door to where the bear stood.

Just as it occurred to him that the bear was afraid of the smoke, Sonny reached forward and opened the hot stove door, exposing the belly of the fire. The bear huffed and lurched back. As they sat there unmoving, the bear—now lit by firelight—lifted her head, swung around and waddled off into the bushes.

The tent was then filled with the sound of long withheld breaths being exhaled, with whimpers and cries, and they all sat there touching one another, making sure they were unharmed, although after a moment they agreed that the bear likely hadn't retreated very far.

Ed stoked the stove, glad he'd brought in enough wood to keep the fire going through the night. Lana sat wrapping Sonny's burned hand in a piece of cloth, although he kept telling her he was okay. The Devine brothers were sitting bolt upright, back to back, while Dottie drifted into a fitful sleep.

At last Frederick unclenched the pipe from his mouth and remarked that the mouthpiece was cracked. He held the broken pieces out to Ed and shook his head. "I wish like hell I'd gotten a picture of that beast."

"Keep your camera at the ready," Ed said, staring out the open tent door. "You may get your chance yet."

Sixteen

Francine stood beside the barn talking to the group of cattle that were lined up against the gate. They were ignoring the hay bales she'd just kicked from the loft and instead stared at her where she stood on the lowest rung of the corral fence. The effect of them gazing up at her dolefully was disconcerting. She looked down at her outfit, and finding it no different than ordinary, put her hands on her hips.

"Go on now," she said, waving a hand at them. "What's wrong with you? Eat!"

They continued to look at her, fighting for a position closest to her until one large cow pushed against the fence, knocking her backwards and onto the ground.

She hit hard and lay there a moment, dazed. Normally Sonny would've been there to laugh and help her up, but now she just had the dead-eyed faces of the cattle to cheer her. They came to the fence and stuck their wet noses against it.

"Well, thanks for you concern, but your mama is alright."

They didn't budge. Just kept staring at her. For a moment she indulged the idea that the cows cared for her, and that she had, nearing thirty and childless, developed maternal qualities and affection for her stock. It was a silly notion. Come spring, the bulk of them would be auctioned and sold by the pound, and although it would make her heartsick, it was a necessity if this place was to stay afloat.

Paying guests wouldn't be coming until then and meantime, she'd have to pinch her pennies. Things still had yet to be settled back east. Thomas had continued to make things difficult, draining their bank accounts, while he knew full well all her assets in New York were frozen until the divorce was settled. The man was slowly trying to bleed her dry. Or, impossible as it seemed, he was hoping she'd come back to him, tail between her legs. And be the good, hush-mouthed wife he'd always wanted.

144

Francine stood and dusted herself off. Like these cattle, Thomas was going to end up making a fool out of her. Regardless, Wyoming was indeed where she was now, and she had no intention of leaving. Even if the bank came and took the land. Her car. Her horses. Or the cattle she didn't even know how to feed properly.

But when she looked over her shoulder, she realized why the cattle were acting so strange. The sky had turned gray, and over the Crooked Mountains, the clouds were darker yet. And low. She had the sinking sensation then, watching them quickly enshroud the mountains, that a bad storm was coming. And judging from the sudden chill in the air, it was going to be snow that fell.

Francine had begun to prepare for winter, but hadn't expected it so soon. Her Farmers' Almanac had predicted it would be a long one, and there was still plenty to do before it arrived. She'd spent the past days going through the cabins, washing windows and scrubbing floors, seeing what of the bedding and furniture would be salvageable come spring. She'd made sure doors were sealed tight, and had put a lock on each one, to assure that she had no more uninvited guests.

At times it felt like a strange compulsion, fixing this old place up and get it going again. But such an obsession was not unwelcome, as it kept her mind off of other things. And only time would truly tell if her wager on this place was foolhardy, or if come spring she'd be flush with guests.

So far she'd gotten by solely on hope and what money she had before her marriage. Back when she still had hope in spades, as most young women do, before life took hold.

Hope. She thought of the word, looking up at the coming storm. As a child, hope had always seemed like something from a storybook. A downy, feathery creature. One that could fly arrow straight from a blue sky into her heart. And there inside her it might flutter, lilt, and pull something—like a silk ribbon—spooled tightly inside, and take it under wing and fly away, where she could but watch and feel the great unspooling, the ribbon dancing in the wind as the bird flew to and fro.

Now, her hope was often more subdued, although at times it still burst out of her unexpectedly, wings flapping madly. It was that very kind of hope which had brought her here, set her to fixing the place up, even while people like Heaton laughed at her. While people in town cut down her sign. Thomas had also tried to take her hope away—she saw that now. New York and its socialite scene had tried to suck it away from her too. And for a time she'd thought it gone, until she set her eyes on this old place.

And there wasn't a damn thing she had left, she told herself, a bitter wind raking across her, her eyes trained on the dark mountains, if not hope. To this one thing, she knew she could not let go.

The wind picked up again and the cows began lowing in the corral. Those left out to graze had congregated in the middle of the valley and she could see them, over the rolling hills, a brown and black herd, roaming away from the coming storm.

When she turned she saw a cowboy on a sorrel come down the trail from the mountain and pause beneath the new metal sign at the end of the driveway. For a moment her heart lifted, thinking it might be Sonny, coming back to check on her. The figure was far off, but she could see him pause to look back at her. When he waved and plodded over, his hand on the butt of an old rifle, she saw that he was not Sonny at all, and her heart sank.

"You that crazy lady bought this old place?" he yelled, lifting the collar of his duster, looking around the ranch. "I barely recognize it now."

She nodded. "You work up at that camp?

"Yes, but my time there was up." His voice was sharp and thin as he yelled over the wind. There were dark circles around his eyes. "You have any work around here needs done? You're going to need those cows out there rounded up before this storm comes. They're liable to try and cross the river and drown."

She looked at him a long time, not particularly liking what she saw. He seemed too young to be so arrogant. And yet there was indeed much to be done. And not just today. She needed a good line rider for one thing, to check her fences and keep her cows together. It would be no problem to let him use Sonny's old cabin, she reasoned, looking him over some more.

"I could always use some help," she managed. "And now's a good a time as any."

"Name's Jake," he leaned over and extended his hand.

She shook his still gloved hand. "Francine."

"Well, Francine," he said, looking over her place. "You need yourself a cowboy, you're looking at one of the best."

Francine came back with some coffee for him, wearing a long oil cloth coat. The wind had picked up, and the storm was still hovering over the mountain. She paused, looking up at it. She still knew little about what was up there. Some kind of fishing camp; perhaps their season was winding down, which might explain Jake coming down the trail midweek, looking for work.

She expected he'd already be off rounding up the grazing cattle, but instead she found him leaning against the barn wrapped in his saddle blanket, the rifle beside him, his legs crossed and his hat covering his face.

"And here I thought you'd be hard at work," she said, offering him the mug of coffee.

He tilted back his hat. "You ain't told me what to do yet." He reached up and took the coffee from her. "That's how this works. If indeed you're the boss around here."

"Well, it seems a good cowboy should know what needs to be done and I shouldn't have to tell him."

He stood up, looking around, and grinned at her. "Well, everything looks pretty good around here I must say."

She laughed. "Then what would I need you for?"

"Company? Someone to keep you and these cows safe. Maybe I could go now and round them up for you, keep them from drowning. Might not ask for money at all. That is, maybe we can work out some other kind of arrangement."

He moved closer and took her arm. She looked down at his hand, then up at him, a frosty chill passing through her, realizing he'd been sitting there while she was inside, planning this.

"Please let me go."

"Why?"

"Because I asked you to."

There was nothing in his tone to suggest he had anything other than success with this sort of approach with women in the past, and nothing in her tone to suggest she, despite having the sensation of a snake gripping her arm, wasn't in complete control of the situation.

147

She ripped her arm from him, spilling his coffee on the ground. Four months working the ranch had given her a strength she'd never known.

She glared at his stunned face. "I think it's time you keep on going down the trail."

He rocked back on his heels and snickered. "Those are big words from a woman living out here all alone. If you ask me, you've bit off more than you can chew and it's just a matter of time before it bites you back." He nodded off at the storm. "And I say it's coming your way any minute now."

"Then you should get a head start."

"I may just have to bed down in the barn here until it passes. Might not make it to town before it hits."

She looked at him, squinting, then casually reached over and picked up the old rifle leaning against the barn, and pointed it at him.

He took a step back. "That's hardly necessary."

"You have trouble understanding things don't you?" She looked down and drew back the hammer. "Like when you're no longer wanted somewhere."

"You should know better than to separate a man from his rifle, Francine." His tone softened. "Come on now, I was just having some fun. Didn't mean nothing. Now give it back."

He stepped forward and she brought the rifle to her shoulder, aiming it right at his heart.

Jake froze, his eyes trained on the barrel. "Figures," he said, then bent and picked up his saddle blanket. "You are crazy. And a fool. Only such a person would buy a God forsaken place as this."

Jim Hickens' truck rumbled up the drive just then, blowing dust as it came to a stop. Francine lowered the rifle as he climbed from the cab. Jim gave a look up to her and waved, then walked up slowly to where she and Jake stood.

"Morning y'all," he said, smiling at them both, seeming not to notice the tension there between them. "Francine, I hate to drop by unannounced but we have some business to discuss." He looked up at the sky. "And there's some urgency here. That storm will be upon us within the hour."

"That's perfectly fine, Mister Hickens," Francine said, her eyes still locked on Jake. "My guest here was just leaving. Isn't that right?"

"Morning Jake," Jim said, turning. "Say, it's only the beginning of elk season yet. I thought you were signed on for the season up at camp?"

"I wasn't getting paid enough, so I thought it best I leave. I don't think they'll have much luck without me either." He played with the buttons on his shirt a moment. "Well, I got to see about moving on. Doesn't seem like any help is needed around here, but I thank you for the job offer, Miss," he added, tipping his hat to her.

Francine bit her lip and together she and Jim watched him mount his horse and head down the driveway.

Jim shook his head, pulling up the collar on his own jacket. "If ever there was a no-good piece of nothing, you're looking at him. Steal your wife, kill your dog, take the money and run. That's old Jake Haggard." He looked at her. "Be glad to be seeing the back of him and headed in the other direction at that."

He finally acknowledged the rifle in her hands. "If memory serves, that was Ed McCann's. Long story behind that old piece there."

"Ed McCann?" The name struck her like a bolt of lightning.

Jim nodded.

"Eddie McCann? I thought he was killed a long time ago. In a rodeo."

"No," he laughed. "He's alive and well, works up on that mountain. Well, most of the year anyway. He owns the land up there you're interested in. Which is why I'm here." He turned and looked up at the darkening clouds. "We best go inside to talk."

"I'm afraid this isn't a social visit," Jim said, seating himself at the long table in the main room. "And I think you already know what I'm about to say." He sighed. "That check you wrote, the deposit. Well, I'm sorry to say it bounced."

Francine shook her head slowly. "I figured it would be weeks before anyone tried to cash it." She set two mugs of reheated coffee on the table and sat opposite him. "I'm still waiting for things to get cleared up back in New York, you see. I'll call my lawyer in the morning and get it sorted out. I'll find the money, somehow."

"Well, it's too late now, I'm afraid. The state is officially in possession of the land as of yesterday, due to the back taxes owed on it. Ed doesn't even know yet." Jim removed his hat and hung it on the chair back beside him. "And I've been informed the land is going up for sale at public auction next month. It'll be listed in the papers, which means our friend Will Heaton will hear about it, and you can bet he'll be there when the bidding starts. And I don't know anyone with pockets deep as him."

Francine looked down at her hands as Jim picked up his coffee and blew on it.

"I'm sorry Francine, but there's not much else I can do here."

"I was hoping I wouldn't have to look out my window and see a chair lift to the top of the mountain, but doesn't look like that will be the case."

"That's not all you're going to see. There will be roads. Parking lots. Buildings. Sure as the sun will rise tomorrow, this town is going to change. And fast."

Francine stared out the window at the coming storm, moving slowly towards them. "I don't suppose," she said, picking up her coffee, "that you know anything about that sign in my front yard."

He chuckled. "Francine, if I'd known it had been cut down to begin with I would've been the first out here, but I'm ashamed to say I know nothing about it."

"I think Heaton did it," she said, turning to him.

Jim laughed again. "That'll be the day." He put his hat back on his head and drank the last of his coffee. "I knew him when he was just a kid. He had a sparkle in his eye then. Not unlike you, when you first came here. Walked around like he could throw a lasso around the world. He was a different person then. The accident changed all that."

Francine set down her coffee. "What accident?"

"Yes indeed," Jim continued, as if she hadn't spoken, "he came here thinking he'd be a cattle king. He's an oil man if you ask me. Buys any land down in Texas when he thinks it might have oil under it. He's a gambler, when it comes down to it. A *speculator*. But he doesn't do things like fix up houses and ranches. If he bought this place he would've razed it and used it as cow pasture…but I guess it was too expensive for him to use it for that. And now, the cattle days are over and so he's got to find a new way to make his money here."

He stared in the bottom of his empty mug. "You're no threat to him. Neither is anyone else in town. If I know Will, he's going to give up on cattle, except as a sporting enterprise. But if he gets his hand on this land here for sale," he stamped his mug down on the table, "he'll have a lock on all the mountains and any development that ever happens to them.

"There's other places in the country that already got the drop on him. Big ski places. He sees the money they're making and wants a piece of it. But if you ask me, he don't need the money. It's all just a game to him. And our town, and these mountains, are the chess board."

Jim leaned back and crossed his arms. "He's already got that airport under way. He has a ski lift, and trails cut on the other side of the range. Even brought in equipment that will make snow when there's none. But what he don't know a damn thing about is *hospitality*. Hell, just look at the Sundowner. Not a shred of hospitality there. So, there will be places for folks like you yet, should you get your finances in order."

Francine sat there looking at him. It seemed to her the entire nature of their relationship had shifted. She was just *folks* to Jim Hickens now. Gone were the embraces from him and Iris, the pistols to ward off bears, the friendly advice. This whole meeting was to show her that she was on the outside of the club now. She was no longer, in the eyes of a county land commissioner, a real player in this latest land grab. Were the land in question still for sale, she knew he'd have gone to Heaton with it immediately. He may have even been sorry he hadn't done so in the first place.

"So what about the accident?" Francine said, lighting a cigarette.

"It was an automobile crash. About ten years ago. Took his wife and young boy, who was about three years old at the time. Truck ran them off the highway down in Texas. Both killed. Heaton was off somewhere, speculating at the time. When he came home and found out about it, he blamed himself. Not sure how a man couldn't. But Lord knows he loved that woman, as much as he did that child. Tore him to pieces, really. Was hard to watch."

Jim stood and buttoned his coat. "Ever since then he's become a very private man, as you know. Makes his money to fill some deep pit inside him. He won't stop until he's got everything. I believe he thinks that will be like having his wife and son back. I don't know. I can figure out his business ideas, but I will never understand that man or his heart. If he still has one."

She stood and walked him to the door. As she opened it, the wind began to howl. "What is it you want this town to be?" she asked, shouting over the noise. "You offered that land to me first."

He just looked at her and grinned. "You best make sure all your animals are inside and warm tonight." He tipped his hat and she watched him drive away, his truck quickly swallowed by the blowing dust.

After it had vanished she looked east and saw that her cows had broken through her fence and were headed towards Heaton's herd, which was grazing by the river.

"Damn it," she yelled, throwing on her coat and running outside, where she hastily saddled her horse. She climbed on and rode hard after them, soon crossing over the barbed wire fence that her cows had positively flattened. They were still over a mile off and moving steadily towards the river. As she came over a rise she saw that Heaton's line rider had noticed the stampede and was doing his best to keep the herds separated.

As she neared she saw that Heaton himself was out there, riding among the cattle, attempting to head them off. When he noticed her approaching he turned and rode over, wearing only a wool shirt and cotton chino pants. It looked as if he'd run out of the house wearing what he had on. Even his head was bare.

"Can't you see there's a storm coming?" he yelled over the bitter wind. "You never let cows graze when a storm is coming. That's when fences get broken." He spun around on his horse, squinting in the direction of the river.

"Well, I don't want my cows mixed in with your Longhorn any more than you do."

He looked up at the darkening sky and sighed. "I have but one man working with me today. Didn't see this storm coming. It's too early for winter."

Sitting there atop his horse, after what Jim had told her, she saw Heaton in a new light. As more of a person than he'd ever been to her before. Her tone softened. "Best we can do is keep them together for now, Will. No sense in trying to separate them until the storm passes. Have your line rider go mend that fence and we'll try and gather them all together."

He grinned at her, as if surprised that she'd so swiftly devised such a sensible plan. He nodded in agreement, then yelled after his man, who rode off quickly to fix the fence.

"Think your cows can bear to spend any time with mine?" he asked.

The joke wasn't lost on her. "I doubt it. But it doesn't look like they have a choice." She picked up her reins and eyed the herd, milling about the river banks.

"I'm going to lose all my calves if they try and cross. And I only have one male left. I lose him and my next season is over." He looked at her a moment, as if sizing her up. "Do you know how to do a proper round up?"

Francine looked over the valley, from where they sat atop a small hill. Behind and to the east lay her ranch, and before her the expanse of the valley, coppery fields stretching into the mountains, divided by the wide trough of the Snake River.

Before she could answer, the first snowflakes fell, small at first, swirling and dancing between them.

"Let's go," she said, prodding her horse, and together they turned and trotted towards the river.

There they encircled the herd, each riding as fast as they could in opposite directions, standing in their stirrups and waving an arm. The herd slowed at the sight of them, and began to group together as she and Will rode around them in a wide loop. At last they drew up together and stopped, breathing heavily, smiling at one another.

"Not bad," he said, sitting back and admiring their handiwork.

It was odd to see all their cattle intermingled. The conjoined herd had stopped on the bluff beside the river, and some, not liking its sharp slope, began backing up the hill. As they did, a few stragglers broke free and continued their charge towards the river, now only a hundred feet away.

"Well, there he goes," Heaton said, pointing as his last calf ambled down to the river, following after a few panicked Longhorn. "He's going to try and cross with them and when he does, he's going to drown."

Francine looked over and saw the rope hanging from the

pommel of his saddle. Without pause, she reached over and grabbed it, then kicked her heels into her horse.

"Let them go, it's not worth it!" he yelled, but already she was underway.

The calf was just entering the water as Francine dismounted, grabbed the lasso and threw a loop just like Sonny had showed her. It happened faster than she could put together. One moment she was atop her horse and the next the open loop of rope was sailing over the swollen river. By some miracle, some stroke of luck, the lasso uncoiled neatly and fell around the calf's neck. To anyone watching, Heaton most of all, she'd just earned her stripes.

She shouted out in astonishment before remembering to draw the lasso tight. The calf was already deep in the current, twisting and turning against the rope, and as the river pulled at it, she leaned back against the rocky shore, but her boots quickly gave way. As the calf yanked her into the frigid water, she gasped.

At the same moment, she heard Heaton behind her. "Let go! Let go of that damned rope!"

"No!" she shouted in reply, even as the calf was pulled further out and downstream. She had a good grip on it though, and she wasn't going to let it go—not after that perfect throw she'd made. If she could just guide him to shore, she knew everything would be okay.

Below her were rapids, heaving torrents of water, and with one final burst of strength, she tried to swing the calf ashore. But it was of no use—it may as well been the river bottom itself for how heavy the calf seemed. As she did her best to hold the thrashing calf there, it went under and didn't come up.

"Let go or he's going to take you with him," Heaton said calmly, drawing the pearl handled knife that he kept in his boot. "Let go, Francine, or I'm going to have to cut him loose."

When she didn't let go, she felt his arms encircle her waist, the two of them now hip deep in the frigid river.

"Let go of me!" she shouted.

"No way, Missy," he said, a shiver in his voice, "you've got me in this now. If you're not going to let go, I'll have to help you pull. Now," he implored, throwing the knife away, "you hold the rope and I'll try and walk us all in."

He held her tightly, pulling her towards shore at a downstream angle. As he did, the calf began to swing out of the current and into an eddy, where it sprang to its feet. They then both sat back on the rocky shore, she in his lap, the rope slipping from her raw hands, but not before the calf ran up the bluff to join the others.

The two of them sat there, laughing and shivering, seeming to forget the embrace they were in. Francine was holding up her shredded hands, cramped into half-closed fists. Heaton grabbed them with his own, warming them, trying to open them up.

"Please don't," she said, looking back at him.

"Would you stop being so stubborn?" he said, snowflakes in his eyebrows and his hair. "You're half frozen. You'll be hypothermic in a few minutes. We need to get you inside and get you warm."

At this she tried to protest, until she was standing and found her lips chattering and her legs already as stiff as her arms. She let him lead her to her horse and help her on it. He then guided them both from atop his own to his barn, but not before yelling at his line rider to bring in what cows he could.

"There will be hell to pay if we mix them up," the rider yelled in reply.

"There will be hell to pay if we don't. That storm is upon us. Get what you can and then get inside yourself."

Heaton was crouched by the fireplace in his wet clothes when she emerged in a bath robe and some women's clothes he'd found for her.

"Don't look," she said, "I probably look a fright."

"You look fine," he said, throwing another log on the fire. "Come sit. I'll make some coffee while you warm up."

"You don't have to. I'll be going now."

"You don't know when to quit, do you? Look out the window Missy, we're in one hell of a storm. You aren't going anywhere, and meantime we need to get you warm."

While she didn't exactly relish the idea of spending an evening there, the fire, as it sprung to life, was perhaps the most glorious sensation she'd felt in a long time. Out the large windows came a wall of blustery white snow, and the wind suddenly began to whistle at the pitch of a boiling tea kettle.

"God help anyone up on that mountain," Heaton said, when he came out with the coffee a few minutes later.

"Thanks," she said, forcing her hands open to grasp the steaming mug.

He continued looking out the window. "You reminded me of someone today."

"Your wife?" she said, and immediately regretted having mentioned her.

Will showed no sign of shock or discomfort. He must've known the way small town people talked. "No. Just someone I used to know. A long time ago. Someone special to me."

He offered no more, and she said nothing else, and as the storm continued to batter the house, they began to talk and tell stories, and at last found they had many things in common. They kept their secrets yet, but found that the other was much unlike who they'd initially thought them to be, and so as the blizzard raged outside, something between them was forged. Like tales of enemies setting down their arms during battle to trade the base necessities of life, they too discovered that they were more alike than they could've possibly imagined.

It wasn't until she awakened, the house dark except for the still blazing fire, a blanket atop her, that she realized she'd drifted off there on his leather sofa. She heard the rattle of pans and knew that Heaton—Will—was in the kitchen making her dinner. The idea made her uneasy until she realized that he was trying to care for her, in a way that no one had since she could remember.

"I hope you don't mind, but you fell asleep and I covered you up."

She shook her head, pulling the blanket tighter around her as he came in the room.

"Well, it came from a can," he said, setting a bowl of chicken soup on the coffee table before her. "I'm not much of a cook."

"You don't have one in the house for you?"

"No," he said, as she picked up the spoon. "I sent her home at the first sign of the storm."

"I was only kidding," she said, taking a bite. "It's delicious, thank you."

A long silence followed, and before her soup was gone, she said that she thought she should be going. Here he offered no protest. The storm seemed to have abated, and he must've figured that she, forever the lady, would not spend the night in his house with him, even were she on her death bed.

He nodded. "I'll have my rider bring around the sleigh."

Sure enough, a horse drawn sleigh sat waiting outside his door only minutes later. It seemed an impossibility, something from a dream, as she eyed the stark carriage and its patient horses. If the evening had suddenly filled with an unexpected spark of magic, there was little she could do to douse it, had she so wished.

She took Will's hand, and after he snapped the reins smartly, they fell in the seat beside one another. The harness bells rattled as they trotted over the snowy, noiseless hills and into the shallow glades, a curl of snow trailing them like smoke.

"I haven't done this in years!" Will shouted, leaning back and laughing as they whisked along the river, the sky the deepest shade of indigo, the moon and starlight illuminating a world gone white.

She was laughing too, warm at last, there beside a man who suddenly felt as if she'd known him all her life. Will guided the sleigh through the barren timber, where the far reaching branches could not have smote the wild wonder of the stars, where there lay more questions than she could ask in a lifetime.

I'll never leave this place again, Francine thought, as they pulled up the lane to her house. As they did, she realized that she didn't want this feeling to end. This was in part due to the rosy cheeked happiness of their ride, where—for but a moment—it didn't feel like she was accompanied by the self-satisfied oil baron she'd first met in that Denver train station, but by a man far richer than his wealth conveyed.

She sat there a moment as the sleigh came to a stop, the horses' flanks twitching in the crisp night air.

"I wish," she said, looking at him, "I'd known some way I could've avoided you William Heaton. Here I started my day perfectly happy, but I think I'm even happier now than I was then."

"Shall I walk you up?" he asked, looking towards her unlit front door.

She looked at it a long time, then back at him, his eyes twinkling in the moonlight.

"I think I better do this part alone," she replied.

"Of course," he said, looking back at her with the same unending patience he'd shown, as if knowing every last detail of her thoughts, since the moment they met.

"How do you do that?" she said, stepping out into the deep snow, facing him one last time, knowing that under the light of a new day, this moment, this feeling, might be entirely lost, never to return. And as she stood there, her words a steam, whisked away into the frigidness, she hoped that she could remain there one minute more. To remember what it was like, the night she and William Heaton laid down their arms.

"Do what?" he asked, sitting back.

"Talk to me like you know what I'm thinking."

"Maybe I do know."

She closed her eyes then, drawing her borrowed robe close to her chin, and leaned towards him. But there, in the darkness, she was greeted only by the chilling wind and the horses' impatient snorts.

"Goodnight to you, Miss Lilley," Will said finally. "You best get inside before you go entirely frigid again."

She opened her eyes wide in astonishment, but Will had already smacked the reins and the sleigh had shot off with a lurch and was now but a distant glimmer across the frozen moonlit landscape, the tracks his runners carved upon the hills the only evidence that he'd visited there.

Seventeen

"I wonder where they could be?" Esther said as Jessica came in the kitchen, took her apron down from its nail and tied it around her waist. "They were due hours ago."

Out in the cafeteria, percolators were running, dinner was steaming on trays.

Jessica gazed out the kitchen door. It was coal black outside, besides the moon, full behind the pines. "They must've stayed down at base camp another night," she offered. "Ed said they would if their day ran late."

"Then by all accounts, they must be eating beans," Esther replied. "And I can't see anyone in that crew liking that very much."

Jessica continued staring out the door. It was cold, windless. There was no sound.

"He'll be here in the morning I'm sure," Esther said, flashing a half smile as she walked out and flipped off the percolators. Jessica knew she meant Sonny, who, if he were there right now, would be the center of attention, if not the man of the hour.

"I think he likes you."

"Well, I don't want you to confuse him. Because I'm not confused about it. I know who I am and what I want. And it's not another disappointment."

Esther was watching Jessica as she dried some dishes and put them away.

"You know," Esther said, "you shouldn't be so cold. He's a good man. And there'll come a time before no one's showing anything but a sporting interest in you, if you catch my drift. No one's gonna say a word if you run off with a man like that and never come back, least of all me."

Jessica stood there quietly, sorting through the dirty pans.

"I've seen the way these men look at you. A girl like you could do real well for herself."

"Well," Jessica said, looking out the window, "I've got competition it seems with that New York City girl. I don't stand a chance. I'm just one of the guys out here to him."

"Yeah," Esther said, snapping a towel at her behind. "I guess you don't stand much of a chance then."

Jessica looked at her and smirked.

"She's just having her fun. She'll be gone before you know it, and will never so much as glance back."

"I don't know. I've seen that look in a man's eyes before. That's the look of a man in love."

Esther didn't seem to disagree completely. "I don't think he's that foolish."

"Didn't see the girl, I take it?"

"Lana?"

Jessica paused and lowered her head. "I dare say she's the prettiest woman I've ever seen. I don't blame him one bit." She was still looking out the window uncertainly. It was very dark and way too still. "And if what you say is true, she's going to break his heart."

Esther pulled a tray of hoecakes from the oven and threw it on the stove. She picked up each one quickly with her fingers and dropped them in a towel lined basket, despite knowing that they'd sit untouched on the table until they went hard and cold.

"It would be good for him. A man needs to know what that feels like. And when she does break that old heart of his, he'll be like a snapping turtle laying on his back. Then that's when you'll move in."

"No," Jessica said, scouring the bottom of a pot. "He's too damn prideful for that. And so am I."

"Well then," Esther sighed, the playful spirit gone from her voice, "best just put it all out of your mind then."

Jessica went and brought the uneaten food back in from the cafeteria. Covered it and left it on the stove in case the party showed up late. When she turned, Esther's apron was swinging on its nail, and she heard her off in her tent, humming a tune.

Sure as hell, she thought, peering out the window again, that eerie silence meant there was a storm coming. And those folks wouldn't be coming back tonight; they'd be covered in snow

160

come morning. Lana included. She could picture her snuggled up to Sonny all night long, and Jessica stood there, imagining the girl's hands roaming over him, until she couldn't take it anymore.

She reached way back into a cupboard, knocked loose a board, and pulled out her bottle of Old Crow that she'd been nipping from all night, and, looking over her shoulder, tossed it back once again. She corked it and placed it in the lower pantry, not sure she could make it through another sleepless night.

They were just nips, she told herself, as she continued cleaning up. But as she reached in a few minutes later and pulled out the bottle again, brazen under the effects of the booze, Esther came in the kitchen and shot her a look.

"I'm going to pretend," she said, hand still on the doorway, "that I didn't see that. I thought I smelled something before."

Jessica shriveled, setting the bottle on the counter. "Just warding off the cold. And besides, it helps me sleep."

Esther stood there, arms crossed, hair drawn back in a tight bun for her bedtime. "I'll explain to Ed what happened here. You'll go down into town tomorrow…take your horse…I'll tell everyone you went down for more supplies. Then you take a day off unpaid, and when you come back you will be clean and sober or you won't come back at all. Six weeks left in the season and I don't need you drinking on the job."

She shook her head. "It's the one rule we have here Jessica. The *one* rule." She looked at her as if Jessica had personally betrayed her. "I'll dock your pay starting from tonight. I'll let you make it up later in the season. Now don't act like I'm being harsh on you. If I was I'd tell you to hit the road now. I hope you find what makes you happy so you don't need that stuff any longer."

Esther waved her arm. "Go on then. I'll finish up here."

Jessica hung up her apron and started for the door.

"Don't you want this?" Esther asked, holding out the half empty bottle of whiskey, looking her square in the eye.

Jessica paused a moment. Of course she should walk out of there, tell her to dump it, but she reached out slowly and took the bottle, and, tucking it under her arm, walked to her tent, where she proceeded to sit there by the light of the stove, taking

161

sips, until Esther came in, at which point she rolled over and was fast asleep.

At first light, Jessica began down the trail on her horse, slipping out before Esther awakened. Her breath came out of her as steam. The sky was an opaque gray, the air biting cold—the kind of weather where animals tend to bed down and not move, and the kind that makes people want to do the same.

Snow had fallen on the mountain during the night. Looking at the dark clouds above, she knew the storm would soon grow stronger, the snow heavier. What had fallen already made it easier to trail animals, and had begin to fill the trees, still filled with leaves, so they sagged low to the ground.

Jessica pushed her hat tight on her head and bundled up her duster. The sound of the snow ticked in the trees and the ground around her. She carried her 30/30 across her lap, still warm from being inside, the flakes melting as they landed on the barrel.

This time, Esther didn't ask her to telegraph back up when she arrived in town—either she'd given up asking, or she didn't care. And besides, Jessica didn't even know where she was going—she certainly wasn't going to Lynn's—although the prospect of staying in a downtown hotel didn't appeal to her either.

She unplugged the bottle of Old Crow and sipped from it as she rode along. It did much to dull her thoughts and feelings, and soon they were as mushy and cold as the ground on which she trod.

A mile down the road she saw a dark shape stagger out of the woods. She sat upright and drew the gun, clutching the bottle under her arm. As her eyes slowly focused, she saw that it was Sonny. Her heart nearly stopped at the sight of him, wet and bedraggled, sucking in wind.

He threw himself at her as she trotted up beside him.

"Give me your gun," he shouted, holding out his hands.

"What the hell is going on?" she said as he drew it from across her lap.

He stood there, breathing hard, aiming her rifle at the tree line. His hands were shaking and his eyes were wide as tea saucers.

"Grizzly. At the camp last night. Then it charged us as we were fixing to head up the mountain this morning. Like no bear I'd ever seen. Scattered the crew when it came out of the woods at us." He drew back the hammer. "She followed me up the hill and I think she's waiting near. The rest are still down there and I think it got at them." He brushed his face with his sleeve. "I have to go back down."

"Hell with that," Jessica said, slipping the bottle in a saddlebag. "We're going back up to camp. We'll use the telegraph and call in help."

"There's no time. That group doesn't know where the hell they are and are probably scattered all around the ridge."

Jessica dropped down from the horse, clutching the reins. "Then I'm going down with you."

"Absolutely not," he said without taking his eyes off the trees. "That bear staged an ambush. She knew where we were going and I'd swear on my life she was waiting for us."

They stood there a moment, just the sound of the wind and the snow falling around them.

"Is this all we've got?" he asked, looking at the rifle in his hands.

"Yes." She nodded. "We should fire off a distress shot. Let them know we're here."

"We need every round that's in it. Ed had the only other gun and he could be miles away by now. And it's just Jake's old pistol he's got."

"Where's Jake then?"

"Long story. But he left us. Took Ed's rifle with him."

Jessica swore and looked up, the flakes falling harder and heavier, as if whatever was up in the sky was about to spill out of it.

Jessica knew the New Yorkers would be scared and confused, and their only hope was that they'd managed to stay together and didn't wander far. Even if they had a compass and a map between them, it's unlikely they'd know how to use them. While they may have accumulated, in the two days they'd been there, some sense of direction, a little bit of knowledge was more dangerous than none at all. The best she and Sonny could hope for is that they'd been too afraid to move.

Jessica descended the mountain behind Sonny, clutching the 30/30 while he held her horse. The rocks were slick. She was dressed in her light duster and old boots; poorly equipped for the cold, although she figured those in the group weren't any better off.

If he wanted the rifle, and might've been more handy with it, were the grizzly to charge them again, he didn't ask for it. He'd somehow determined before their descent that it was hers to carry and had returned it, hammer cocked and ready to fire.

He paused midway down the mountain and held up a bare hand.

"It happened just below us here," he said. "Ed went north with Lana, towards the river. The rest went west. At least I think so. It happened quite fast."

"How far do you think they ran?"

Sonny scanned the opposite ridge, now blanketed with snow. "How far would you run if a bear was chasing you?"

"I would've seen them if they headed up the trail. Which makes me think they climbed to the nearest high ground, hoping it was the same way they'd come down yesterday."

"Well," Sonny said, blowing in his hands, "nothing looks like it did yesterday. Our trail is already covered. And so are any tracks they've made."

Jessica pointed to the opposite ridge line. "Once they get there, they'll be looking for the trail to camp. When they can't find it they'll keep going, thinking it's just a bit further." She shook her head. "No gun. No map. No warm clothes. No sense of direction…"

"And a grizzly trailing them."

Jessica looked at the rocks below, already slick with ice. She should've warned them of the bear, as there was little doubt it was the same one. It lived in this valley, threatening anything that came near.

"This is some fine mess we're in," she said, wiping snow off the rifle.

"I'm guessing that thing holds six rounds, but it doesn't have that many in it." He looked at her. "Does it?"

She didn't lift her head. She worked the lever and expelled three rounds into her palm, and when no more came, stood there holding them out to him. "I'd say you figured right."

The shells were dull and mottled; she couldn't recall when she'd bought them. It may have been her father who had, years before. She slowly slid them back into the rifle.

"And I wouldn't think," he added, "that a distress shot would sound like much to someone over on that ridge in this weather. Which I figure is about two, two and a half miles from here?"

"I'd say you figured right there too."

"And I don't suppose I could tell you to head on down the trail with your rifle, wherever it was you were going, and forget you walked into the middle of this?"

"Right again," she said. "I suppose we're in this together now, like it or not. The only way out is to find those folks, and before dark...which will be in about six hours."

He shook his head. "I sure don't like our chances here."

"I don't either."

They were quiet a long time; as much as she would've preferred to be in town already, she was glad Sonny had found her. She wanted to try and make this right.

"I'd take your leave now if I was you," Sonny said.

Jessica leveled her eyes at him. "You know I can't leave you this gun any better than I can take it with me. And where am I going anyway?" She racked the lever. "So let's stop this talking and get moving."

Any thoughts of what had happened between them in the preceding days, even after she followed him down the mountainside, making switchbacks with the rifle leveled, was only dimly present in her mind and likely in his. It was sheer bad luck that had forced them into this, and as they entered bottom land where the initial charge had occurred, they were struck by the eerie stillness of the scene.

Broken photographic equipment lay strewn about. Packs had been dropped where those carrying them stood. The bear had torn them open and smashed their contents into the dirt. Footprints scarred the clearing, doubling over themselves, before trailing off into the woods.

"I don't see any sign of the horse at all," Jessica said, breaking the silence. "Just people and bear."

"Jake," Sonny said, toeing a shattered camera lens. "Bastard took off with it yesterday. Left us here with nothing."

Jessica pressed her fist to her lips, considering how poorly equipped the group was to handle this disaster. She stroked Jack's neck when he began to whinny. He sensed the bear too. Perhaps it was nearby, waiting in ambush, or maybe it had retreated into the woods. There was no way to know for sure unless they followed its trail.

She glanced at Sonny, who understood their situation as well as she. He wasn't unfamiliar with being both hunter and hunted. But whatever toughness she possessed would soon be tested, because as far as she was concerned she was responsible for what had happened here, the violent traces of which was quickly being covered with soft, wet snow.

"What now?" she said, scanning the edges of the clearing, alert to any sound.

"Well," he muttered, "which way they went is anyone's guess now. The real worry is the cold, and for that, they may as well be bare-assed."

He looked at the north facing ridge, a cut that ran through it up to higher ground, nearly a mile to its summit. "We have to head that way. Should be able to see them from there if they didn't get too far last night."

Jessica knelt and pulled something from the snow. A checkered wool sweater, belonging to one of the Devine brothers.

"That should hedge our bets," she said, dropping it and wiping her hands on her jeans. "If they happened upon the camp trail, then they're safe right now and we're the missing ones. But if they went up that ridge, which is more likely, then they won't last the night in this weather."

It was quiet a moment. Just the creaking trees, and the sound of snow ticking against her duster.

Sonny removed his hat, squinting down at her as he brushed the snow from it. "Where were you headed this morning anyway? There was no reason for you to be down there, leaving Esther all alone."

She'd have given anything not to have to answer, and in fact, on the entire hike down she'd been more afraid of such questions than she was the cold, or even the bear.

She spit it out quickly: "Esther caught me drinking last night and sent me off for the rest of the week, without pay."

He put his hat back on his head. "Ed and Esther don't kid

around."

"No, they don't," she said, standing. "But I suppose I deserved it."

"Why do you drink so much anyhow?"

She turned and gazed up at the north ridge, taking Jack by the reins. The snow was falling steadier now, nearly obscuring it from view. The trail of footprints leading into the woods was nearly gone too, but she began walking beside the soft dimples still visible through the snow.

"I have my reasons," she said finally, but when there came no reply she turned and found that Sonny was no longer there.

He was gone.

Eighteen

Jessica stood in a panic, scanning the wooded valley. She was about to shout out when at last she spotted him a hundred feet ahead. Standing on a shelf of rock, gazing down into the swollen stream bed. The stream ran along the base of the mountain, falling steeply over red boulders as it rushed eastward into Cutthroat Lake. How he'd gotten down there so fast, she didn't know. She pinched her temples and shook her head quickly, trying to free herself from the hazy effects of the whiskey.

As she approached where he stood, Jessica noticed something unusual and squatted beside the stream.

"That's our bear," she said, running her fingers over the remnants of a footprint. She looked up as Sonny came and knelt beside her.

"Fresh," he said, before eying the rest of the sandy bank. "There's more over there."

Several footprints marked where the group had paused before crossing. It must've been a brief rest, knowing the bear was behind them. But there were at least three people in this group by Sonny's count, if not more.

They gazed across the tumbling water, wondering if the group had crossed and then wandered down into the valley, or gone straight up the adjacent mountain thinking they were on the trail home. Hoping the bear wouldn't follow them, although it seemed it was —as if by plan—pushing them deeper into the frozen wilderness.

Jessica sat there beside the stream, considering the situation. She was shivering, and when she looked back, Sonny had his jacket gripped around his throat, his nose red and dripping. By the expression he wore, she knew he was thinking the same thing she was. Both of their eyes returned to the frigid stream. Another day of weather like this and its edges would be crisp with ice.

"How deep is it, do you think?"

"Hang on," he said, mounting Jack and wading out to the center of the stream. "About three feet or so."

That would be to her waist, she thought, before Sonny rode back and lowered a hand to her. She looked at it a moment before climbing up on Jack behind him and wading across, the gun clutched to her chest as if it was radiating some kind of warmth. When they reached the opposite side he had to grab her rigid arm to help her dismount.

Standing on the bank, teeth chattering, she realized that if the bear was to come charging from the woods at that precise moment, she wouldn't have the ability to shoot, let alone hit it.

Sonny took the gun from her with a steady hand. She relinquished it easily, afraid she might drop it anyhow. As she sat heavily on a log and removed her snow slogged boots and wrung out her socks, she realized that they were truly in this now. Deep. It was already past noon and they were too far from camp to make it back by nightfall. Come morning, she thought, slipping back into her boots, the two of them may also need saving.

"Let's get a move on," Sonny said grimly, and she stood and proceeded after him, shaking the snow off her hat before it melted. She felt her hair and found it dry, but the braid that fell over her shoulder was wet and starting to freeze.

They found a foot trail beside the stream, not a few hours old, judging from its depth in the snow. They followed it, heads down, noting the different footprints and the patterns they made. At first, the spacing between them appeared careful and measured, but soon they began to spread apart. As if the group had started running.

Suddenly, Sonny halted and put his finger to his lips. He shouldered the rifle, sweeping it around the woods as he walked ahead, one foot crossing the other, combat style.

Jessica sucked in a breath and put her hand over her mouth when she saw what had made Sonny stop: blood in the snow. Before them, not thirty feet ahead, were the signs of a struggle. The ground was torn up, the snow stained a pinkish hue. A waterproof camera bag lay in the mud, torn open, its contents spilled about. A long pointed stick lay shattered beside it, one end honed into a spear.

Sonny stood there, looking back her way, before moving forward again. Jack shook his head and snorted. She gripped the reins tighter.

"C'mon," Sonny whispered, waving his arm.

Jessica followed. Soon she stepped over the sleeve of a blue sweater, not unlike the one they'd seen earlier. Only this one was soaked with blood.

"Harold's," she said, remembering he'd stepped off the plane in a similar sweater.

"Poor bastard." Sonny shook his head. "Take what you can from here. See if there's anything we could use."

"I don't think I can," she said, looking down at the camera bag sitting in the bloody snow. It seemed wrong to loot the site when Harold's body might not be twenty feet away, hidden behind a tree.

"You have to. The bear might still be around. *Hurry*."

She knelt slowly and reached into the bag and found a pipe and a lighter. She took the lighter and a packet of crackers, then unhitched the bag's strap, soaked in blood. The contents of her stomach, mostly whiskey, threatened to come back up.

Sonny, she knew, had nothing at all on his stomach—but he didn't ask for the crackers, which she slipped into her pocket along with the lighter. There was also a wool blanket nearby and she rolled it up, lashed the strap around it, and threw the roll over her shoulder.

Jessica knew that before the day was out she'd see more blood. Scenes worse than the one she'd just witnessed. The thought closed around her like a steel trap. And, just as she often did when things seemed interminably bad, she moved forward and tried not to think about them.

They left the bloody scene behind them without ceremony. It became clear to her, with each footprint that passed beneath her, each of them twice the size of her own, that they were no longer following the group, but the bear now. That their aim was to hunt it down and kill it before it harmed anyone else.

The wind blew indifferently through the trees. Jessica gave one last look at the groups' footprints, leading to higher ground, before they continued on the bear's trail. As they did she felt something pressing down on her, so hard that she fell on her knees in the snow and cried out. She'd never felt anything like it, and try as she might, she could not bring herself to stand back up. She feared it was a heart attack, or that the bear itself was upon her. But just as the pressure became so powerful that she feared her bones would snap, the sensation was gone, just as quick as it had come.

Sonny grabbed her arm and yanked her on her feet. "You're

nearly hypothermic and starting to body cramp," he said, thrusting his hand into her pocket, something no man had ever done, and, his fingers probing just an inch away for her most private parts, which seemed as distant to her at that moment as the Galapagos Islands, he pulled out the crackers, tearing open the wrapper with his teeth.

"Eat," he said, thrusting them at her. "All of them. That'll light a fire in you."

As she chewed, Sonny studied the sky. Already daylight was growing faint. Staring at the cold dimness settling in around her, out here miles from town, she thought of Lynn. Her sister was, of course, completely unaware of her situation. Jessica could nearly hear Lynn screaming at her for not walking away when given the chance. Telling her that this wasn't her job, that she wasn't responsible for any damn bear. And that she should come home right now, while there was still time.

"We should make camp early," Sonny said in a cracked voice. When she followed his eyes to a windbreak fifteen feet above them, in a jagged cut in the mountain, she knew that she'd be spending the night there, may Lynn be damned.

The small meal enlivened her some. She tied Jack to a tree, took the blanket they'd found and climbed up to the windbreak. Sonny gathered dry kindling and pine boughs from beneath the rocks and soon had a small fire burning. It flickered amber and gold, the one bit of light and warmth in the dark wilderness, where the two of them sat huddled with their backs to the mountain, hands reaching for the warmth of the flames.

Sonny scanned the woods, the rifle across his shoulder, listening for any sound. Jack stood beneath them somewhere in the dark, snorting and pawing at the ground. As night set in, the fire began to die, and she found herself inching closer to Sonny, her eyes growing heavy.

Before she drifted off, they heard the muted but distinct crack of a gun shot. Unsettling the still night air. They both sat up and peered out. As far as they could tell, it came from where the main camp was. Nearly five miles away.

"That must be Ed and some of the others," Sonny said. "They've probably been back at camp and waiting on everyone to turn up."

"At least they know we're out here," Jessica managed.

"They don't know you're here. And they won't come looking for us until the morning. I hope the whole group is with them, but I have a strong feeling they aren't."

"If Ed made it back with at least one person, that would make five in the party we're following," Jessica said. "After wading through that stream, and without this here blanket and lighter, and one of them injured, well, it seems pretty bleak."

"We'll find them," Sonny said, sinking back against the rocks. "Dead or alive, we'll find them."

He didn't seem too concerned with this notion, but she knew better. He liked Lana a good deal and was worried about her; of this she was quite certain.

His eyes narrowed as he gazed off into the darkness, from where there'd suddenly come another, more terrible kind of noise. She prayed it was the lost party, but as they sat listening to something large crashing through the woods, circling their camp at a distance, pausing now and then to sniff the air before continuing on, she knew it was the bear. And that it was hunting them too.

"Sonny," Jessica said. "I have to tell you something while I have the chance. I can't have it on my conscience any longer."

"What?" he said, still scanning the timber for the bear.

"A bear charged me last week, coming down the trail."

He looked over at her a moment, then back out at the woods. "And you didn't tell anyone?" He seemed as distressed as he was mystified. "This is probably the same bear. And this whole situation could've been avoided. Why?" He shook off the blanket. "Why didn't you tell?"

She sank deeper into the blanket, afraid that he would scold her further. "I was afraid they wouldn't let me ride into town alone anymore."

He stared at her for what seemed like a minute. "That's no good reason."

"You're right. I should've told." She sat up. "But how would you like it if someone was always making a fuss of where you were and where you went, and all you wanted to do was just to go where you wanted to go, and do what you wanted to do, and didn't want anyone telling you that you couldn't?"

Jack neighed softly and pawed the ground.

"Well," she added, "I was wrong. But Ed saw signs of this bear too and he led folks into these woods anyway. And you and him know these woods better than me. So this all isn't on my damn shoulders. I just wanted to tell you what happened. That's all."

He tipped his hat over his eyes and settled back into the pine boughs. He grabbed the blanket and tugged it back over him. "I can't say I blame you then. My own folks always had a say in everything I ever did. The day I finished school I thought I was finally free." He looked at her and laughed. "Then I got drafted."

The fire was just a bed of coals, the night growing even darker around them.

"This is the first time I've really been free I suppose. And here I am, stuck out here with a bear." He stirred the coals with a stick. "But Lana said she wants me to come visit her." He chuckled. "And if I get us all out of here, I've decided I'm going to go. To see New York City."

The place sounded foreign and strange out here in the wilds. "You're half in love with that girl, and you only met her a few days back." She felt something cold and unpleasant wash over her and pulled the blanket up tighter.

"No. But I like her. More than I probably should." He tossed the stick on the coals. "And I like the idea of getting out of here. Came back after I was discharged to clear my head. But I haven't been doing a very good job of it."

For a moment it felt as if they were somewhere else. Somewhere safe. Jessica knew they'd blocked out what they'd seen earlier. But as night settled in around them, their chatter was the only thing keeping those images at bay.

"Everyone here seems to think," she said, "that this is where you belong. And I think they're hoping you'll make a stand for this place. So it doesn't go away if Ed loses it."

He chuckled again. "If I'd done everything everyone expected of me, I wouldn't be here now. I'd still be in the Army. Miserable."

"This ain't miserable?"

"No," he said, looking up, "this is nice. I'm alive, and I'm free."

"Well, when trouble hit, this is where I came," she said, sinking deeper into the pine boughs until her backside hit rock. "If I could be anywhere in the world, I'd be right here. And I'm never going to leave here."

"You don't know the meaning of trouble."

"I know what trouble is all right," she said, closing her eyes. "I know it all too well."

Jessica fell into a fitful sleep, unable to stay warm, until at last she moved up close to Sonny. When she looked up she saw the fire was down to ashes. Jack stood on the end of his tether, not more than a few steps away now. The valley was quiet, save for the wind twirling and tumbling through the trees, and although she figured it was her imagination, she thought she heard the deep and wet sound of the bear breathing nearby.

"If I die," Jessica whispered, unsure if Sonny was awake, "I want you to keep that rifle. It was my dad's."

"If you die," he replied with a shiver, pulling her closer to him, "I die too."

She closed her eyes, warm at last, and awakened at first light with Sonny breathing on her neck and his arms wrapped tightly around her. He was likely dreaming she was someone else, as she could feel a part of him pressing insistently against her. Instead of feeling cold and raw, she felt a warm flush and didn't pull away. It was only when she remembered the bear, and the cold that awaited them, that she whispered his name.

His eyes opened and, remembering where he was, he slipped his arms from out of hers. "Sorry," he said, looking away.

"It's okay," she said, "I know I wouldn't give you that reaction anyway. I'm not some New York fashion model."

He muttered something she couldn't hear. The sun was out, offering a bit of warmth that hadn't been there the day before. She picked up the rifle and checked the chamber for a round, as she had nearly a dozen times in the past twenty-four hours.

"What's that?" she asked.

"I didn't want to wake up," he repeated.

"Well, that won't be the last dream you have. You'll be with your Lana soon enough."

"If she's alive," he said, studying the woods, which were stock still at this hour. "I hope to hell she is. I hope she's pressed between those men and as warm as I was."

"Well," she sighed, "if we don't find them by noon, we're going to be in a real pickle ourselves. We can't spend another night out here. And I," she added, pulling the blanket from him and folding it up, "have done my duty beyond a reasonable measure. And that includes me enduring a night with you."

She tossed him the folded blanket and picked up the rifle and went and untied Jack.

"I'll lead today," she said, stroking his ears.

"Okay, boss." Sonny stood and stretched. "Let's go find them."

Nineteen

They didn't talk as they plodded along, the pale sun shining through the trees, Jessica atop the horse and Sonny walking beside it, holding her rifle. She was hungry and tired and knew he felt much the same, still with a mountain to climb and descend before noon. Neither seemed confident that the party was on the other side, and although neither said it, she knew that it would be easier to surmise they'd made it back to camp. That the shot they'd heard the night before signaled they were all safe, and that Sonny should end his search.

But as they reached the mountain summit and looked down, the view was indistinguishable from the previous morning's. And at this point they agreed that the panicked group was not in camp, but lost somewhere in the land below.

They paused halfway down the opposite side of the mountain. From there, they could still see the jagged snow capped peaks rising into the sky, one after the other, until they faded into the horizon.

"My," Sonny said, hands on his hips, either admiring the view or considering the mess the missing party was in, or both.

Jessica glanced at her watch. Its crystal was cracked and smeared in dirt. She cussed and looked up at the sun, a white disk just above the mountains.

"It's nearing ten," she said, scanning the valley and opposite ridge. The wind picked up and she shaded her eyes.

"The point of no return," he said. "We take another step, and we're spending the night." He turned. "At this point I'd be happy to get you home safe."

"Uh-uh." She waved her hand. "You don't have to worry about me. I'll say when I've had enough." She picked up the reins. "Those folks are out there, and they're scared, injured and half frozen."

"Or worse," he said, cradling the rifle. "I don't know if they could've made it this far. Especially not after what we saw yesterday."

"Well, you should worry about them then. I'm just fine." Jessica tilted her hat forward to block the sun. "I think you're just afraid we'll keep going and find it was your girl who got torn up."

To this, Sonny said nothing.

Jessica sighed. "There ain't no point of no return here, is there Sonny? Because you and me, we already passed it, didn't we?"

Sonny studied her a long time. She'd never told anyone at camp about her past, but he seemed to understand that bad things had happened to her as well. She'd walked through the fire too, maybe not like he had, but she'd also come out on the other side, alive and free.

"If you were to turn around now," he said, staring at her, "I'll turn around with you."

"Honey," she said, snapping the reins, "you talk too damn much."

They stopped when they reached the valley floor. The wind picked up as they stood there staring into miles of sparse pines, their branches casting thin shadows on the ground.

Jessica was about to move on when Sonny grabbed her reins and pointed ahead. Two hundred yards away, on a jagged outcropping of rock not unlike the one they'd slept in the night before, was a piece of shorn blue fabric.

Her heart lifted as they approached. When they untied it from the branch, it was clear that it had been hung there as a trail marker.

"It's wet and half-frozen," Sonny said, balling it in his hand.

"Must've been from yesterday."

Sonny tied it back on the tree and resumed cradling the rifle. Jessica dismounted and walked behind him as they followed a vague trail of footprints over a mile through the woods. Judging from how fresh they were, the group wasn't far ahead of them.

Soon they came across an empty pack.

"They're shedding weight," Sonny said. "There's at least three of them, and they're lost. If not delirious."

"But they're alive," Jessica said, hurrying through the woods, ducking under overhanging branches, the trees thinning as she came to an unexpected ridge and stopped, gripping Jack's reins.

"Whoa," she yelled as Sonny came over a rise, only to notice the steep slope leading down from the ridge, beyond which the earth abruptly seemed to end.

"There's no rocks here at all," he said, as he inched his way down the slope, holding onto the tree trunks as he lowered himself to get a better view.

Jessica watched him stop, not ten feet ahead, clutching the base of a small aspen.

"You're not going to believe this," he said, staring over the ledge.

"What?" she asked, trying to peer over, but lost her nerve and returned to her crouched position. "What do you see?"

"It's the lake." He turned back to her. "Cutthroat Lake."

The thought hit her like a blow to the face. Had they been that turned around? Were they that lost?

She lay Jack's reins over a tree branch and inched her way down until she was beside Sonny. He looped his arm through hers and held fast.

"Look," he said, as she leaned forward and saw the lake, sparkling in the sunshine. After admiring it but a second, she drew back, a sickening feeling passing over her.

"You afraid of heights or something?" he asked, looking at her shaking hands.

"Only when I'm up high," she joked, looking as far south as she could from where she sat. Because of the lake's kidney shape, a belly of shoreline obscured her view of camp. "Are you *sure* that's Cutthroat Lake? There's a lot of lakes up here."

"Shoot," Sonny said, his eyes suddenly growing wide, "why sure it is. This is the *spot*. This is the spot the Sioux named the lake after. *Jump* Lake."

She peered over the edge again. "Those Indians tell some tall tales. I don't think a person could survive that fall. Must be over a hundred feet."

"Well," he said, "you must have the story mixed up, because the way I heard it they didn't survive. And it's a hundred and twenty feet down if it's a foot. And there's no telling how deep that water is. Five, ten feet?"

She sat back, disturbed by how truly disoriented they'd been.

How lost, and how foolish. As she sat teetering on the ledge, she pictured the earth beneath them giving way, their bodies tumbling into the ice cold water. Suddenly she was afraid she couldn't stand, that she might need Sonny to drag her back up the hill.

But as they sat there, Jack gave a whinny and a shake, and when they looked up, they saw a large shape moving through the trees behind him.

Shit, she muttered, as the bear calmly came towards them. She remained perfectly still, wondering if it had seen them yet, but knew it made no difference. It had *smelled* them, and sure as the sun would rise tomorrow, it followed its nose to where the three of them sat on the edge of that cliff.

Sonny and Jessica looked into the other's hands, to see who was holding the rifle. And it was only when Jack spooked and turned to face the bear, that they saw it buttoned in the scabbard. How it had gotten there was as inexplicable to her as how they'd gotten themselves in this position.

What was said then, there between them, were words unrecognizable. All she could understand was how helpless her horse was. Jack didn't panic easily, she knew, but here he seemed to understand the severity of the situation better than any of them.

And that's when the bear lunged with a speed she'd not seen before in nature, opening its jaws and latching onto Jack's neck. His eyes bulged as he spun around to face her, as if asking what she could do for him.

A moment later, the bear let go, took a step back, and grunted. Rivers of dark blood began to stream down Jack's neck and Jessica cried out, her voice sounding to her as if it had come from a bottomless cavern. Sonny grabbed her arm as the bear started towards them, growling.

"Jump!" he yelled at her, and when she turned one last time the bear was feet away, jowls flapping, yellowed fangs covered in Jack's blood.

This is the day you die, Jessica thought, as she jumped from the cliff grasping Sonny's hand. The torrent of wind, the sickening feeling of weightlessness. After flipping over once she straightened out, enough so that she could see the sparkling water, so very far away, rushing up at them.

It was bitterly cold. She was elated to realize that she felt the water at all, and as she plunged deep into it, her legs hit sandy bottom and buckled, pressing her knees into her chest. She coughed in pain before mustering one great upward push. Bubbles streamed around her as she burst into the blinding sunlight, gasping for air.

Sonny grabbed her waist and pulled her towards shore. As he did she looked up and saw a dark shape tumbling towards them, and when she covered her head to shield herself, she heard a concussive splash. After a wave passed over her, she saw that it was Jack, and that he'd fallen with them, or—she preferred to think—that in one last feat of loyalty, he'd leapt along with her.

"Let me go!" she cried at Sonny, and swam back to run a hand over Jack's mane, as if to calm him one last time.

"Thank you, Jack," she said softly, unsheathing the rifle from the scabbard before he began to sink.

"Can you swim?" Sonny said when she turned, spitting out a mouthful of pink water.

She kicked her legs and looked at her hands, surprised to find that she was intact. That she was alive. As she swam for shore with the rifle, she gave a look up at the shadowed cliff, dirt tumbling from it still, as the bear retreated into the woods.

"A hundred and twenty feet my ass," she said after they climbed ashore and stood on the rocky shoreline, dripping wet.

"Felt like a thousand." Sonny smiled at her, working the lever on the rifle, expelling the bullets into his hand. "One in the chamber is dry, the others, I don't know."

"Will they still fire?"

He laid them and the rifle there in the sun and began peeling off his coat and shirt. "I hope we never have to find out."

Within seconds he was bare-chested, and Jessica noticed a bandage around his arm. He threw the soaked jacket aside and began to wring out his shirt, then flung it on a rock in the sunshine and unbuckled his pants.

"Strip," he said to her, as she stood there, teeth chattering. The water had been, as near as she could figure, about forty degrees. Another month and the lake would be iced over. "No time for modesty. We need to get dry."

As she turned and slowly began to peel off her own clothes, she saw the last of Jack sink into the lake. Their situation, she realized, had suddenly become grim. The only good news, she thought, as she stripped all the way down to her bare feet, was that they could follow the shoreline back to camp.

She wrung out her clothes and hung them on a tree branch in the sunshine. Sonny had assembled what he could of kindling and leaves, and was crouched there in the nude, trying to get the lighter to work. When it wouldn't, he opened the casing and removed the butane soaked cotton stuffing, then struck the flint starter directly against it.

The fire was small and smoky when it came, but the two of them held their hands to it, stealing glances at the other while pretending not to. She didn't mind. She had nothing to be ashamed of. And even some things to be proud of, as did he, she thought, as he stood and checked on their now steaming clothes.

The devastation of losing Jack, the thrill of the leap and of having dodged death, did little to diminish the errand that lay before them. The instant they were sufficiently warmed by the fire and sunshine, they threw their still damp clothes over their bodies, and assembled what of their gear remained. Sonny was careful to load the driest round in the rifle first before handing it over to her.

"Don't you want your jacket?" she asked, glancing back at it, still bleeding water on the rocks, but he didn't look back as he proceeded into the shadowy woods.

There would be but one hour to find the missing party, as already the day was growing short, and they weary. As they walked along, her wet boots felt as if they were encased in cement, and they had soon rubbed her ankles raw.

"There was nothing you could've done for your horse," Sonny offered.

"I know," she replied, looking at the wet ground. "I miss him already."

As they paused in a sunny clearing a mile east of Cutthroat Lake, Jessica saw something which she at first did not believe. She blinked and narrowed her eyes. No, it was not her imagination. Several figures were huddled together under some pines, not a hundred years ahead. They weren't moving, she realized, as she trotted towards them, and it was only when she was upon them that one of them looked up and, pushing back an overhanging branch, smiled in a dazed sort of way, unconcerned if she was human or the bear herself.

They appeared to have collapsed in a shivering huddle, not three miles from camp. As lost as she and Sonny had been not an hour before. The smiling man was one of the Devine brothers. Stephen. He nudged the other three, who were not so much asleep as hypothermic, and who seemed at first, when their heads appeared from the boughs, both perplexed and annoyed by the disturbance he was causing them.

Sonny came running up as the others in the group began stirring. Among them was Lana, who appeared unscathed. It was Frederick whose arm was tied in a sort of makeshift sling. He had blood on his forehead and matted in his hair. The other Devine brother, Harold, also had scrapes on his arm.

"Are you alright?" Sonny shouted, standing there looking at them with an astonished expression, as if surprised, not only in seeing them alive, but in their discovery of them, when at last they'd given up hope.

Stephen stood first, who looked to be in a trance, smiling drunkenly at Jessica as she helped him up, thanking her, as if she'd just handed him a cup of coffee.

Sonny helped Lana to her feet and hugged her.

"You found us," she said groggily. "Thank God. I thought we were all done for. The bear," she said, burying her head in his shoulder and sobbing. "That damned bear."

Jessica then helped Frederick up, who cried out as his pack slipped from his arm.

"My camera and film!" he exclaimed, picking it up and clutching it to him like it was his child. These he'd managed to save by way of the rubberized pack they were in, and he smiled sheepishly as he realized that he was making such a fuss over them.

The group then recounted the story of the first attack. How Dottie and Ed had scattered one way and they the other. Then how they'd somehow fended the bear off with a makeshift spear, only after it had swatted at Frederick and Harold.

They then stood shaking their heads, as if too exhausted to explain the rest. They were smack in the middle of the wilderness. Wet and bedraggled. Just miles from camp, but thousands of miles from New York. Not much longer than a day had passed since they'd gone missing, and yet they looked like they'd been lost a week. There was no telling what misery another day would've brought them.

Jessica considered how she'd found them and realized, that whether the group knew it or not, with no fire or shelter, they'd sat down to die.

"We need to save our breath," Sonny said, "and get moving if we're going to make camp by nightfall." Sonny grabbed Stephen and threw an arm around him.

"I don't need help anyway," Lana said, turning away. "It's not like I'm nearly frozen to death."

Stephen's lips trembled, as if to give thanks to Sonny, but no words came out.

"What about the bear?" Frederick whispered as they fell in line. "He followed us."

Jessica cocked the rifle, making no mention of the attack that morning. "If it comes back," she said, looking at him, "I'll kill her."

As they started their hike back over the mountain, following closely along the lake shoreline, her mind turned to thoughts of a safe, warm bed. Frederick led the way, removing the camera from its pack without breaking stride. There was a keenness in his eyes as he adjusted the lens and hung the camera, at the ready, by its cord around his neck. But he began to falter as they braced the mountain. When Jessica couldn't help him and keep lookout with the rifle, Sonny grabbed him with one arm and Stephen with the other as they began their climb.

Frederick looked back at Jessica, his eyes frenzied. "I regret that after all this, I've not gotten one single photograph of the bear. Even if he gets me this time, I shall have my picture of him."

The walk back to camp would indeed take all day, and as Sonny fell to the rear with Stephen, who was beginning to talk nonsense, Jessica took lead with the rifle, seeing them safely down the opposite ridge.

By then, it was well into the afternoon. They paused briefly there, and Sonny began shaving off cottonwood bark for the horse, before remembering Jack was no longer with them. He looked at Jessica and tossed it away.

As they continued on they heard the sound of rushing water, and soon they were standing beside the stream that fed into Cutthroat Lake.

"Hold still," Frederick said, aiming his camera at Jessica, and when she turned, there on the rocks before the waterfall, the sun in her face and lighting the frothing water, she heard its shutter working.

"One more," he said, winding the camera, and then, leaning against a tree to steady himself, snapped another picture. When he was finished, he stood there grinning at her. She was filthy, by all accounts. Her hair was a mess and there was mud on her hands.

"That's the kind of real picture I came here for," he said, nodding slowly.

Lana sneered at him, her hands on her hips. "Oh no, you didn't drag me out here for nothing." She climbed up to where Jessica stood, slipping once, before wrestling the rifle from her.

"Go on now," Lana said, nearly spitting as she held up the gun, "I came out here and nearly died, so go on, take my picture."

Frederick smirked at Lana, wound the camera slowly, and obediently took her picture.

"There." Lana shot Jessica a look, thrust the rifle back at her and huffed to where Sonny stood, still holding up Stephen.

"I'm not going to be shown up by the *cook*," Lana said, looping her arm through Sonny's.

Sonny didn't look at Lana, and instead smiled at Jessica, standing there beside the stream in the misty light.

Jessica smiled back at him and turned to lead the group across. As she did there came the sound of branches snapping and heavy footfalls, beating against rock. The group froze as the bear rushed from the outcropping of pines on the opposite bank. Without pause it charged into the water, fur bristling, eyes trained on Jessica.

Her heart, she was quite sure, stopped beating as the bear

exploded from the stream with its head cocked, lips crusted with blood, to rip out her throat as it had Jack's.

There was little time to think. She shouldered the rifle swiftly, waiting until she saw her reflection in its eyes, which quickly grew until all that remained was her face, the mountains beyond, and the bore of her rifle.

Jessica closed one eye, held her breath, and fired.

The rifle bucked against her shoulder. Whiff of cordite. A piercing whine filled her ears. She stood gripping the gun as the grizzly's brains sprayed onto its back and the animal collapsed mid-stride at her feet.

The rifle went tumbling, and she with it, her mouth opening to scream, but no sound came. Gun smoke swirled about, and then came the smell of the bear. Rank. Fecund. Its wound spilling on her boots. Tears streamed from her eyes and she breathlessly tried to stand and get away, but she couldn't move.

Sonny knelt beside her. The rest of the group was gathered around her within seconds, and they watched as Sonny ran his hands over her to check for injury, as shocked as she how fast it had happened, and that she hadn't been killed.

At last Jessica was able to fill her air with lungs, and she let out a wail, rocking there in the lapping, bloody waves, until at last they lifted her up and carried her across the water. Harold tried to calm her while Sonny walked out to collect her hat before rushing back to her side.

"A grizzly charge," Frederick said under his breath, looking down at his camera. "And I got every single frame of it on film."

Twenty

Ed had wired down into town the day before to spread the news that a group was missing up by camp. Over at the Sundowner, he was to learn, Griff had rounded up her own group of searchers by offering drinks on the house to those who would help. And only with a break in the weather the following morning did the ramshackle search party assemble outside the bar. Those who'd drank for free the night before, as they all piled onto the bed of an old truck, with Griff holding her shotgun and shouting at them to hurry the hell up, appeared to have second thoughts about the agreement.

Ed had spent the previous night at camp with Dottie and Esther, firing off the occasional volley and using the telegraph to try and call in the float plane. Esther sat in wait for a response while he went out on horseback and glassed the valley with his binoculars. Snow, sleet and rain beat against him, and as he sat there, his horse snorting, water filled his boots. And yet he kept watch until dark, his heart lifting when he saw someone's camp fire, far out in the snowy wilderness.

He came back that night through a soaking rain, wet and coughing. Esther stripped him down as Dottie stoked the fire, then put him to bed with a slug of tonic. He awoke sometime that night, sweating. Like a rope bringing up water from a well, a vision had come to him. It was the man in the bottom of the lake. Ed had been sure to get a good look at him this time. He had black snails for eyes, wisps of weeds for a beard. On his lap sat a wooden lock box.

"I'm waiting for you, Ed," the man said, tapping his fingers against it.

Ed continued to stare at the man. "Who," he asked finally, "*are* you?"

The man smiled. "I think you know, Ed."

After a minute, the old man looked down. Beneath him was a crevice where the lake suddenly grew deeper. Ed knew it was Cutthroat Lake, and he the old hermit who'd once lived there.

Ed looked down; a thousand feet down, maybe further. From far below him came a faint pulse of light.

"Come with me, Ed," the old man said, holding out his hand. "But first, you must let *go*." The old man ceremoniously lifted the lock box and let it drop. It opened as it fell, spilling gold coins, which went fluttering into the deep.

"Come," he said at last, standing slowly. "We're waiting for you."

"There's some things I have to take care of first," Ed replied, and awakened at the sound of his own voice. He looked around the tent and set his head back down, glad the vision was gone.

At dawn, Dottie snoring in a cot beside him, a flashlight and a dime store novel laying on her chest, Ed rose and, wheezing, slipped on his damp boots. Esther was stirring behind him, but before she could complain that he shouldn't be going out alone, not in his condition, he'd saddled his horse and packed another and was in the process of heading out with the two of them, when she ran after him.

"You know I'm not a scold," Esther said, standing there with her coat clasped around her. "But you have your own self to worry about."

"Esther," he said, lifting his hat and leaning back in the saddle. "I love you, but I've got to go."

He was still on the trail when he saw the plane fly over the valley where he expected the group to be. Its engine whined as it dove low over the trees, crossing over the lake and circling back again. Ed knew the group had already extinguished their fires, and had no way of signaling the plane. But after the pilot had made several low passes over the valley and gave no indication, by a wave of his wings, that he'd located the group, he started home.

As Ed watched it head over the northern ridge, his heart sank. Once again he could hear the plodding of his horse's hooves, and as they descended into the valley, he felt that they were very much alone.

He made base camp in an hour and rode south on a game trail another mile, coming to a broad clearing that he'd paused in many times before. He stopped there, patting the horse, looking for sign, but found none. The air was sharp and clean, and it blew steadily through the trees, making them sway. This is what he'd miss most, were he never to see it again. To feel the sun, to see the mountains, to be on the trail of something living. It was, even in the darkest moments of life, as he snapped the reins and continued south, something that still felt new to him.

When he reached the southern end of the valley, he found it filled with sunlight. He didn't sit there long, looking through his binoculars, before he saw shapes heading west across it. He held his breath as one by one, six figures appeared from the brambles and thicket, and came into a clearing where they stopped to rest.

As he lifted Jake's pistol and fired a shot into the sky, they turned in his direction. Ed smiled, and although they were far off, he hollered out as he rode on to greet them, firing another shot as he descended into the clearing. When they saw that it was him, they all fell down on their backs, except for Sonny and Jessica, who held up their hands and waved as he rode up beside them and gazed down at their shining faces.

As the group crested the mountainside, they heard the grinding of gears as an old flatbed truck worked its way up the trail, following Ed's old Jeep tracks. The truck must've not been making much headway, because the search party was on foot ahead of it, and the ragtag bunch shouted and pointed when they saw the group appear from out of the woods.

Although they'd arrived too late to find the missing party, there was still plenty to do—including taking care of six hypothermic patients. Ed helped them load Frederick, Lana, Stephen, Harold, and at last, Jessica—shivering and pale—onto the flatbed truck. They all reached down for Sonny, but he pulled away and stood by Ed as the truck rolled down the hill, leaving the two of them standing there with the horse.

There was a moment where it seemed something needed to be said. Of what had happened, and how lucky the group had been. But they both seemed too weary, too tired to rehash it all.

"I'm signing the papers on Monday, turn this place over to the government," Ed said, slipping off his worn work gloves. "Maybe it's the end of the line for a place like this."

"Don't be foolish, Ed. Heaton's a buyer. He'll give you what you need for it. You know it."

"Maybe the government will just leave it be a while. Turn it into a park or something."

"You know there's no chance of that. They didn't put those heavy taxes on you to turn it into a damn park."

"Maybe." Ed coughed, gazing down the trail. "Maybe not."

"You go on ahead up to camp," Sonny said, looking at him with a concerned expression. "There's something I need to get while I'm down here."

"You need company?" Ed said, coughing again.

Sonny waved him away, same as he had the hands that had reached to pull him onto the truck headed to the hospital.

"I have to do this part alone."

Ed gave him his horse, then watched as Sonny wandered southwest into the valley, the horse's tail snapping as they worked their way through the trees, until at last they disappeared.

Upon his arrival at the hospital that evening, Ed learned that each of the five patients from his camp were indeed suffering from hypothermia, and that Stephen had the onset of frostbite on his toes. The rest of the hospital was quiet, except for this wing, where there were several newspaper reporters milling about, some who'd come from as far as Cheyenne to get a story on the missing New Yorkers who'd been hunted by a bear.

The members of the group all had adjoining rooms, and as Ed stood in the hall with his hat off, covering his coughs with a handkerchief, a nurse walked up to him.

"Sir," she said, placing a hand on his arm. "Maybe you should see a doctor too?"

"I'm just here to see my friends."

The nurses eyes were a cold blue. "Visiting hours are over. Only family now."

"My daughter," Ed said. "Jessica. I'm here to see her."

The nurse furrowed her brow. "She's your daughter?"

Ed nodded, running his hat band through his fingers. "Yes,

ma'am."

As the nurse pointed towards her room and walked away, Ed slipped inside and stood by the doorway. Frederick was in the same room, reclined in a bed with the sheets pulled tight over his slight body. He told Ed that Jessica was in a state of shock and only in the last hour had she lost the fight against the sedative and fallen asleep. Ed could see the drip bottle hanging above her arm, and as he moved towards her, a reporter shoved his way into the room and the same nurse came and chased him away.

Ed lowered himself into the chair beside Jessica, watching her sleep.

"That's some woman there," Frederick said softly. "I took some mighty fine pictures of her today. May turn out to be the finest of my career. Perhaps that's the saving grace in all this."

He smiled and sat up. "Spoke to my editor on the phone after I got here. Your girl here may be on the cover of LOOK Magazine if those pictures turn out half as good as I think they will. I don't suppose that will impress her much. But her stock will go up, as will yours."

Ed shook his head, continuing to run the brim of his hat through his fingers.

"As for my wife," Frederick chuckled, "she hasn't even come to see me. Jessica's family has come, been a better family to me than my own. But as for Dottie, well, I bet I could guess where she is right now, and I bet you could too."

Ed nodded slowly.

"I suppose you think I deserve it," Frederick said, waving his hand in the air before Ed could answer. "Well, I'll be seeing a lawyer when I get back to take care of that. And you know I'm going to be sued as well." He nodded his head towards the room where Stephen Devine was staying.

Frederick looked over at Jessica, then at him. "I think this was my last rodeo, as they say out here. Sounds like, from what I've heard, this is yours too."

"I suppose it is," Ed said, sitting back. "Almost thirty years running that operation out there. But now I have no say in what happens to it."

Frederick nodded, studying Ed, whose eyes hadn't left Jessica since he'd stepped in the room. "It seems like our girl Jessica here is the type used to worrying people."

"That she's an expert at," Ed said, nodding.

"I have two boys like that. Grown now. They were always in trouble. You have any kids Ed?"

"No." He shook his head, looking at the floor. "Wasn't in the cards for me and Esther I'm afraid."

Frederick looked at him a long time.

"I have a feeling you're taking a picture of me."

"No," Frederick said, looking up at the ceiling. "I was just thinking. About angels. You believe in angels? Not the type with the wings and all that. But angels. Here on earth."

Ed didn't answer. It seemed peculiar that a man like him would believe in such things.

"Well, I never believed in them until today," Frederick said, looking over at Jessica.

Ed looked over at her too, sleeping soundly. "Well, I better let her rest," he said, standing and putting on his hat.

"She cares about you. Seems women always fall for you cowboy types." He looked at Ed, his face having grown serious. "I may have caused you all more trouble than I'd ever wish, Ed. That Lana of mine. She's troubled too. But she's like a daughter to me. Seems she may have taken a liking to Sonny. Expecting him to come visit her or something. You see that he lets her down easy for me, that is, if he's so inclined."

"Sonny is a man used to handling his own affairs."

"Spoken like a true cowboy," Frederick slowly nodded his head, looking at Jessica. "And, if I may be permitted to speak like one for a minute, you take care of this one, Ed. She's something special."

Twenty-One

Lynn threw an afternoon picnic at the house when Jessica came home from the hospital a few days later. It was an unusually warm Sunday. She'd put on a dress she bought in Laramie but had never worn. Yellow. After the shock of what she'd gone through, and several days in the hospital, the air smelled a bit sweeter, the sunshine warmer. In the distance stood the Crooked Mountains, and she gazed at them as she came and sat at the table and brushed back her hair, unable to shake the feeling that—although the sky was a clear and brilliant blue—there was a gray shadow cast over her.

Lynn had made a whole spread. Deviled eggs. Roast beef sandwiches. Even a lime Jell-O mold. Ed arrived with Esther in his Jeep, both of them beaming as they hugged Jessica, Esther balancing a pie she'd brought in her free hand. The kids were off playing and Scott was lassoing their feet with a rope, while Lynn stirred a pitcher of iced tea and called everyone to the table.

"To Jessica," Lynn said, raising her glass, "the girl of the hour. Who I must say we are awful glad to know. And that we are awful glad it's her and not the bear coming to join us today. Thank the Lord."

"Amen," Ed said, and everyone echoed him, holding their glasses high.

After lunch, when Jessica had a moment alone with him, she confessed that she'd seen the bear before. That it had charged at her before.

"Well," Ed said, "under ordinary circumstances, I'd fire you for that. But seeing as I'm as much to blame as you, why don't I pay you for the rest of the season and let you go so you can rest up. You've already done more than I ever could've asked. And I think I'm going to shut down early anyway."

Jessica sat there, gazing up at the mountains. After a pause she turned to him. "Have you seen Sonny since then?"

"He's leaving today," Ed said, lighting a cigarette. "Headed to

New York as I understand."

"To see Lana," Jessica said, looking away.

There was another long pause. Ed looked over at Esther, as if for help.

"Men are funny, Jess," Esther said, placing her hand on Ed's arm. "They don't know what they really want. Sometimes it takes them a while to figure it out. But they always do. In the end."

Lynn came back over with the family and they sat in the cool sunshine behind the house, the mountains framed behind them. An ice bucket full of beer had appeared and Scott opened one and set it before Jessica and she just looked at it a moment before she pushed it aside.

As Ed and Esther stood to leave, an old black truck pulled up the drive and Sonny stepped out. He didn't have on a hat, his hair was neatly combed, and his shirt was clean and buttoned all the way up to the neck.

"Who invited him?" Jessica asked, but everyone just looked at one another and shrugged. Lynn winked at her and Jessica shot her a scowl.

"Hi Jess," Sonny said, walking up and standing by the table.

Lynn cleared the plates as the kids stood and went back to play. "Help me with these, Scott," she said, and he stood slowly and gathered some and followed her inside, his beer tucked under his chin.

Ed and Esther waved a quick goodbye and slipped away, until at last it was quiet and it was just the two of them under the shade of the tree.

"Ed told me you'd be here too," Sonny said, watching the trail of dust their Jeep made as it turned onto the main road. "I think people think we have some things to sort out. But I just wanted to see how you are. What happened up there," he squinted at her in the light. "Well, I never have and never will see anything like it again."

She pulled at the tree branches, looking at him. "Is this what you want Sonny?" She spoke flatly, quietly. "To turn away from all of this? From Ed? The camp? From Wyoming?" She shook her head. "I'm sorry, it's not really my business."

He reached for his hat, but remembering it wasn't there, ran his fingers through his hair.

"C'mon," he said, grabbing her hand. "I brought you something."

She followed him across the gravel driveway as he opened the tailgate on his truck and pulled out her father's old 30/30 rifle.

She looked at it closely and smiled.

"I hope you don't mind," he said. "I went back to the river that day and got it for you." He looked at her. "It took the biggest bear ever killed up there." He broke into a wide smile. "That was some shot."

He'd refinished the wood, re-blued the metal.

"Here," he said, handing it to her. "It was a mess. Had started to rust and all, after being so wet. Careful now, the varnish on there still needs time to dry."

She smiled at this, turning it over in her hands. It looked brand new. She worked the lever and the spent casing came out in her hand. She held it up in her fingertips, inspecting it.

"What if I'd missed, Sonny?"

He grinned, shaking his head. "There was no way. If I'd been holding that gun, we'd all be goners." He shook his head. "But there was no way God would've allowed you to miss."

She stood there holding the rifle as he climbed in his truck and leaned out the window.

"Good luck in New York City," she said, disappointed in the way the word didn't sound so strange now. It felt right in a way. Sonny was a man headed for bigger things. Bigger places. She could see that now.

"I'll be seeing you on the cover of LOOK next month. I heard from Lana that they're rushing it to print."

"Yeah, I guess you will then." She shrugged.

"If I send you a copy, will you sign it for me?"

"Sure," she managed, shaking her head.

"Well, I've got a train to catch." He tipped his hat and she lifted a hand to wave as he drove away.

She understood why a guy like Sonny wanted to see all they could of the world. Life was short; no one understood that better than he. And Lana was beautiful, a woman in all the right ways. She couldn't blame him. In a way she was glad he'd gotten out of that fix in the woods and in the end, he was going to be happy.

But of course that wasn't the truth. She watched as he drove

194

down the lane and pulled onto the road, then looked down at the rifle and felt her nose suddenly start to run.

Lynn looked up when Jessica came back into the kitchen, looking for a tissue. She'd clearly been watching from the window.

"The man fixed that old gun. Went and did all that for you, and all you did was keep backing away from him. I watched it." Lynn handed her a tissue. "The world is doing you favors and you won't even meet it halfway." She turned back to the dishes, shaking her head. "He's different than the rest of them. Too good for someone like me. Too good for that Lana girl. But not too good for you."

Jessica turned and placed the empty brass case on the windowsill above the sink, where it gleamed in the light. "I'm nothing special."

After looking at her a long time, Lynn dried her hands and reached up into a cupboard, pulled out an envelope and handed it to her.

"It came while you were in the hospital. I opened it. I was going to bring it out at the picnic but I didn't want to embarrass you or something."

Jessica turned the envelope over. *Wyoming Forest Service.* She pulled out the letter and began to read:

We're pleased to inform you that you've been hired on for the Winter 1946-47 Season . . .

Jessica shook her head. "I don't understand. I never mailed this."

"Lee Ann found it stuck to some barbed wire. I just mailed it for you. And this was long before everyone from here to Denver had read about you shooting that bear."

Jessica held the letter out, reading it again. "I don't believe it." She sat heavily in a chair, eying Scott's sweating beer that was sitting there.

"Everything you wanted is happening, Jessica. It's time for you to go too. Don't back away from this like you did Sonny."

Lynn turned and took their father's old rifle and hung it where Jessica always put it above the door. She then came and kissed her cheek as Jessica was reading the letter again, and started walking out of the kitchen.

"Thanks," Jessica said.

"For what?" Lynn said, turning.

"For everything."

Twenty-Two

Francine reached the mountain summit first, and sat there atop her horse, looking down over her land and the cattle roaming it. The ranches below were pieced into vast quadrants, land that had been grazed or soon would be. Thin clouds passed over the golden valley, and she could see the road cutting a stripe through it, a lone car fading silently into the distance. The sun warmed her as the clouds parted, and she squinted as she looked up at it, so close it seemed as if she could reach up and touch it.

She'd looked at the mountain all summer before deciding, at last, that it was time to climb it. Seeing things from up there, she thought, might put things in perspective. Below stood The Flying U, the twelve restored cabins and the main house, and to the east, the trail up to The Cutthroat Lake Lodge; to the west stood Will Heaton's ranch, which she quickly looked away from so as to not spoil her mood.

Her skin had grown tan over the summer and her muscles firm from hauling hay and feed. What Sonny had shown her about ranching was enough to fill a book, and she found herself surprised that there, across the country, she'd found a cowgirl in herself that surpassed those in the dime store novels that she used to read.

Francine heard the drumming of hoof beats and a moment later, both a rider and horse appeared over the summit.

"Damn it you ride too fast," Dottie said, as she pulled back the reins on her chestnut horse, spinning once before sidling up next to her.

Francine watched, her brow furrowed. It was the most unlikely scene she ever could've imagined. Dottie—the beautiful, loud, brassy New Yorker—out here with her, riding a horse. She'd been with her but a few days, after the incident the whole town and much of the state had heard about, of the party gone missing in a blizzard, and the girl who killed the bear.

Her husband had already left town; the details were still murky, but it seemed Dottie would soon be in her same situation, alone and divorced, and Francine couldn't turn a friend away in a time like that. Of course, she'd tried to talk her into going home, but Dottie wouldn't hear of it. Francine liked to think it was their friendship that had kept her there, but she knew better. The way she borrowed the DeSoto to run errands in town and came home with nothing; there was someone else in the picture, someone Dottie knew she wouldn't approve of.

"You've done mighty good, Frannie," Dottie said, looking out over her ranch. "More than I can say for myself. All this time, I was secretly hoping you'd turn tail and come back home."

"Out here," Francine said, "everything can just be wiped clean."

"Well, I'd say you've been wiped clean too."

Francine laughed, scanning the valley. "I'm just doing my best to fit in."

"Boy," Dottie said after a moment. "I feel like I've been here before. Déjà vu. You ever feel like that?"

"Almost every day," Francine replied, pushing back a wisp of hair.

Dottie began whistling a tune under her breath. She stopped and looked at Francine, who was smirking at her. "It's a trail song. You know, songs cowboys sing on the trail? Learned it up at camp."

Francine looked up towards Cutthroat Lake.

"It was beautiful up there. Have you been? It's closed for the season now. May be closed forever. You should go see it before it gets sold off."

"No," Francine said, a chill passing through her. "I don't think I will."

Dottie looked at her with a puzzled expression. "Why's that?"

"I tried to buy it. But Thomas hasn't yet signed off on the divorce."

"Shoot," Dottie said, gathering up her reins. "You earned every cent you made living with that man. I hope you can buy the whole damn valley."

"May be too late then. I'm afraid people have other ideas for this town. And I don't have any say in it without money."

Francine sat there, her eyes settling on Will Heaton's dark

mansion nearly two miles away. The Snake River winding just below it. The day of the snowstorm was a week past, but she could still feel the frigid river, and the warmth of his fire. And yet, she hadn't heard from him since. The day after the storm, her fence was mended with her cows all safely inside it, and that was the end of it. Like it never happened.

But Heaton had revealed himself to be the good sort after all. Even if just for one day. He hadn't been at all haughty that evening. Not one bit. He'd been—dare she say—likable. In fact, for one fleeting moment after she stepped out of his sleigh, she would've let the very man who was going to ruin this town take her to bed, had he so wished.

She shuddered again, and beneath her, her horse did too. "Let's get going," Francine said, leading Dottie quickly back down the mountain. As they rode, she told herself that the whole town could change around her—as it inevitably would—but as long as she was alive, she'd never sell The Flying U to Heaton or anyone like him. As long as she could find paying guests the next spring, it would be here to stay.

That evening, Francine set the table for dinner. She and Dottie were cooking a roast. There was far too much food for two people, and Dottie asked if she could call a friend. Francine watched Dottie's eyes light up at the suggestion, and so, Francine relented.

Thirty minutes later a truck pulled in the drive. Dottie left the door hanging open as she sprung down the steps and into his arms, and Francine stood there smiling until she saw who it was.

"Francine," Dottie said, beaming. "This is Jake. Jake, this is Francine."

"We've met," they both said, nearly in unison.

She wanted to tell him to leave right then and there, but Dottie was already showing him around, and before Francine could get a word in, she had Jake seated at the head of the table.

Francine listened to Jake talk all through dinner, telling stories of his adventures as a hunter and cowboy, and Dottie sat holding his hand beneath the table, her food untouched. Jake, on the other hand, ate most of the roast, and as soon as he was finished with it, stretched and stood, scratching at his belly.

"You're not going, are you?" Dottie said, looking up at him. "Surely you can stay here tonight. In one of the cabins, right Francine?"

"Well, I wouldn't want to intrude," Jake sighed, "but it is getting late."

"Can he?" Dottie asked. "Please?"

Francine shook her head disdainfully. "Whatever you think is best, Dot. I can't tell you what to do," she said, eying Jake, "or who to spend your time with."

After the dishes were cleared, Francine sat reading a book by lamplight, Dottie beside her leafing absently through *Cowgirl Ballads and Trail Songs*. She kept looking out the window at the light in Jake's cabin, then over at her.

Francine knew what she was waiting for. "I think I'm going to turn in early," she said at last, although she wasn't tired.

"Oh really?" Dottie sat up and snapped the songbook closed.

Francine had no sooner washed her face and brushed her teeth when she saw Dottie running across the field in her bare feet towards Jake's cabin.

How she'd let that man sleep on her property, let alone with her best friend, was beyond her. But she supposed he was just your run of the mill, everyday bastard; essentially harmless as long as he was getting what he wanted. And anyway, she was helpless to try and stop Dottie from being with him. Better she have her fling here under her watchful eye than over at his place, wherever that was.

Dottie had always been impetuous, if not licentious. And here she was with a man that she clearly must've known, even in her desperate state, was—like Frederick—no good for her. Francine liked to think Dottie would've wised up by now, but she hadn't, and probably never would. And yet Francine knew, watching Dottie run, that no one was going to watch over her if she didn't. Like sisters, they were stuck with one another.

Francine flipped out the light and lay there in the dark, unable to help feeling a bit envious of Dottie's carefree spirit. Were she a bit more like her she might know, for once in her life, the pleasures Dottie was experiencing at that very moment. And not be here alone in an empty bed, with all her principles and hang-ups, and thoughts of tomorrow's worries and responsibilities already closing in on her.

Francine awakened before sunrise, knowing what she had to do. She dressed quickly, then went to the barn and saddled her horse. She packed her old pistol as well as the old cavalry rifle she'd taken off Jake the week before, and rode by the cabin in time to see him, half-naked, leaning against his window smoking a cigarette and grinning at her.

She rode past him and stopped at the trailhead to Cutthroat Lake, looking up at the old wooden sign that hung there: *Cutthroat Lake Lodge and Bungalow Camp.* Her horse pawed the ground, waiting for her to move, but she didn't. She sat studying it a long time, the old rifle across her lap. *Eddie McCann.* The name summoned memories of her first time in Braxton. And while of course her feelings for the cowboy she'd fallen for years ago had faded, in hearing that he was alive—were it indeed the same man—she knew she owed him this favor, even if he didn't remember her at all.

The horse snorted impatiently, but still she didn't move. Her heart had been pulled in so many directions over the past year, she could no longer trust it to guide her. And so, how long she sat there exactly, she didn't know. This is a practical errand, she reminded herself, nothing more. And yet, her heart was beating quickly, her hands were sweating, and when she moved at last, it was to go back home. Yes, better to do that, she thought, but then at the last moment she turned and trotted up the trail.

There was nothing to mark it as it wound up the mountain, except for a thin telegraph wire strung in the trees. She felt entirely alone here, and yet she was not afraid. She tentatively crossed a rushing stream two miles later, where she paused on the opposite bank to drink and let her horse rest. The air was changing as she ascended. Thinning and growing cooler. The trail widened the higher it wound, and soon she saw tire racks in the mud and wondered what kind of vehicle could've made it that far.

Brightly colored leaves fluttered and fell around her, twirling and twisting in the air. A cool breeze blew down into the valley, and for a moment she grew lost in the rhythm of her horse's gait. Soon the ground leveled and through the trees she saw Cutthroat Lake, shimmering in the sun. Through the aspens, it appeared calm and flat, and the trail followed its shoreline for a mile or so until it veered off into a clearing.

There she saw a stable, a wooden building which must've been the lodge, and a dozen tents surrounding it. Francine pulled back on the reins when she saw there was a man there, carrying lumber from the trailer attached to an Army Jeep. He wore a red bandanna around his neck and he was hatless and sweating, seemingly too old looking for the work at hand. And at this, he dropped a piece of lumber and coughed deeply into his closed fist.

She sat on her horse under the aspens, watching him begin nailing a board to the framing surrounding a tent. The sound of the hammer blows echoed across the lake and then back to her. Her horse busied itself eating the grasses that grew trailside, and it was only when it whinnied did the man look up from his hammering and notice her.

Francine didn't move. She watched him standing there a moment before he lifted a hand to wave. She plodded forward on the horse, dismounted, and walked beside it up to where he stood.

The man wiped his face with the bandanna. Instantly she recognized him. Nearly twenty years had passed, but there he was, just as she remembered. He was older now, of course, as was she. Time had worn him down some, as it did to those in the line of work in which she now found herself. His shoulders were stooped and he seemed shorter, but perhaps only because she'd since grown.

As she approached she was quite sure that he wouldn't remember her at all.

"I'm Ed," he said, looking at her. "And you're Francine."

She stared at him a moment, startled. "How is it you remember me?"

"How could I forget?" He laughed. "Heck, you were the only guest that ever sent me postcards. Used to tickle Esther pretty good."

Francine blushed. She'd completely forgotten about them. Had never considered how obvious it may have seemed to him, or his wife, how she'd felt.

"Besides, I heard a woman named Francine bought the old

ranch and I just knew it was you. My, you were just a little thing then. A bit in awe of this place too as I recall." He wiped his brow with his sleeve. "Say, what took you so long to come back then?"

Francine shook her head. "I'm afraid I got a bit waylaid by life in general."

"You easterners have a way of doing that. Of making everything too damn complicated."

He removed his glasses and wiped them off. "I spent over seven summers working there. Was a shame to see it sit there going to rot. Glad to see someone is trying to bring it back." He paused and lit a cigarette, and offered her one, which she took and lit by his still burning match.

"I believe I have something of yours," she said, removing the old rifle from her scabbard.

He nodded, looking at it. "I take it you met Jake Haggard then?"

"He's shacked up with my friend Dottie."

"Well, he's sure made a mess of things, that's for certain," Ed said, flipping open the trap door chamber, then closing it again. "Well, thank you for bringing it back."

Francine crushed her cigarette under the toe of her boot. It seemed there wasn't a whole lot left to say. She cleared her throat. "Looks like you're fixing the place up."

"Well, I don't know about that. It's up for sale now but only man who can afford it is…"

"Will Heaton," she said. "He's my neighbor."

Ed shook his head. "I just wanted to finish it the way I always saw it. Even if the state comes and tears it all down."

"Well," she said, staring off at the lake. "It sure is beautiful up here." She turned her eyes slowly back to him. "Can I help you with that?" she asked, pointing to the lumber.

"I thought you'd never ask."

He took her horse and tied it up at the stables, and together they began nailing the remaining boards to the framing. Somewhere in the process, she mentioned that she'd tried to buy his place too, but things had fallen through back east, although they were expected to be resolved any day now.

Ed looked at her and declared that if she wanted the place, he'd sell it to her on a handshake. They quickly agreed her best option was to borrow against The Flying U to secure a down payment for the property Ed owned, nearly three hundred acres, including the lodge, the lake and the adjacent Six Mile Hole.

"That's a big gamble," Ed said, holding out his hand. "I wouldn't make this deal with anyone else. I just don't want to see you lose your rear end if that money doesn't come through."

"I know what I'm doing, Ed. It'll come through by law," Francine said, shaking his hand, but even then she wasn't so sure.

Ed smiled, adjusting his glasses. "I must say you've made an old man very happy. When I get back into town I'll go over to Jim Hickens directly and have the papers all drawn up. There'll be some other things to do on my end. Bank wise. May take some time."

He shook his head. "I like to think all they want is the tax money, but what they really want is this land. It's a gold mine for developers. I figure they want to do here what they done in Colorado. Bring the tourists back into the state."

"Well," Francine said, "I'm betting they'll come back to Braxton for just what it's always been."

They parted ways as the sun was touching the treetops on the western side of the lake. Ed gave a look at the pistol tied to her pommel and went and fetched the old rifle.

"Take this back down with you. When I come to collect it I'll tell you the story of who it belonged to." He showed her the initials, carved into the stock, of the soldier who'd owned it. *M. Keogh*. The rest of the rifle was covered in Indian markings of some sort. "It's a long story, but it's a good one."

"Ed," she said, before turning and riding away. "By some odd chance did you have anything to do with the big electric sign there on my property? I'll be damned if it isn't the greatest mystery."

"Wasn't me," he said, squinting up at her. "Although this is a backasswards town, people here can still surprise you. And sometimes, when you least expect it, one of them shows up and saves your skin." He winked at her as she turned and rode off.

Twenty-Three

That afternoon, Jessica sat in the kitchen holding her letter from the Wyoming Forest Service, looking out the window at the kids playing in the yard. Lynn saw her and waved, and Jessica slipped the well-worn letter into its envelope, tucked it in her pocket, and went out to join them.

Around the same time, she was to hear later, Sonny arrived in New York. He'd gone to Lana's place directly, wandered past the uniformed doormen and rode the elevator up to her floor. There was some sort of party going on, there in the middle of the afternoon, and as he wandered through the well-dressed crowd in his Levi's and cowboy boots, he spotted Lana. Wearing a silver dress, holding a highball glass, laughing at something someone had said.

For some reason, she looked like a fish to him then. A cutthroat trout, standing there in a cocktail dress. Jessica would never know if Lana ever saw him, but as she heard it, Sonny had simply turned and walked out of the party.

He wandered into the lower parts of the city, Chinatown, then walked the filthy Bowery, where he felt he fit in a bit more. There, he found a store window filled with western cowboy gear. Things he recognized from home, there in the shadowy parts of the city where it stank of dead fish, and beggars openly asked for money.

It was a mystery to him, why such a place was there, until the owner, a fat man in a leather apron, came out and looked at him.

"I'll give you ten dollars for those boots and that belt," the man said.

Sonny eyed racks of worn cowboy boots, of all sizes and styles, all carefully crafted and no doubt with many stories to tell.

"No," Sonny said, blinking at him, "they aren't for sale."

"That's what you all say when you first come to town," the fat man said, turning. "You all come from where there's no work, and find there's none here either. Come back in a few days when you change your mind."

Sonny found himself in an all night cafeteria, seated by the window, where he could watch people coming and going. Their dark clothes, the sharp way they talked, the way they walked right past him, nodding off there in a booth with a cup of coffee and a piece of pie.

"Wake up there, cowboy," a voice said, and when he stirred, a young waitress in a blue uniform was looking down at him. "This ain't no hotel." She pointed a pencil stub out the window. "There's one across the way that's cheap."

Sonny lifted his head and apologized, but she'd already slapped his check on the table and walked away. He set down a dollar and change and stumbled out into the street. The sky was still bright at that hour, a haze of artificial light, and he retired into the stuffy hotel room, twelve floors up, where the city below, muted and distant, was still not far enough away.

He awakened to a pounding on the door, and finding it was nearly noon, he made a long distance call to a friend back in Braxton, perhaps on instinct, or just to hear a familiar voice, and it was then that he first heard the news of what had happened.

As Jessica understood it, Ed had just returned from a week long trip up to camp. Despite Esther's wishes, he'd gone back up after closing early for the season, saying that it was the mildest fall he could recall, and he wanted to take advantage of it. She hadn't given him too much trouble about it and even offered to go up with him, but she had the house to pack up and ready for sale, and so he'd ventured up alone.

They were moving to Texas. Down to warmer weather. Of course, it was his last season, so there was little point in fixing up camp. The Braxton winters were intolerably cruel, and he'd come to face the grim reality that he could not endure another. Esther had come to the same realization, but she let him go on his errand, foolish as it was, especially since he hadn't rested much in the past days.

He loaded up the trailer and Jeep with tools and lumber and headed up. Even if a match was taken to the lodge and camp in the end, she knew Ed wanted to at least be able to say that it had at last been a proper camp when he left it. That he'd made a good go of things up here.

The season had ended on a low note. Guests had been notified, deposits returned; Cutthroat Lake Lodge and Bungalow Camp was officially closed. Perhaps Ed was thinking, as he drove up the trail, of all that he could've done differently. And that he had, in his old age, finally lost his good judgment. Lost control of things that a man in his position needed to have a handle on.

He returned a few days later, tired but jubilant. And the tune he was whistling as he hurried into their kitchen, and into her arms, told her that he had good news to share.

"The old camp will continue on," Ed said, telling her all about Francine, who she remembered as an innocent girl who'd sent him postcards of the Liberty Bell, and Ben Franklin, twenty years before.

"I'll go see Jim Hickens in the morning and have it finalized." He smiled as he stood there looking out over their pasture and into the Crooked Mountains.

"I sure hope Texas has mountains like them," he said, and to this she'd laughed.

He'd gone out to put the tools from the Jeep away in the barn, and it was there Esther said she found him at dusk, sprawled on the dirt floor, his eyes closed, hands grasping a hammer and a set of chains, and as she cried out and knelt to hold him, she found that he'd already gone cold.

Twenty-Four

Jessica stood outside the church a few days later, greeting folks as they came inside. Of course, news had traveled fast. Had brought people in from far and wide, and everyone who passed by seemed to have memories of Ed that were as fond as her own. As she stood there looking out at the growing line, she hoped to find Sonny's face among it, but she knew the chances of that were slim.

He'd left Ed. Left the camp. And left any thought of her behind for some girl he barely knew. Jessica stood there atop the stairs, looking out over the parking lot as the church bells began to ring. Organ music spilled out the open doors, and suddenly she was ushered to a seat. Esther was sitting beside her, facing a framed photo of Ed as a young man, which stood beside an urn and a vase filled with flowers. Indeed Ed had been something to see in his prime, Jessica thought, gazing at the photo.

After the service, there was a brief burial ceremony outside the graveyard, as Ed's ashes were to be spread, per his wishes, up on the mountain. There was then a luncheon with drinks at the Sundowner, and Jessica sat by Esther the entire time, as she stoically accepted each hand and condolence offered to her, as if it was all an unpleasant but necessary formality that she was eager to put behind her.

Slowly the bar cleared, until at last it was just the two of them and a straggling guest. Soon he too stood to leave, and although she didn't know him—an older man with wire spectacles who hadn't said a word all afternoon—she envied him. That he could just stand up and leave this all behind.

The summer had changed her in ways that she didn't yet fully understand. Even there, in that dingy bar, it had filled her with a grief she'd not have otherwise known.

"Jessica," Esther said at last. "I can't make the trip up to camp again. For many reasons." She pressed a handkerchief to her nose. "I just can't."

Jessica watched through the window as the man got in his sedan and drove away, leaving her there with Esther and of course Griff, who came and brought her a beer and set it down before her.

"On the house," she said, looking out the window at the trail of dust left by the departing car.

As Esther continued to sob softly, the beer sat sparkling in the light, until Griff drew the curtains against the coming sunset, and the room went dim, and the neon signs shed their glow on them as she stood and walked Esther out to her car without looking back.

Jessica drove her home and saw her into the house. Someone had come and brought all the flowers from the church and they filled the den.

"We have a lot to figure out," Esther said, walking inside, as if Ed was still there. She looked tired, and for the first time Jessica had ever noticed, confused. Jessica took her in the kitchen and made coffee. Esther sat there, hands balled up in her lap, too young to look so old and empty.

"I feel like he's still talking to me in a way," she said. "Helping me through this. Telling me that everything is going to be okay."

The coffee percolator burped and out the window the clouds began to part, and it filled the room with a golden light.

"Like that," she said, looking up. "Just like that."

The next morning, Jessica packed a bag, saddled Scott's other horse and told Lynn and Scott that she was heading up to camp. They were still asleep and murmured their goodbyes from their bed, but then Lynn popped her head up from the sheets.

"You okay, kid?"

Jessica nodded, knowing better than to tell them of her errand.

"Want me to make you some coffee?"

"No. I've got a long ride. Should be back by nightfall."

She didn't need coffee now. As she climbed on the horse and looked at the smoldering sunrise, it also felt good not to have to squint at the sun until that first drink of the day.

She rode slowly until she picked up the trail, the polished 30/30 across her lap, the weather still unseasonably warm. When she arrived in camp around noon she saw, to her surprise, that Ed's horse was tied up at the stables. She kept her hands on her rifle as she slipped from her own.

The cabins had been sided since she'd last been up. Rather crudely, she noticed, but there were no longer those moldy tents. All else looked the same, from the lodge, the fire pit, and even the old crumbling well. She'd try and fix that herself today, she told herself, as she crept towards the lodge with her rifle at the ready.

For a moment, it seemed the last few days had been a dream. That Ed was still there, closing the dining room for the season. But of course he wasn't. Couldn't be. The urn was tied closed with rawhide cord, packed deep in her saddlebag, and had come with special instructions from Esther to spread them on Cutthroat Lake.

As she approached the lodge, the 30/30 on her hip, she called out. When there came no answer, she slowly walked inside, but stopped after only a few paces. Hanging on the far lodge wall was a large grizzly pelt. She absently set her rifle on a table and stood there, her mouth hanging open as she studied it.

It was *her* grizzly. And it's pelt nearly covered the entire wall. There was a scar where the head had been sewn up, and as she tentatively ran her hand over its fur she noticed a wooden placard beside it which read:

GRIZZLY. 985 lbs. Shot by Jessica Gladinger. Six Mile Hole, Fall 1946

"Oh Ed," she said, tearing up, but grabbed her rifle when she heard a noise behind her.

Sonny was standing in the doorway, hands on his hips. Sunlight spilled in the open door, into the empty room that only a month before had been filled with voices.

"The old man fixed up the place some," he said casually, looking around.

"He didn't quit," she replied automatically, unable to keep from sounding surprised at his presence. "No one could take that away from him."

As he stepped into the room, motes of dust twirled about. "Would you look at that bear? I still can't believe it."

She quickly wiped away a tear, gazing up at it.

"I don't know if that day will ever get out of my head," he added. "Haunted me the entire time I was away."

She glanced at him, then the bear. "Me neither."

Sonny chuckled and she did too, and then came a long pause. Something about him being there felt natural, and she knew that in a way, Ed had somehow arranged all of this.

"Shame that this will all be gone soon."

She shot him a look. "What do you mean?"

"It's going up for auction."

"No," she said, "the woman down the hill, who owns the Flying U. Francine. I saw her last week and she told me she was buying it from Ed."

Sonny stood there, shaking his head. "Just talked to her on my way up. Papers never got signed. It's going to auction next month. Seems the state's champing at the bit for their money."

Jessica didn't speak, and Sonny just stood staring at the bear, moving closer to it, until he was standing beside her.

"Ed would've told that story time and again. Would've proudly told everyone that it was you that shot it."

He turned and faced her, and as he did, she felt a sudden flash of anger. Of course, word had reached New York too late for him to make the funeral, but he never should've left to begin with. That night they spent alone out there in the woods had felt more meaningful than anything she'd ever experienced. And it had clearly meant nothing to him.

And now, just when she'd come up here to grieve alone, he'd decided to show up. She thought he hated this place. Hated her. As far as she knew, he'd wanted nothing but to get away from Ed, her, the people who cared for him. For a moment, her feelings about him funneled into one distinct emotion that she was able to drop at her feet, as simply as if it were a rock.

A lone gust of wind blew into the room.

"Why are you here, Sonny?" she said coldly. "No one expected you back."

The question hung in the air. He looked at her a long time before answering.

"I just had this feeling. Like I had to come up and see this place one last time."

"No, I mean, why are you in Wyoming?"

"This is my home. Where I belong." He looked at her. "I guess

I had to go to New York to find that out."

"What about Lana?"

"Lana." He shook his head and looked at her. "There's nothing to tell."

She looked at him a long time. For what, she didn't know.

"Well," she said finally, clutching her rifle and giving him a half smile. "Ed would've appreciated you coming back. Now," she added, "I'm going to go have a look around and see that it's properly shut down for winter. That," she said, walking out the door, "was why I came up here."

She went down by the lake, and Sonny didn't follow. She hoped he'd head out, so she could spread Ed's ashes in private. As she passed by the well she noticed some of the rocks surrounding it had spilled. She sighed and began re-stacking them neatly. As she did, she tripped and a stone tumbled down the hole. She cussed and waited for the splash, but none came. She leaned over and peered thirty feet down at the oil black water. There wasn't even a ripple on its surface —it was as if the stone had simply vanished.

She stood quickly and found the cap to the well, a rusty piece of corrugated steel, slid it in place and set some rocks on it. As she did she heard someone speak. When she turned, Sonny was hammering a protective wooden door over the lodge's entryway.

"Did you say something?"

He furrowed his brow, shook his head, and removed the nail he'd been holding between his teeth. "I'll be out of your way soon enough."

"Well," she said, walking up beside him. "I might not be seeing you around then."

He tossed the hammer at his feet. "What do you mean?"

"I got a job, with the Forest Service over in Yellowstone. Headed that way shortly."

"Esther told me," he said. "I guess congratulations are in order."

"You saw her then?"

"Right when I got back into town. She told me you'd be up here." He moved closer and she took a step back. "And so I thought I might come and help you. If you wanted someone to help row the boat, that is."

"You've helped me enough, Sonny." A tremor slipped into her

voice. "I can handle this just fine on my own."

She went to turn but he took her hand and stepped closer. When she looked up at him, there were tears in his eyes.

"Why couldn't this have been easy times?" he said weakly. "I came home after discharge and I was tired of fighting, Jessica. So very tired."

"I'm not fighting you."

"That's not what I mean." He shook his head. "I saw things. Did things. Things I've been trying hard to understand. And I thought everything would be clear to me when I got home. But nothing was the same. I wasn't the same. And to think that this was all going to become something I couldn't recognize. Well, I just couldn't bear it. I had to get away."

Jessica looked at him a long time, standing there so close to him. She slowly reached into her pocket and pulled out his war medals, which she'd been carrying around, planning to mail them off to him someday.

"I know," she said, holding them up by their ribbons. "I know the things you did. It seems the Army did too."

"Where did you get those?" he asked, looking down at them. "I threw them away."

"Francine. She came by the place and gave them to Lynn." Jessica opened the clasps on each of them. "She must've known we were friends. Thought we'd know how to get a hold of you.

"It seems," she added, pinning them beside one another on his breast pocket, "that everyone in this town, hell, in this world, is doing their best to tell us something." She smoothed the medals down and stepped back. "There. That looks nice."

Without a word Sonny leaned forward and kissed her, and as he did she closed her eyes and felt herself falling. Tumbling backwards, over and over, although this time she knew there'd be no earthly end. In that moment, the entire summer replayed in her mind, from start to finish. And at the end, she saw the two of them standing there beside the lake, the wind tracing over a blue sky, golden leaves swirling in the lodge doorway, and the door Sonny had just nailed to it, which Ed had freshly painted red.

Twenty-Five

Francine drove to the auction in Cheyenne the following month, the first time she'd left Braxton since the previous spring. Dottie sat beside her, smacking gum bubbles and checking herself in her compact mirror, fiddling with the radio as she did. It was a long drive, and in many ways felt a rather useless, but necessary errand. The divorce had at last become legal, and while the money had started to flow, it wasn't as much as she needed, and had been slow to move through the necessary channels. Thomas still had, over a year since she left him, long reaching arms. Here he was on a lone stretch of Wyoming bi-way, still trying to hold her back.

Mountains gave way to rolling hills, then prairie, and when they reached Cheyenne and found the Capitol Building, they parked and walked inside, wearing their finest Fifth Avenue dresses. They listened to the hollow clatter of their footfalls echoing off its cavernous interior, the sun shining through the grand windows, down onto the polished marble floors.

The place seemed deserted until at last they heard voices. When they turned a corner, it seemed that there, at eight o'clock on a Sunday morning in November, was everyone she knew in Braxton. There was Sonny, tipping his hat to her, Jessica beside him. There was Griff too. Even Jim and Iris Hickens. They sat huddled on one side of the room, while alone on the other sat Will Heaton, leaned back in his chair, hat low over his eyes. She glared at him as she found a seat with the others.

"How you like your new place, Dottie?" Jim asked, leaning over a row of chairs. He'd found her a cheap house in town, where she'd been shacking up with Jake.

"Oh I like it just fine, thank you," she said, patting down her hair.

"Damn shame about Ed," Jim said, turning to Francine. "The papers were at my place, just waiting for him to sign them. If he hadn't bought that land before he was married, Esther could've sold it to you. But we'd have to wait on the courts then, and the state had no patience for that."

"I think everyone here is still grieving too much to be concerned with the loss of that deal. All except for him," Francine said, nodding in Heaton's direction.

Just then, the officials stepped into the room—two older men in dark suits—who found their place at the podium. The men sighed, looking at the half-empty room, and promptly began the auction. One rubbed his eyes while the other raised his hand and in a tired voice, started the bidding at twenty thousand dollars—the value of the taxes the state had levied on the land.

Perhaps the auctioneers were disappointed that anyone had shown up at all, and as they glared out at the room, it seemed clear they hoped no one would be able to meet this rather lofty bid. The necessary legal notice for the upcoming auction had been but a small block in the back of the previous Sunday's paper. It seemed that the state, even more than Heaton, wanted this land.

Jessica was the first to place a bid, which Heaton quickly countered, not even lifting his hat off his face to raise his hand.

Soon Jessica and then Griff dropped out and Sonny entered the bidding. Had he that kind of money, she didn't know, but Heaton countered and he soon dropped out. Jim eyed Francine, then made the next bid. He stayed with Heaton up until twenty-seven thousand dollars, and then he too fell away.

Francine made the next bid, narrowing her eyes at Heaton. Twenty-eight thousand. He raised his hand to counter each ensuing bid, still not moving from his reclined position, until the bidding reached thirty-one thousand—more than she had at her disposal, including a bank note which would name The Flying U Ranch as collateral.

Francine bit her lip and lowered her hand as the two auctioneers assayed the room. One raised his gavel and in the same tired voice, began to close the bidding. Heaton went to stand, as if the auction was finished, when Jessica turned to the group.

"Why don't we pool together what we have and split the land? Whatever percentage we put in, that's how much we'll own," she said. "It's our only chance."

There were but seconds to decide. The group looked at one

another and nodded in agreement, and then Jessica turned to the auctioneers and raised her hand.

"Thirty-five thousand," she declared. It was a ridiculous sum, and every eye locked on her at that moment seemed to know it too.

Heaton, in the midst of buttoning his coat, pushed his hat back on his head and, for the first time, looked over at their group.

"Thirty-six," he said haughtily. "And it ain't even worth half that."

He sat down again, seeming to grasp what was happening on the other side of the room. Francine noticed that whatever imposing presence he'd commanded at first had now withered away. She glanced over at him, sitting there with his chin in his hand. Had she not known the real him, as she had for a brief moment that one night, she might've hated him.

But now she only felt sorrow for him. The man didn't have a friend in this world. Not without paying them, like he did his line riders, his gardener, or his cook.

"Thirty-seven thousand," Jessica shouted, and turned to the group with a concerned expression. It was more than anyone wanted to spend and they all sat there restlessly, looking across the room at Heaton, holding their collective breath in hopes that this would be the end of it.

Heaton pushed back his hat to reveal his sweating face. It was clear that this no longer made business sense to him, but that it too had become a personal matter.

He sighed and grasped the back of the empty chair in front of him. "Might as well make it forty-thousand then."

A pall fell on the room. The auctioneers were no longer stifling their yawns. When Francine turned, the others behind her were all shaking their heads, and Jessica didn't move to raise her hand again.

Francine stood, glaring at Heaton with what the others there later described as atomic rays. Distinct beams of fiery red radiation seemed to shoot across the room at him. Whatever it was in their chemical make-up, it was enough that Heaton unbuttoned his sweat soaked collar as he looked back at her.

"Damn you, William Heaton. Have you not one shred of decency?" Francine wasn't sure what angered her more at that precise moment, his actions or the fact that she had to shame him.

"We all know you have deep pockets. Big damn deal. But don't you know when you see something special? Can't you have faith that good things can still happen in a place like Braxton? That maybe *one* place there can remain as God intended?" She paused, panting, and took one step closer to him, and for a moment, her voice lowering a register, it seemed as if they were the only two in the room. "Don't we deserve better? Don't I? Or is your intent here to drive me off too?"

Heaton hung his head. The room was still for what seemed like minutes. Finally he looked up, slipped off his tie and waved it in the air. When he glanced over at Francine again, he at last seemed like the man she'd known that one night.

"Excuse me gentlemen," he said, standing and lifting a flask from the breast pocket of his suit. "What have I bid up to again, I seem to have forgotten?"

"Forty-thousand dollars," the auctioneers replied in unison.

"Forty-thousand for a musty old camp." Heaton laughed, uncorking the flask. "My, my."

They asked if he'd been drinking, which he answered by taking a long swig. The auctioneers then looked at one other, shaking their jowls.

"It seems," Heaton said, looking at Francine, "you all have a dream of this place. But I do too. That's no crime. There's more people in this world every day. And you all think nothing's ever going to change." He shook his head slowly. "All my life, everywhere I've turned, they're building something. Where there were fields, there are now houses. Where there were wild rivers, there are dams. All I want to do is build something of my own. Something people will enjoy. While you all hope that things will always stay the same. But things can never be what they once were. No one should understand that better than I."

He capped the flask and sat back unsteadily.

"I apologize, gentlemen," he said, looking up towards the podium. "But I seem to have come in here in not too good a shape. I thought if I drank some I wouldn't feel too bad for anyone, myself included, but it doesn't seem to have worked."

The room had fallen quiet. He took off his hat and brushed back his hair, revealing his bloodshot eyes. He looked over at Francine and then the others. "I retract all the bids I've made this morning."

"You can't do that," an auctioneer said, standing and leaning over the podium. "Your bid is a contract."

"I assure you, gentlemen, that by law it is not. Especially not by a man who's spent the night drinking spirits. So now, I will recuse myself of this matter in its entirety."

Heaton stood without fanfare, and after tipping his hat at Francine, quickly exited the room.

The auctioneers noisily conferred with one another. After a few moments of deliberation, one of them spoke: "This is highly unusual. But being that we can't very well accept bids by an inebriated man, we must start the bidding again. At twenty thousand dollars."

Nearly every member of the group raised a hand, but after a moment they all looked at one another. Francine slowly lowered her hand. Griff followed suit. Then Jim lowered his, and finally, looking closely at Sonny, Jessica too dropped hers.

Sonny sat there eying the group with a stunned expression. "What are you all doing?"

They all sat staring back at him, arms crossed.

"It's yours, Sonny," Jessica said evenly. "It always was."

Sonny looked at each of them as they nodded in solemn agreement.

"There are no other bidders then?" The auctioneer asked, staring at the group, and then at last sat back, exasperated, and declared the land sold.

"I know how Sonny got his money, but when did you manage to scrape up twenty-thousand dollars?" Jim said to Jessica when they were all standing in the empty hall.

Jessica reached in her back pocket and pulled out a folded up LOOK Magazine. On the front cover, in full color, was a picture of her standing on a boulder in the middle of a stream. *The Girl and the Bear*, the caption read. When she flipped the magazine open, there were over a dozen pictures of her and Sonny during their adventure in Six Mile Hole.

"Dottie here made sure we got paid handsomely," Jessica said, passing the magazine around.

"Well," Francine said finally, looking at Sonny, "no one deserves that place more than you. I'm sure Ed sure would be pleased."

"Thank you, Francine," Sonny said, turning to her. "I won't forget this."

"I've got my hands full with the ranch anyway," she replied, slipping on her overcoat.

As she said goodbye and started down the stairs, Iris took her arm and pulled her aside.

"I shouldn't be telling you this, and not even Jim knows, but a couple months back one of Will Heaton's hands placed an order with me for shielded electrical cabling. The kind someone might use to install an electric sign." Iris winked. "But loose lips sink ships, ain't that right?"

As her headlights whipped over the snowy Braxton streets, the place no longer felt foreign. It was home now. Still full of that unending sense of hope. Like a spring it flooded a part of her that had once been completely dry. And at last, there in that unlikely place, where even in winter, with its starry sky and white-washed landscape, she was filled with a sense of contentment that she'd never known.

She stopped in front of Dottie's place, a two-story cottage a few blocks from the center of town. Jim had sold it to her cheap, even throwing in an old sawed off shotgun, in case any bears got in. Francine knew Dottie wouldn't be here long, that her real place was back in the city, but Dottie had yet to realize this herself. She was in love with Jake, who seemed to have made promises of marriage and starting a family. Much to Francine's chagrin, Dottie had believed him.

Already their relationship had gotten notice in town. The wild late night parties they'd thrown, full of whiskey and gin, and seedy types who never seemed to want to go home. Dottie didn't even seem to mind the women who hung around there, as long as they were gone by midnight, and Jake was ready to wait on her in all her desires.

But there'd been fights. Heated spats that had the two of them yelling in the frozen street, waking up the neighbors in the early hours. The police had become a common fixture there, coming and going with such regularity that they were all on a first name basis.

But, as Francine pulled up to the little house that night, all seemed calm. She walked Dottie inside and helped her turn on the lights. The place was quiet except for the odd sound of a needle stuck in the end groove of a still running Victrola. As Francine went and shut it off, she noticed an open liquor bottle beside it with two glasses, one with lipstick on it. In a shade that was decidedly not Dottie's.

As Dottie picked it up and examined it, Jake wandered from the bedroom, bare-chested, rubbing his head. He stopped at the end of the hallway and squinted, as if surprised to see Dottie there in her own home.

"It's you," Jake exclaimed, coming quickly with his arms held open. He embraced and kissed Dottie, slipping the glasses from her hands and tossing them in the sink. He then emptied an ashtray full of butts that were smudged with the same color lipstick. "Always someone to clean up after here."

Francine stood there with her arms crossed, shaking her head. As Dottie's lips parted to speak, a girl—not more than twenty—wandered from the bedroom wearing Jake's plaid wool shirt.

"Who are you?" the girl asked, looking at the two of them. She was rubbing a clearly visible protruding belly. "Jake? Who's this? I thought you said no parties tonight."

Dottie's mouth was hanging open as the girl continued to rub her belly.

"It's not a party," he said, turning to face the girl. "I didn't expect her back so early."

"I own this place," Dottie said, crossing her arms. Forever to her credit, she was entirely calm as she saw her affair with Jake crumble right before her eyes. The humiliation was evident. Not from the betrayal itself, but because everyone but her had seen it coming.

She placed her hands over her eyes and suggested the girl get dressed and leave, and that Jake should too, before she lost her temper.

"Fuck," Jake scowled, leaning forward, "you."

The young woman looped her arm around his waist and chimed in. "Yeah. It's his place too. Ain't it, Hon?"

Francine was so very pleased that Jake had finally revealed his true character, but even she hadn't expected this. He was the man who'd ended Dottie's marriage, had proclaimed his love for her, made promises that he was not equipped to keep. Not with Dottie anyway.

What happened next was something Francine would never forget. Dottie didn't flinch at being cussed at in her own home. Instead she simply went to the fireplace mantle, removed the double-barreled shotgun Jim had given her, and turned.

She leveled it at Jake and cocked both barrels. Within an instant, their two half-naked bodies flashed across the room and ran out the door in their bare feet. Francine looked out the window at them dancing in the winter air and locked the door, then collapsed with her back against it.

"Men are the same here as in New York," Dottie said, lowering herself against the wall until her legs spilled out from under her, the gun still gripped in her hands. "A bunch of no good louts."

Francine stood there looking at Dottie, wondering how many cowboys there would be, how many wild parties, how many nights the police would need to be called before she got bored and went back home.

"No good louts," Dottie repeated, staring blankly at Francine as she came and took the gun from her and set it on the mantle.

As Francine left Dottie's house that wintry night, she saw the girl and Jake still standing there in the road, half-naked and shivering. Francine passed through the gate and got in her car, yelling out through her open door: "Get in."

The girl climbed in the back and when Jake tried to as well, she pointed her gray eyes at him. As she did, he must have recalled the way she pointed Ed's old rifle at him the month before. As she revved the engine he backed up, flinching when she yelled "SCREW!" at him and peeled away.

The girl lived far out of town, near the new airport. She sat there staring coldly out the window as Francine drove her to a small house in a ravine, where an old woman stood in the lighted doorway holding up a hand as the girl slipped inside without so much as a goodbye. Francine then turned and made her way slowly back to town. As she did she passed the airstrip, and noticed it was now alight, Will Heaton's Duesenberg parked at one end of it.

He was sitting on the car's hood wearing a sheepskin coat, looking out over the runway as she parked behind him. He didn't turn at the sight of her headlights shining on him, even as she cut the engine and shut her door. Beyond him lay the hangars he'd built and the polished aluminum faced terminal. *BRAXTON AIRPORT* glowed in neon blue letters above the entrance, the familiar *H* emblazoned above it on a metal sign.

Francine's eyes swept over the entire complex, nearly complete, and quite neatly put together. She pictured him overlooking the entire project, assuring that every last detail was attended to.

Will still hadn't turned, but resumed looking off into the starlit sky, even as she came and stood silently beside him.

"Who knew?" she said quietly, pulling the collar of her fur coat tightly around her neck.

"Who knew what?" he said without looking at her, tossing his cigarette on the yet unused airstrip.

"That you were a good man."

He looked at her finally and managed a half smile. "Well," he said, "just don't tell anyone. I have a reputation to keep."

She stood there with him a while, looking at the western mountain face, his lighted chair lift leading to the top of it like a string of Christmas lights.

"I guess it will all never come to be now." He laughed softly. "A beautiful airport and no reason to come here."

She moved closer to him. "The town needed an airport, Will."

"Maybe," he said, resting his hands on the still warm cowl. "I think a dirt airstrip would've been just fine." He looked over at her. "I went all in here, Francine. All in. And now I'm bust."

She slipped her arm through his. "Well, you didn't see the latest LOOK Magazine I take it?"

He shook his head. "Can't say I read that particular publication."

"Well, there's reasons to be looking up, I assure you," she said, and sighed. "My, this sure is a nice place to be at night when it's all lit up like this."

"Maybe I can sell tickets to it."

"C'mon," she laughed and pulled closer. "Don't be so glum. Join me for dinner? I know Braxton well."

He smiled as he slid off the hood and held out his hand. "I thought you'd never ask."

"You drive," she said, as they walked arm in arm. "The Sundowner?"

"No," he said, laughing, "that place is terrible."

"This town does need a decent restaurant."

"Now there's an idea," he said as they slipped in his car and stared at the headlights shining on the open runway. The row of orange lights lining it, growing closer in the distance. He looked over at her and smiled, then put the car in gear. Instead of turning down the lane towards the exit, he began to drive along the runway.

He drove swiftly, until the lights and painted stripes were flashing by. The pavement was smooth and didn't seem to end. Perhaps it goes on forever, she thought, as they reached a hundred miles per hour.

Will looked over at her and grinned. Landing lights flashed against his face, the motor roaring loudly. Soon of course, the pavement would end and he'd have to slow; and soon they'd be laughing breathlessly for the exhilaration of this newfound thrill. But in those precious seconds it seemed—speeding between those mountains, there in that forgotten town—that something magical could happen. That with a pleasant lurch, the wheels might leave the ground and they'd begin to fly. And there together, free of the earth, they'd see all of Braxton below them, and find that the stars that shine so brightly on Wyoming weren't so far away after all.

Owen Duffy's fiction has appeared in various journals such as *Passages North, New South, Storyglossia, New Delta Review, PANK, and Hawai'i Review*. This is his second novel. His first was also published by Livingston Press. Its title is *The Artichoke Queen*. He holds an MFA in writing from Rutgers-Newark and currently teaches and mentors young writers. He lives with his family in Vermont.